New Suit
for
King Diamond

Peter Cowlam

Author Publishing Ltd
61 Gainsborough Road, Felixstowe,
Suffolk IP11 7HS

ISBN 1 898030 47 2

Copyright © 2002 **Peter Cowlam**

British Library Cataloguing in
Publication Data available.

Produced in Milton Keynes
by Lightning Source

For Jack and Katie

Contents

lx

A note to my successor

I can't think of a more instructive set of case notes, whose subject – or at least the name – won't be lost on you – for after almost twenty years on his hill farm, a greying Ryder Twill has returned to the entertainment world – specifically the McGregAir studios. What we want to know here is *why*.

Alas that question forces me to clear to its gloss the vast plateau of my desk, whose sheen I only now revive as a walnut or amber, depending on the light. I would like to say there is something slightly aloof in marshalling my papers so – yet that would be too optimistic. I am (I insist) about to retire, and but for the prospect of all that rambling idleness, it weighs as a burden that the *whole* document, and not just this preamble, is a 'note' to my successor. I dictate its various parts without at any point knowing who my successor will be.

Be that as it may, I did, with the changed air of autumn, some days ago hand over all my voice transcriptions, which have now been returned to me (on good, traditional paper). It means I begin to judge more certainly the size of the project, which I know you will one day inherit. As I have said, my desk is host to this last remaining file, for whose neatness and precision of keystrokes I can thank my ever willing Miss Ashley, who is herself due to retire. (Not for the first time today, the distant zub of a helicopter engine, and the swish of rotor blades, disrupt the slumbers of autumn.)

Let me explain the more important aspects of my job – which after all will be *your* job – or what theoretically it means to be the Federation's 'unofficial' monitor – by which I mean of course *media* monitor. Not unnaturally, my department forms a wing of the Data Protection Bureau, and owes its coherence to that spinster I mentioned – the greying Miss Ashley, who was born on the southeast coast of England, and who keeps me strictly to my diary. Through all the years I have known her, Miss Ashley has remained so very punctilious about tea and coffee breaks, and has marked these times in particular when entry to her carrel is strictly by invitation. Yesterday there was for example Danish pastry, and once – about a year ago – she passed me her holiday snaps (of a cloudy ten days in the Baltic).

I am all but transparent, and make my presence felt only among a few handfuls of public persons, or because these are mostly media people, I ought to say 'personalities'. Even then this is usually via the crescents of my virtual stamp, a little personal touch I brought here myself. The office you will find is a far from democratic resurrection of its British precursor, the Lord Chamberlain's, whose failure was not in its aim, but rather in its inability to act on amoral impulse – so essential to stage and statecraft. In that light, it is so much more astonishing to me that Twill could ever find the means to rouse my suspicions, and is doubly hard to take given the interests he has. But we'll come to that...

1

Allow me to show you round the castle here at Ix, a domicile that goes with the job. It's a reconstruction, and goes back to the last century, and owes much of its current state to a prominent English family. You probably know the trio of movie directors, or the name at least – a father, son and grandson. Their line culminated in a fourth, whose break with tradition was final and spectacular – for here was a man preferring the roulette table to almost a century of family toil (in fact he flirted with *all* those casino games). His name no one here can ever take lightly, though it is purely coincidental that with the dawn of his birth, that procession of fathers before him had systematically trawled the Internet, and through zipfuls of genealogical information had compiled a plumpish-looking dossier. That, as I say, is as may be – for there's much more to it than that.

Their surname was Martin. That, they discovered, gazing late in the night at a glow of URLs, had links with other clans whose origin was French – to the ear more a *Martan*. That does not explain why his ancestry was briefly intertwined with that of a Swiss composer, though it probably *is* why our fourth in line was called Aimé. But more on that later.

Monsieur Martin spent the greater part of a decade raising cash and running up debts, in an effort to fund the world-wide travel underpinning his pursuit of the right marriage candidate. It is I think ironic that the vital union was conceived on a blustery day in Whitechapel, where oil and rain in one of those darkly slated back streets had merged into several spirals of the spectrum (this I lifted wholesale from the memoir *Our Love Affair With Ix*, by Emma and Aimé Martin).

Aimé's want of cash for many years involved the auction of family memorabilia, which usually meant signed drafts of scripts the three directors were known to have had a hand in. Of antique value were the written ones, attributed to Aimé's great-grandfather. Patchworks from a Remington you could identify with *his* son, while the third in line – Aimé's father – graduated from a golfball typewriter to a pre-Microsoft wordprocessor. Here, the artefact for sale was always an 'original' diskette – Aimé a man always possessing a library full of these. I use that punctuation advisedly, well knowing the story attached to one batch – which was hastily withdrawn, on the suspicion of fraud. In outline, a last sci-fi blockbuster, *Night of the Coelacanth* (in part it *could* explain the silence of Andrew Martin's last ten years of life), was never satisfactorily authenticated. Technicians from a Swedish laboratory failed to verify its various electronic date stamps, and furthermore could not agree that the antiquated file structures fitted any known historical model. Aimé, who at that time had a taste for fast cars, quickly receded, in a blur of British racing green, over a continental horizon.

Yet these were only slight setbacks, invoked in *Our Love Affair* in much the same glow as Aimé's Tequila beach parties, or bankrolls bet on the turn of an ace or king, or with Aimé himself at his 'most at home', among the thunderclaps of Bayreuth.

2

What Aimé was up to in Whitechapel was a point speculated on, on *Our Love*'s first appearance. The fateful Chapter Two, with a lovers' vines ensnaring a large, bold, and scene-opening A, began so:

"Aimé had dropped someone off..."

...or in fact had left some person unnamed in one of those dampish back streets. This was via the rear of his limousine, a black, diplomatic car, which came with a liveried driver, a convenience Aimé could not at the time of writing recall the reason for. A fun lady of leisure, all sunny highlights and pimply areolae, in a mildly repugnant article – or rather inset to a two-page photo collage – claimed *she could* recall the reason. This merely provoked in Aimé a protracted silence, which in turn prompted a sequel – long, colourful disquisitions, musing on the exact disposition of his briefs. That was as restraint for his ankles, and no doubt helped his companion earn her ride home, palpating the rage of his phallus under the hard point of her tongue. The car pulled up, just as she'd mopped his copious fountain.

Yet there was still no response. Did Martin simply not read that sort of paper? Whatever the reason, Aimé kept his counsel. In time five others like her made substantially the same claim, to the point where the trail went cold (so vindicating the Martin legal team, who couldn't possibly comment throughout).

Whatever had been the exertion, Aimé had worked up an eleven o'clock appetite. He instructed his driver to park up and read the horoscope, and trotted off for a plate of eggs. This was in Leonardo's caff. At about this same time, Emma (née Wilding) – heiress to an American textiles empire, and much photographed as an art historian – was having troubles with *her* car. In fact it was stolen when her own driver, a man stupendously bored, went off to look at a bookmaker's shop front. (It turned up on a trading estate in Orpington, at seven a.m. the following day, having all night been driven through hoops by teenage joyriders, and finally set fire to.)

4

Emma however could never be despondent, and anyway had other things to occupy her mind. No inclement or slightly inconvenient Tuesday in London could dampen hopes of adding to her Impressionists, a collection she kept sealed from daylight in a Sacramento vault. She emerged from her present venue – a dove-grey, corrugated warehouse, sheeted in rain. She marked her catalogue with one, decisive tick.

As Aimé later discovered, that tick was for Melanie Klopp, whose body of work encompassed the Whitechapel piece. Not exactly innovative – for much the same had been done in Berlin, by a rival, months before – Melanie's contribution to the currents of debate was nevertheless a Perspex cylinder filled with cabbage leaves (her Berlin rival much preferring cauliflower). Appreciation, as the catalogue explained, you derived from organic changes over time – necessitating frequent revisits – for which one jaded critic personally recommended breathing apparatus.

3

Aimé knew a *distinguée*, in the cut of a coat or the tinct of a tiny brooch. He wiped the café grease from his mouth, and concealed his paper serviette. He picked his way carefully through a patchwork of oily puddles, whose ruts and craters peppered the street. No one, with quite such alacrity, could have registered Emma's look of loss, or bowed in that stupid English way (which was slightly, from the waist). She told him that somehow her car had gone, and in doing so mishandled then completely dropped her cell phone. He picked it up, shook it, examined – and himself got only the same dead tone when he dialled for her chauffeur.

"Dear me," he said. Then he called for his own car, which in an instant purred round a corner, its wiper blades sluggishly cutting two fine arcs through a violet film of rain. He drove her to central London, and escorted her up the hotel steps, thence to the concierge's desk. He passed her his card, should she require his help in any way again. A day later he received a bouquet of foil balloons, all plump with helium, and firmly secured to a magnum of champagne. Attached to this was a handwritten note of thanks. That, in a trailing hand, signed itself off as a slightly amused postscript, and told him that eventually her car *had* been found – alas a burnt-out wreck. The driver – a really cute blond boy working his way through school – hadn't been located.

He called her up. Emma wasn't there. He left a message with the concierge. Then *she* called *him*, with an invitation. This was to Melanie Klopp's laser installation, opening that night on a scrub of industrial wasteland, somewhere on the fringes of Camberwell.

That really clinched it. In the brief courtship that followed, Emma records – and again I allude to that memoir – so many of Aimé's eccentric English ways, to her a charm and delight. For example, he reserved the ascent of restaurant steps for the final caress of his pockets, only to discover, belatedly, that his wallet must have been left in the creases of yesterday's tweeds. Or how many times had she been in a cocktail lounge, among friends, with Aimé, picking up the bill, then folding in it on the salver the last of his gold-plated credit cards, which the waiter returned only moments later... Cough! "Beg pardon, sir... your card has expired – "

"Good heavens, so it has!"

4

Portraits that once adorned the interiors of Ix, and are now safely in a local vault, show Martin to be tall, lean and baggy-trousered (or 'troisered', as Aimé would say). Emma is floral and dreamy. The wedding was a society do, with the reception taking place at one of her daddy's several mansions – this one in upstate New York. Incidentally one of the faxes, read out by Balliol old boy Sir Christian James (one of Aimé's student partners in an abortive property deal), was from that cute blond holiday chauffeur, who having read the notices in the London press wished the couple well (without explaining how he had lost Emma's car, and what he had done afterwards).

As usual, on the honeymoon cruise, Aimé was caught without cash.

5

Emma insisted that the marital home must offer scope to the interests and stimuli the partnership had sparked. Various ruins in southern Europe were looked at (with no disrespect to the English climate), with nothing at all suitable cropping up until – incredible luck – the changes wrought on that particular continent delivered her the perfect playpen. The ancient family Maqueda – at that time headed by Javier Maqueda – who for centuries had lived under the mountains of Ix, fell foul of a bureaucratic tangle in Brussels. One of those many commissions – at that time prevalent and powerful – decreed that the mountain spring water that was treated, bottled, given a hint of peach, and distributed from the Maquedas' factory at Ix (an industry that had long assured employment for hundreds, if mostly indirectly), did not meet the multiplicity of standards set out in the official slabs of Federal documentation. Javier, who by then was a seedy fifty-year-old, and not inclined to change his ways, went on with his processes just as before, to the point of refusing the visiting inspectorate one inch of room over his threshold (I use that measure nostalgically). Notices were served. Javier not only failed to back down, but formed his own political party, with a manifesto declaring as its central aim the restoration of all Europe's sovereign states, the return of a mysterious English concept known as subsidiarity, and eventually full autonomy for each member nation. Sadly for him his family coffers were not sufficient for what became a lengthy campaign. As a conclusion – after all the many years that this dragged on – Europe's free press apprised us of one thing only. This was nothing more than Javier's own spiteful obsession, driving him into the footnotes of history, where he died in penury, a man socially unfulfilled.

6

I find my detachment wavers, approaching that industrious phase of the Martins' memoir, a book these days acquired *only* through the well stocked libraries of Ix. By this I mean those early years of restoration. High levels of unemployment all over the civilised world meant labour was cheap. You wouldn't think so, when both Emma and Aimé insist that electricity charged their surrounding air, with happy bands of workmen – all dedicated to Emma's ideal – all plying their rosy trades. These were her stonemasons, carpenters, wrought-metalworkers, not to say fine artists in filigree and gold leaf. (It has to be said too, as a matter of observation, there are a great many floor mosaics and ceiling frescos here at Ix.)

Aimé called on another of his Balliol old boys, Anthony Purefoy, MBE (anachronistic titles were allowed to remain, for the lifetime of their holders – as I am sure you know). Stylistically, Purefoy engaged an unusual if charming blandness, his sights set infallibly on the genteel coffee tables of the then United Kingdom, and produced a book – with sumptuous colour plates – recording the renovation and 'great experiment' that 'bore the name' of Ix. Again I refer to the prodigious libraries not too long a walk from my office door, and find that our own copy – whose title is *The Restoration Of Ix* – yields a handwritten epigraph from Purefoy himself, clearly penned a great many years after his labour:

Emma – re-living that privilege called Ix. Fond memories. Your Tony

In the book's introduction, Purefoy notes that a commission that should have taken him no more than two years, in fact took twelve. I imagine a great deal more research was involved than he at first anticipated, a task *anyone* would weary of. Evidently, some of his sources, and most of their authors, didn't quite have the necessary grasp, relying too much on a vague if hopeful architectonics, with terms like 'superb Gothic arch', or 'fabulous rose window'. What he does understand, and is very tactful about, is the Martins' aesthetic, a couple who, taking on the Maquedas' ruin (perhaps dampish even in Javier's reign), rebuilt it Disney-style. Therefore what was once developed by Moorish workmen under Christian supervision, is now a kind of catalogue of Hollywood eclecticism – Bavarian towers capped off with slate cones, medieval courtyards, abundant enamel decorated *cloisonné*, an emphasis on twisted columns, sweeping stone stairways awaiting only swashbucklers and camera crew… and so on.

Emma's advances into human science saw the conversion of state and function rooms into studios and lecture theatres, and where the floor plan allowed, into stage and auditoria. Where the Maquedas' retainers had had their quarters, the Martins installed up-to-date plumbing and all the latest bedroom fitments, so that, within a decade, when Ix began to flourish – and as more or less complete in its major refurbishment – it offered a wide range of residential courses. Here are just some whose titles appear in an old sales document I have come across:

1) Harmonising Relationships

2) Circle Dance, Song, Community

3) Art and Psychodrama

4) Yoga for the Over-50s

Another, 'The Sacred Art of Clowning', is advertised at half-price. A typical day is described so:

> Early morning: meditation, exercise, yoga, dance or similar. 9.00-9.45 a.m.: breakfast. 9.45-10.00 a.m.: community meeting. 10.00-1.00 p.m.: course group session. 1.30-2.30 p.m.: lunch. 2.30-6.00 p.m.: free time. 6.00-7.00 p.m.: group dance, games, exercise, singing or other complement to main course. 7.30-8.30 p.m.: dinner. 8.30-late: free time.

The disenfranchised – those at that time without work, and accordingly without economic power – perhaps had to be excluded additionally by the presence of castle machicolations. For there has been no civil war in Federal Europa. Nor will there be (you can bet your bottom Eurodollar).

7

Aimé's slight unease I attribute to his rootedness in the English system of establishment, which had shown its flab for several generations, and was all but moribund, once the royal family

9

decided to retire. That, I recall, if only a boy at the time – with Euroleague soccer predominantly on my mind – was amid scandal and recrimination, and all took place in the shadow of two teenage suicides. This was the so-called 'woodland pact' or double hanging, that little fork in history by which the problems of succession happily neutralised themselves. In the end it was academic anyway, protocol surrounding a third sibling and potential boy king naturally fizzing out.

Did this play on Aimé's mind? I know only that the last male Martin publicly applauded his spouse's endless energy, though I suspect watched darkly from an upper casement while she barked out her orders over the building sites of Ix. Under the brashness of all that megaphonic Americanness, huge landmarks of human potential mushroomed into life. A procession of visiting professors – still only ever the representatives of one social group displacing another – preached a new-style entertainment for the benefit of all their paying students, here to liberalise themselves in the punctuated grind of office life, with its pension and mortgage commitment. I can frame Aimé's ascent to the summit of one of those stagy stairways, all lit up in an angular evening crossbeam, under the slight tremor of a chandelier, and ask myself how often would he hear some Orphic chant going on, careful to avoid the filter of lemon light cascading from an open studio door, thence trickling across and up a stone wall.

8

Despite Aimé's distance from London and its life, his first plan for a new theatre – a Bayreuth of its day – attracted attention through that city's press. His own rough sketches were passed to Emma's architect, on the unseen condition that, with *her* intervention, his design was transposed from its original (nineteenth-century) to her own (post-millennium) rationalisation. I have seen both blueprints. Here I interject, because, among the many photographs available for inspection in the Martin archive, none is more puzzling than that married pair, each with a foot to the theatre's foundation stone. There is a hint of false authority in Aimé's slight stoop.

Emma's straight spine is a model of rigidity. Her arms akimbo are a vanquisher's. The sun is in her hair.

Aimé planned a *Ring* for the theatre's May opening, and was not overridden – though to Emma, Wagner, if quaint, was *passé*.

9

Nor did Aimé wait to be solicited. He sorted through his best morning suits, and pursued, through his web of social contacts, a first English Wagner – man he wished to see wreathed, and on a pedestal, and in a niche, and somewhere here, in his Ixy Bayreuth. Best candidate was Sir Oscar Barb, who incidentally, with the official stamp on Europe's full integration, renounced his New Year's honour (though by a bureaucratic gaffe left its mark on his letter heads) – then vied successfully for post of EU Composer Laureate. The appointment proved a great tonic for the far-sighted Emma, though I am certain Aimé had reservations. Barb's scores were known for their textual ingenuity, while bearing a parallel seed – not so common now as then – that made them hugely complex for the listener.

Barb's Ix *première* was a time-based piece, an operetta called *Hawking*. It has seen mixed fortunes since. It isn't much played, but survives under the assiduous lamplight of students and musicologists the world over. It was scored in nine sections (or IX, as Oscar frequently corrected), and involved wind ensemble, dustbin lids, pre-recorded whale song, plus a great deal of pantomime (one male, one female, one indeterminate – all garbed as Harlequin). A series of dissonances – unmistakably Oscar – accompanied the trio, who sat, or rather writhed, in suspended hoops, which in accordance with Oscar's performance notes were arranged on the three points of an equilateral triangle, vertex uppermost. At the mid-point of Section V the vertex is lowered, so that the triangle now has its *base* uppermost. From this point the score is repeated, backwards (how one clashes dustbin lids in reverse is difficult for the untrained musically – persons such as myself – to comprehend, though I'm sure it can be done). The technician at the control desk, whose sole charge is those whale tapes, has a feat of co-ordination (rendered much simpler in later years through digital techniques). I may add that there is, not surprisingly, a literary precedent, which is fulsomely acknowledged by Oscar himself, a nice geometric piece by JL Borges, called *The Plane Serif*.

Sir Oscar's tenure at New Bayreuth (as he himself referred to it) was long and influential. A school developed under the Barb name, taking in students, who were mainly Japanese. A generous EUA fund ensured that many working-class Europeans passed through his portal, some of whom turned out scores that the maestro himself would *première*. He produced one new opera per year, directed a *Parsifal*, a *Tannhäuser* (twice), an 'experimental' *Meistersinger* (Emma at this time interested in stage lights and nudity), and conducted briefly at Ix's first festival of new music. (All this in addition to his other engagements.) On that same festival's tenth anniversary, Florence Martin – fruit of Emma's forty-year-old loins – was a babe of six months. Sir Os kept up his attendance to that one infant of wonder all through those early years and beyond, and waxed at his most poetic when dedicating numerous opus numbers to her alone. One-four-six is, for example, a book of songs, whose collective title reads: *For my itsy-bitsy Ixy pixie* – in my opinion lieder not quite suited to the nursery.

The whole thing got over-complicated when, as a robust girl of fourteen, he insisted on visiting her Swiss mountain school, where he coaxed her out of hours, usually with rum-coloured milk-shakes and a particularly sickly chocolate gateau. Emma regarded such niceties as charming, on reading of these in Florence's perfectly formed hand, though of course Aimé grew morose. He finally levelled certain accusations, which, to coincide with those tabloid revelations I have already outlined (that dignified response to the newly published *Our Love Affair With Ix*), resulted in only a sharp rebuke from Emma. (In her view, Aimé must have considered that limousine trick plain dirty, since in all their years of married life never had he asked *her* for oral favours.) In the blazing row that followed, it came out that perhaps Sir Oscar was merely showing natural paternal love. All this took the form of rumour (various ex-retainers of Ix published articles and even in some cases books), which as a hard-working thirty-five-year-old I took little notice of at the time – even though as gossip it was spectacularly fuelled.

There was an eighteen-month separation, for professional reasons, which was all later, and meticulously explained. Nothing must despoil Ix's mythology.

10

I shan't tax you with too much more of this. The point I have to make is one of communication. In human terms – I mean as generation speaks unto generation – the Martins parcelled everything up as a legacy. I am expected to whisper, as the 'key' for all common stock, and in the cloistered chambers of history, after so many things where the name Emma shall touch my lips. What is infinitely more remote is that whole groups should garb up mystically, to shout hosannas into the vaulted height of Emma's 'new way'. That, apart from its arts and crafts, and the assumption of Aimé's family pedigree, finally found its perpetuity through the refinements of Florence's education. Florence, the prototypical being, whose mission would be one of promulgation.

There are several things wrong with moments like these. Firstly the Martin 'experiment' was not unique. Case in point is this, that as much as three years before Florence was born, the media king Craig Diamond came in as a late entrant to the Benbrook College of Performing Arts, where many of Emma's 'ideas' flourished independently. Second – and I will stretch these objections no further – by the time Florence came to have *her* say, the whole rig-up must have looked brutish and medieval. At the age of twenty-four, that golden girl was a multi-linguist, operated finance over all five continents, could quote Shakespeare (unlike her ma), had had serious fallings-out with Sir Ossie, and was on the point of earthly marriage. This was to a corporate lawyer, a man who invested much of his self-made wealth in cereal products. 'Art', it has to be said, was altogether a different kind of lottery.

Florence was moved, I have no doubt, at the temporal precision of her mother and father's death, a last conjugal event that occurred across a span of five years. Aimé went first, Emma followed, that length of time later – both at the age of sixty-six. *His* demise was after a last painful thrashing at the hand of hostile fates, when a kind of animal verdigris, or highly disfiguring cancer of the skin (Aimé too much in the sun) finally carried him off. Emma fell serenely asleep on a bench in her azalea dell – that place a concentration of mollis, Ghent, Kurumes and Exbury hybrids – with three lines and a trailing ellipsis freshly written in her notebook. From these is formed an inscription, chiselled in a whirl of shadows, over the plunging steps to the family vault:

I hope I shan't have to say so again

11

Florence called an end, by which I mean that the engines and the many personnel subsumed in the Martin 'plan', were dismantled or disposed of. All permanent lecturers received a golden pay-off, even those who had faked their qualifications. I was not myself party to talks, which on Florence's side were led by her, and called to the table an entire retinue – such is her office, such are her specialisms – and whose negotiations ended in the purchase of Ix, by and for the state. I did spend one joyous afternoon being escorted – though not alone with Miss Martin – round the grounds and through much of the interior. Precious hours of conversation! Even now I can't help reflect (twelve years on, in a pinkish glow of satisfaction) that the rare education her parents had heaped on her, for the purpose of advancing Ix's arts, had in fact curtailed them. At some studio or other, where a light was detached from its rig, she fingered its amber filter, and declared that the next shade was red. She was solemn, when she came to a certain bench, that last point of vantage from which a worn-out Emma surveyed the solids of her vision. Sole scion of the Martin line, her natural auburn having turned to bronze at a recent Alpine resort, she became slightly ashen on skirting the family vault – in all its rococo scrolls – a place where she herself would never come to rest.

There were other poignant moments. I found none more enigmatic than those bound up in her links with Sir Oscar, person known to be highly displeased at her decision to divest herself of Ix (or perhaps more tellingly, of all that Ix represented). Certain props backstage at New Bayreuth had obvious secret meanings. I remember she blushed slightly to her ear lobes on finding, upended, the well crafted model of a huge gilded fireplace, the kind Sir Ossie often used as dramatic focus, his technique so very minute in its demand for historic transplants – which saw for example an eighteenth-century salon displaced into the nuclear world of his music. She sneezed at the reddish dust on an Attic backdrop, this, as I later found out, intrinsic to what were called the 'Maastricht-Nice' scenes in his operetta *Bazar*. She scoffed, visibly, at the fractured arm of a plaster Pan. She recoiled at a photographic reproduction of Olympia (the Manet one), whose black cat is much like one I have seen in those family albums associated with Florence's early years in Switzerland. She lit one of her short cigars abruptly, and in a brief flash of gold snapped shut her lighter, on stumbling on a canapé, where perhaps Oscar had dandled her on his knee – once, when Florence was a girl, and his hands were free to roam. Yet, there was no more significant gesture than the one in the foyer, all square pillars and free-standing ashtrays, where she called immediately for the removal of a brass plate, a little tarnished by then, but still clearly inscribed: OPENED BY OSCAR BARB, IN THE PRESENCE OF CHANCELLOR SCHEIDT.

Oscar's theatre itself, far from the red plush, woodwork and stucco, or the tiers of regal balconies Aimé conceived, we planned to adapt as a seminar room (perhaps resembling one of those old public cinemas). I invited Florence back, when I had thought up a first lecture here – what with all kinds of virtual aids – to be delivered by our own team of architects, on the proposed restructuring of so many of Ix's chambers. I wanted her to have the chance to voice objections. In her prompt and very polite reply, she declined.

It is regrettable, but I have not met Florence since.

12

I owe this latest revisit (to your handover notes) to Miss Ashley, whose qualities of organisation are impeccable, and for whom dictation is also a matter of study, not merely the translation from one medium to another. (Therefore thank you, Miss A!) She points out over one of her marvellous Danish pastries that certain loose ends, in my account of the Martins here at Ix, have still to be tied up, and for that reason what would have propped up that 12 (above) is deferred to 13. This is a number that haunts me.

Let us take them in order:

1) Martin, a defunct Swiss composer. I refer to Frank Martin, 'defunct' in the sense of his present absence musically in Europe's major performing venues. Under the general strains of the world's Oscar Barbs, not much else gets a look in, coupled with the view that things of the past are things that are done with. Even so, there is a vacuous ring to it when one neophyte or another sounds the same cliché: Aside, please! The future is me! However this is all beside the point. When it became known, through whispers and rumours, that a man called Aimé Martin was about to build a New Bayreuth, somehow it got to a sloppy press office that this must be a descendant of Frank. Our apologies to that other line, should it still thrive.

2) Emma's blond chauffeur (or rather nowadays a distinguished shade of snow). His name is Malcolm Polloon. I once met him, in his capacity of Director of the Institute of Genetic Copyright, in Basle, though it wasn't till Emma's obituary appeared that I was able to make that connection. Among the many bouquets and tributes following her demise, was a paragraph by Dr Polloon, in which he referred to that Whitechapel episode. In my references above, it's this that I've paraphrased.

3) Anthony Purefoy, MBE. I would not myself have viewed the absence of this note as an omission. Miss Ashley mentions that Purefoy composed Emma's funeral oration, though didn't so much as attend Aimé's interment. Purefoy died last year, and was entombed in his native Berks – a village whose name escapes...

4) A filter of lemon light. On my many lone escapades among the redundant studio spaces of Ix, I have often puzzled at the predilection for lemon filters (apropos of the lighting rigs) that must have been common to the many teachers of theatre and dance. Florence Martin herself – although in quite a different context – obliquely referred to this, shading those filters amber, according to *her* colour charts – doubtless for the linguistic association with stop-light red (her emphasis being *stop*).

13

Now. A slight blow to my plans. And is it that 13 that haunts me? The minister, who is only now in transit – between Strasbourg and, as it happens, Lisbon – tells me she's not been able to take the necessary soundings concerning my (or your) post, which I'm shortly to vacate (and you commence). She puts it down to pressure of work. Furthermore her choice three candidates cannot for either personal or professional reasons make themselves available for interview. This, I understand, is a temporary situation. I am nevertheless invited to a private view of what she not quite accurately terms 'Louis XVI artefacts' – to include, according to an attached inventory, a silver soup tureen, 'apparently made for Don José of Portugal, by François-Thomas Germain'. This is the kind of event at which much of our business is discussed. That tureen by the way is highly ornate. Perhaps this is an appropriate point to pause, with a little background sketch, say…

Background and history of monitor's post

My name is Anno, and only my mother is English. My father, until his life and career were tragically cut short by a bomb, had connections with German diplomacy, and had applied for a post in the EU Trade Commission. His refined, if severe physiognomy, was in contrast to his large peasant hands, which were calloused. He was a committed European, which (indirectly) was the reason for his death. By chance he was striding across the lichened flagstones of the Europlaz, in rebuilt Berlin, away from its leonine fountain, and towards a pharmacy (which must have meant one of his migraines). What was ostensibly a decorator's transit van, packed not with paint but explosives, did its work on the stroke of one, bringing down three façades plus a rain of concrete, onto the square. There was, I recall from the news flash, a burst water main, or background slash of silver, and a chorus of shop sirens. As a matter of indifference to the newscaster, there were twelve fatalities, and later, in hospital, a thirteenth. That was the 'miracle', according to one spokesman, who in a hard yellow hat and astride the rubble offered his retrospect for an early evening magazine programme (a man accustomed to higher tolls). I therefore locate to this precise moment, aged ten, and wearing lederhosen (all stitched oak leaves and red and green piping), my first mental notes on the numbing, and ultimately destructive power of the media.

1

We revisited my mother's roots. Here she returned to first school teaching (after what I now suspect could not have been an easy re-training programme, the politics of education having changed it over time). Our quiet hamlet in the southeast of England was still at that time untouched by the flamboyant satellite mogul, whose name... whose name I shan't have to refer to, in one of those ancient year books (example of which Miss Ashley has found anyway, a red glossy)... whose name was Robbie McGregor. The polychrome empire that that New Zealander spawned is now in the hands of his two introspective grandsons, whom I personally have no dealings with (nor would I, given the labyrinthine structures of commerce).

My own schooling, in the shifts of further policy change, was largely inconclusive, and was granted in a sprawl of flat-roofed buildings. These I was able to view in miniature from the pliant, and often windy tip of a sycamore tree, organ having outstripped several other saplings under the banks of our terraced garden. My preoccupation was my mountain bike, which, for a life run generally in isolation, made remote villages accessible, and so also made possible a circle of friends. There were, of course, the last vestiges of public provincial transport, which subsisted at the rate of approximately one passenger per bus, owing to the prevailing fare strategy (at the best of times a star-lit phantasy). My obsession was news – or rather truth, as one divined it from the news. (Such is the offended morality of youth.) From my perspective now in Ix, I know this had its origin in the half-dozen years that now clumped by, without, as they fell away, any satisfactory explanation as to that bomb. I had anticipated – and not as pawn, as a much higher denomination – some unifying piece, whose square was a central square, and whose command was the entire chequer board, by which I was apt to make sense of the world (which inconveniently wasn't black and white). There were leftist groups, just as there were factions of the Right, and there was always speculation as to the various strategies adopted at the Europhobe extremes. However. That bomb was the first of many. Initially, no one claimed responsibility – then every lunatic imaginable phoned the press.

2

Was there a need to be rescued? Strangely that was more a maternal question, to which house parties were an attempted resolution. All I recall is a festoon of lime and sky-blue crêpe, and a range of vegetarianism – eggish and mozzarella flans, pasta salads, rice and cucumber cubes in whirls of mayonnaise. At the centre of each dressed table was an ornamental carafe, with peach water newly imported from the mountains of Ix (whose distant blossom I had dreamed of only). Under day- or porch-light, a not very adoring son marked the usual procession of portly business people, other grey teachers, youngish or oldish couples. These were from our neighbouring chalets, whose arms were intertwined or who tottered on sticks. There was a different dark-eyed beauty every time, from the campus and faculties of Canterbury, whose coat or knitted cardigan I removed to a divan in the spare room upstairs (where I think I was half-expected to unleash my young manhood, one day soon).

I did not, even under that bright empyrean, have any new inclination for tertiary education, whatever the nubility of Canterbury, and however visceral a modern pilgrimage would be. Yet that crisis did resolve itself, one sullen afternoon in spring, when with the vague suggestion or sniff of salt in the air, news of another bomb, more destructive than any hitherto, interrupted our screens. Politically, this meant nothing (to me). Psychologically, I found it unbearable.

The target, the ENN Tower (London), later rebuilt on the Isle of Dogs – bigger and better equipped than its continental nodes – had somehow drifted into various breaches in security, the bomb being a car bomb planted in the basement, a parking zone supposedly reserved for network personnel. I thought this all through, rather aimlessly, in the wooded lanes of Capel, and entered (even then I thought foolishly) an ill-chosen syllabus. That gave me my first degree (in media studies), and took me, suspiciously, and under a pseudonym, a long way from home. By then no one of course escaped the sticky marine tentacles – how that name oozes out of me now, now that I've allowed its first trickle! – those false limbs tacked to that moral entrepreneur, who called himself, but not his television empire, Robbie McGregor. That man had a screen and decoder in every club or hotel, which at the swipe of a credit card slurred into choreographed life, some gold-encrusted singer, or the sunshine flicker of trans-continental field sports. Nor did

McGregor's deep urge to communicate preclude him from our insulated English squares, later all our village greens, and almost at once my own college refectory – where those empowered by the largesse of parents and the slops of a collective mind, tuned in to studio quiz shows.

Great days.

3

I hate to intrude like this. Yet I cannot help operate, in all these crossed t's and dotted i's, through the levers of hindsight. There is apparently nothing, in all the green retrospects of campus life, with its sprinkle of old stone and new concrete, the end and the destination of a long winding driveway, whose single track has its passing-points for cars, is pastured through its ascent, and is lined with mature beech trees to the opposite bank, to the declivity. Nor did I play my active role in its smoke-filled lounges, all a litter of ashtrays and plastic coffee cups, under the wings of various handwritten obscenities, penned as the defiant annotation to practically every missive pinned in good faith to the notice boards (often remaining there for months). Here I did no more than probe an atmosphere, thick with the dissenting gloam of student politics, its pockets of resistance, its rebels both leaders and led, all of whom turned out in the same energetic logogram, and who signalled their fraternity in fatalistic hand-to-wrist clasps. Oh yes, I do so hate to intrude (yet could not have planned for my future life in any keener way). I raised problems, not for the child politicos – all of them in any case unclear, and driven by English classism – but for what I gradually saw revealed.

This wasn't an easy time for our prevailing propagandists. For institutions like mine, that meant an augmenting team of assessors, all of whom had been secretly staffed externally. I remember just some of those moments. For example a late night in the technology centre, a facility impossible to book during the hours of daylight. All students were ranked as secondary, and could or would not impinge on the private curricula of college 'research'. This was no more than a handful

21

of tutors, formed as a loose collective, and inspired by the many new opportunities in a pan-Europe marketplace. Here as ever only a glass screen separated my lone (if reflected) person from the moonlit gardens and courtyard (silvered salvias, wooden patio furniture magically powdered white, etc.). What caught in my peripheral vision, first as a Nabokovian moth, helplessly attracted to the light, then as a drunken intruder having blundered from the bar, in fact was a visitor specifically looking for me. It was a good night for nothing. He told me his name – something like John Frame – but not his occupation, though I guessed it as tweedy and academic, from the dun of his sports jacket (which under the dimmed spots over the control panel was flecked with blue indigo). My proposal for the work I was doing now, an audio debate, with my own massaged voice adopting all four parts (three male, one female), had been passed from my tutor to him, and had not come back from his office without discussion. 'Which office is that?' I might have asked – this the forerunner of many such questions (to which for a whole term the answers were evasive). As such there were 'no objections', I was so glad to hear, to my chosen parameters of debate, whose programme title was *Terrorism and the Shaping of New Europe*. Though a taped copy of my final piece would be listened to without censorship, implicit was the shadow of scrutiny, the obvious fact that all I now did would be monitored.

My next 'interested' party was glamorous and behaved coquettishly, and had a propensity for half-zipped or partly buttoned blouses. Her snakish tongue cleverly protruded in a rouge of strawberry at one or other corner of her mouth (which it was, depended on the moment's profile). She had 'looked at' my playlet – *Europe, or Zeno's Half Measures* – a witty fabrication of politics and geometry, a point not lost on her. Here on this particular occasion she offered further insight into those zips and pneumatics, complement bolstered by the specifics of her undergarments, in themselves a feat of engineering, which I did later look at – rather gloomily – when she enticed me into her lair, and had her wicked way. On that cloudless night she vouchsafed but one scent of lust among the many tilted mirrors round the powder keg of her couch, on the radiance of which she groaned and articulated – the climax well chosen – to the effect that the Zeno dialogue had not a comparable thrust. It was, she said, socially impotent – 'though nevertheless we're watching…'.

That one warm night under the starry glow of her skylight offered no presentiment of the series of cold mornings that followed, the first of which was slightly damp. Here I saw ushered in a pallid henchman in the John Frame mould, a man whose dawn ritual inflicted a cross-stitch of nicks on his large square chin, which otherwise was closely shaven. He was, I recall, wonderfully clean, boffin-like and tribal, casual in his casual wear – that official garb through which he prinked himself. The jacket, in cream and navy checks… A rubiginous necktie, with sandy seaside stripes… There was, I now muse, a maroon tint to his spectacles, two shady pools of light, in some way preternaturally detached in the shop reflection by which he adjusted himself. A rusty heap at the roadside was his. For my part, I'd cycled into town (this was my same Capel mountain bike, which I ensnared on a lamp-post). The shop where I encountered him – or rather the threshold he followed me across – was an antiquarian bookseller's, place where I always came to raise money, on this occasion with a pannier of tenth-hand Nietzsches. He flicked through them on the counter so soon as I had exchanged them for cash (sum I drank away that night, in a dive called Gossips, a wine bar where I wrote my monthly letter home), and informed me immediately that now he knew by what means I had fabricated my last essay, which had not strictly speaking conformed to the brief. Seminars at that time were under the general rubric 'Cultural Studies', all with a media slant.

That letter home is again in my possession, and shows that by this third visitor – John Frame, the nymph, the sartorial Frame-ite – I knew them not to be 'assessors' in any academic sense, but agents of the state (on the lookout not, as I had assumed, for subversives, rather for recruits). I asked him for ID. He gave it. I told him my Nietzsche piece was a trite web of puns, taking for sport the second law of thermodynamics, in combination with that insane notion of recurrence the German had put a theory to, and which whole bundle I had offered up only as a test to the gullibility of the marking tutor.

"I shall ensure you get a low grade," he said, but laughed.

One other letter in my possession, in the deliberate, ardent hand of my student years – and in a slightly faded turquoise ink – lingers suspiciously on what it appears was precisely the reverse result.

I can remember watching him disappear, towards the newly rebuilt state highway (the E38, should you have your map), in a rust-coloured cloud of exhaust, with its explosion of timing faults. I cannot remember the car exactly, which was green, and a cabriolet, and belonged to the last century. It bore one of the then new Euro licence plates. He knew, I think, that all roads lead to Ix. I hardly need say that correspondence in the other direction – i.e., from Capel to Benbrook Height – advised caution, since one had to set against the colourful backdrop of almost any 'exciting' era (my mother's cadence falling short of the obvious 'witness the Europlaz')… or what she meant to say was this: I had, hadn't I, to be aware, at least of the possibility of danger, however remote it seemed, and also be sure of at least one hot meal per day, what with winter round the corner…

4

The procession of Frame-ites culminated not, curiously, in one further sample of that caste, but with a genteel, thinly haired, middle-aged, and paternal representative of its team (where seniority in years was not necessarily seniority of rank). He wore a green woollen suit with a centre-button waistcoat. He calmly seated himself at the window table I had chosen for myself one late lunch-time in the refectory, with its wintry panorama over the naked shrubs outside. Through the irregular smears where I had dabbed and wiped at the condensation, I made out more distantly – since at first I ignored him – the white confection blanketing the hilly farmland enclosing the college boundary. Term had not yet ended, although already scores of students had made their

24

way home for Christmas. Only other company was a trio of sophomores, at a table slopped in spilt milk, who passed round the hot belated butt of a last cigarette, and had somehow got an old Charlie Chaplin cartwheeling idiotically on the McGregor screen. Odd guffaws. A rotund char in a voluminous white cape and matching hat, and with two cherry blobs of kitchen heat gummed to her cheeks, emerged from the swelter of her habitat and watched that clown for a minute or two, before returning, a slight shudder of laughter shaking the flab of her shoulders. Cue for my grey angel of destiny, who smoothed a slightly curved palm over the thinning strands of hair brushed back from his forehead, and remarked on the view – or what a bucolic retreat this was, complete with peasantry. He put down his fake ID on the table.

"Oh," I said. "You're one of them."

He replied: "That *could* be to your advantage," though this I doubted. "What, Anno, we don't want," he said, talking academically, "in fact what we never want, is too complete a graduate..."

"Who's "we"?"

"Do call me John."

"Who, John, is "we"?"

"Never mind that now. A solid 2:1, Anno, is to us more attractive than a first, which tends to bring with it all the problems of individualism."

"I'll try, John, to bear that in mind... How did you know my name is Anno?"

Quite how seriously it was intended I should take this did not become evident – and anyway dissipated itself in the absence of any further visits – until the close of that academic (and my last) year. My dissertation, whose subtitle I settled on more or less at the outset, and which never changed (*Hieratic vs the Demotic*), prompted several unscheduled meetings by the assessment board, which I assume were chaired by a Frame-ite. First job I shouldered, under my introductory heading – so to speak to set the pace for the sixty-odd thousand words that followed – was a clear distinction of the two (the hieratic, and demotic). Ironically I achieved this through reference to a care-

25

ful selection of late twentieth-century novelists, such as held sway through the English broadsheet review pages, who as fraternity had intentionally confused the two. I can behold even now the spectre of all these dynastic writers, trash I identify in the kind of articles already glossed over in the Martin family, whose position is secured not by any qualitative criteria, but by the thoroughness of a marketing strategy. The demotic – or from my standpoint, the *shoddy* (book or film) – becomes the hieratic, by virtue of an accepted, strictly mercantile priesthood, a kind of secular henotheism, to which the whole fraternity of writers, publishers, promotions and newspaper people belong (and who form a cultural conurbation, incidentally, that they come to believe in as central). However. This is getting off the point. The problem for the board (as I surmised) was how to award a 2:1, where a first was merited. When, later, I appealed (at the inevitable 2:1), the reply bore the stamp of officialdom, and an illegible signature. This reached me in a Bavarian guest house where I had come for a fortnight's rest, and caused me mild amusement one morning over my warm crispy breakfast roll. It was thought that although my whole student oeuvre demonstrated certain insights, my inability to stick to the brief must, in the final analysis, count against me. The thing closed off with a *Yours sincerely*, in part obliterated by a spiral of pen strokes, dashed down on the page in a mortician's black ink.

5

I regretted my choice, madly, sadly, profoundly, if at all times it seemed informed – that's to say, the study of 'culture' having evolved to the formulaic analysis of one or two popular artefacts – the TV script, similarly the blockbuster 'novel', should it have movie potential. At this point my mother remarried, and moved from Capel to Elsinore (Colorado). I wasn't invited to the ceremony, which was low-key – though I nevertheless sent her best wishes by fax. In reply she ringed in red crayon a handful of ads she had detached from a weekly appointments page. Dutifully, I prepared my CV. Later I applied for, and was astonished to be offered, a position in the ENN newsroom (Paris) – which akin to field events took me through three rounds of interview. Perhaps predictably this line of work didn't really suit (I lasted less than a year), my argument (my lost argument) always being with one or other pipe-smoking editor, who upheld policy unswervingly, by which I mean that the accent on even the most minor news story had to fall in line with McGregor diktat. This was the market avatar whose lexicon of commerce, at least right across Europe, we saw as something not new, but – by means of his own satellite network – ubiquitous (and as it now turns out not quite omnipotent, so many competitors having emerged over the years). In recent times he had changed from Right to Left, Toryism generally seen as fatigued, and flawed by its decades of power and cynicism. A new political artifice was on the horizon, over which McGregor's pristine sun should also rise (flag being already there, four white stars on a radish-coloured backcloth).

6

There were certain compensations – or rather there were two – i.e. the brace of tickets passed to me in a chalk-blue envelope for the men's final at Roland Garros, marked WITH COMPLIMENTS. The laurel was contested that year by the five-times champ, the Dutchman Patrick Muhren, and an American upstart, a sour-faced Artie Rensburg – son of a son of a soap star. My companion for that quiet Sunday, who smiled to be offered my second ticket, was a mousy-haired, inquisitive girl from the communications centre at ENN – whose name I recall as either Hildy or Hilde. She had gorged herself on certain rosy dreams, all of which had imprinted in her mind an ideal, strong, and very wiry Muhren – who for once shaved for the big occasion. I discovered, earlier in the week, under the swags of a café awning, how slightly Hildy's forecast had to do with his slow-surface pedigree (Muhren, virtually invincible on clay), and was fabricated on the openness and honesty of his features, and of course the bed-time lure of his athleticism.

In the first set, not quite won to love (6-1, Muhren, for which again I owe thanks to Miss Ashley), Hildy had no reason to doubt the anticipated outcome. Rensburg – whose coach for that first twenty minutes or so sat there quietly depressed – made consistent errors on the many half-court balls, which – tactically correct – he continued to force wide off Muhren's backhand, not at its best for that entire fortnight. How predictable it got, the drive off Rensburg's sun-filled racquet, with hardly sufficient topspin to dip the ball inside the baseline. At last it occurred to him that something new was called for, and to facilitate the psychological re-start his new approach demanded, he changed his shirt between sets, one baggy lime-green number for another, trimmed with the same scarlet flashing, and the same loud chevrons attaching to his sponsor. One group of spectators below me caterwauled, while the rest of us merely marvelled at the depth of his tan. This was a shade of cocoa his promoters urged on him all year round, either in Monte Carlo or Florida, or in lieu of these through a private solarium.

In set two his inability to reach the net cost him several lengthy rallies, the one course in practically any encounter that would play to Muhren's strength – the Dutchman, a prosaic baseliner, but superfit. Rensburg nevertheless took it on a tie-break – this after an escalation of disputed line calls – which ended in a code violation (racquet abuse), and the sort of fine that matched my annual wage. The crippled racquet incidentally was one of several articles (his scarlet bandanna, his lime-tinted wrist bands being others) that he tossed to an adoring crowd on rounding off those gruelling five sets, which saw Muhren deposed, and heralded his early retirement, and which according to Miss Ashley read 1-6, 7-6, 7-5, 6-7, 10-8 – a statistic I vaguely recall through a Parisian haze of sunset. The racquet turned up, as it were in aspic, at an auction only a couple of years ago, when a 'decent' period had elapsed after Rensburg's death, which was reported world-wide. This was in Arizona, in an air traffic accident, at the tragically early age of sixty-one. Miss Ashley has flashed up the various accounts on her screen, which – all either lurid or sentimental – I certainly shan't refer to.

28

Hildy could not let the thing rest at match-point, which was taken by Rensburg with a mis-hit. That spinning yellow ball ballooned off the frame of the young pretender's racquet, completely wrong-footing a sullen-looking Muhren. Yet here Hildy found as unexpected soul-mate the rampant Robbie McGregor, for the sake of whose extremely lucrative satellite deal the tennis authorities had agreed to re-paint the courts a shade of nectarine, with the two alleys a complementing peach. The surrounding area was a very dilute pink. The screens were a silky vermilion. However, the occasion is more famous now not for its TV livery, but for a prototype system of undercourt sensors digitally linked to an off-site battery of microprocessors, and they in turn to a data storage system, to which Hildy had access. On the Monday she patiently downloaded Lord knows how many megabytes to her own office system, then roved round the network in search of proprietary software. By the Thursday she was able to reconstruct every ball played, and so compare each actual point won or lost with that awarded. She dragged me downstairs and planted me before her monitor, with a "There! You see!" and a painful smile, which animated all these labours. To her credit, those dubious line-calls, a mere blur of yellow over a fuzzy white stripe when replayed photographically, had favoured the well-behaved Muhren at uncritical moments only. For Rensburg they erroneously sealed two of his three sets.

"Okay. Fair comment," I said. "But. The world-weary Muhren was ready to fall." I knew this because he had overcome his twelve-year superstition, walking across and not around the tramlines at each change of ends.

7

At approximately 9.30 on the Friday after Hildy's moratorium, having spent one long and agonised evening in her studio apartment, to console the loss – over endless mugs of coffee, over a mountain of diced coconut – I drafted my letter of resignation. This I committed to the uncertainty of our internal mail system at the start of business, on Monday next. No response by Wednesday left me slightly tense; by Saturday, bemused. On Sunday I did get a reply (regrets, etc.), when I scanned and printed off my mail. I had decided first that I wouldn't, then that I would make this a possibility, through the network node I had long been urged to install at home. The comms outlets went under the skylights of my attic – a warm, sunny, pleasant place to work. Unusually (as it seemed) this had its origin (this memo had its origin) in the ENN Rome office, where I knew my co-ordinating director happened to be located – a man several echelons above me, whose likeness I knew only from a handful of photographs. In virtually the same transmission, I received 'confirmation' of my invitation to the château de Corveau, a misnomer left unexplained even when the card – its edges wavy, its lettering gold – arrived with the Monday morning post. There were also some bills to pay.

The château, noted for the flamboyance of its architecture – Gothic and Renaissance – offers an intricate façade in a lacework of granite, with its dormers and twisted posts. The occasion was a private exhibition of furniture and candelabra *à la Régence*, one of those many rich seams in European living that until now I had tried to avoid. One of several other guests was the political aide to the cultural attaché, who balanced his saucered slops and a very awkward cup of tea in his watch hand, while gesticulating with the rolled tube of his programme notes in the other. His features were gloomy and fierce – a sharp nose, a pout, a jutting chin, a Romantic melancholy moodily lighting his muddy brown eyes. He tried to ensnare me in conversation – once, under the sculpted panels of the dining room; a second and third time over some astonishing examples of marquetry and Chinese lacquer-work. When I left, under a hail and cloudburst, and a shower that darkened everything, he offered me a lift in his official car, which crooned up alongside us so soon as the words were uttered. I declined. His driver touched the peak of his cap, a salute he repeated several kilometres later on the F17, where *their* car overtook mine, at a point where I slowed for a turning to an *hypermarché*. At the checkout, about thirty to forty minutes later, with my few provisions for the evening, I saw that same caparisoned flunkey, checking his watch and scanning the customer notice board. He helped me to my car, carrying the baguette and cheap bottle of Muscadet I'd bought. That barrage of clouds, having gathered itself at Corveau, was now suddenly singed at the fluff of its fringes, and gave way slowly to a stream of yellowish sunshine, which at least one grateful citizen collected in the palm of his hand. Into mine, that chauffeur pressed his master's card.

8

Artie Rensburg turned up again, first at Barons Court (having paid the price in the previous year for flirting with grass, without any real preparation), then in late June at Wimbledon. Miss Ashley says he'd successfully defended the French. This I make relevant only in learning of delays, initially in finding, and now in appointing my successor – or you. (There is a memo on my desk I need to reply to.)

There's much I know I forget. I had though been briefly reunited with my mother, who had found a range of new interests in Elsinore, and had flown to London for a Bletsoe retrospective, painter whose immortality rests in a series of well rehearsed 'revivals'. I chanced on some of the supporting documentation through my investigation of Ryder Twill – which I still have hopes of passing on to you. "Some hopes!" – to quote Miss Ashley. But enough!

I had, soaking in the centre court drizzle, just now completed my second degree, at the School of Social and Cultural Studies, University of London. My tutor, a divorcée from Long Island, whose specialism was Eastern Europe (her papers included *The Rise of Belgrade*, which is still considered a classic), had seemed destined to manoeuvre me into the virginal whiteness of her boudoir, a chamber I frequently glanced into, through its open door, positioned as it was across the corridor from her kitchen, where after parties and soirées I found myself perched on a stool, as one of the stragglers. Once she held an open-air lunch, among the terracotta patios and the entwined green arbours dotted round her pool, or rather that sky-blue facility shared by all other tenants in her and in several other blocks of flats – orange façades and tinted glass. She insisted, a glossy mag protecting her face, that I rub barrier cream into her thighs, then that I take off my shirt (for how could I bear this heat!).

One spring morning we did loop arms, during a carefree ramble among the beeches of Chorleywood, where in a rising mist we exercised a young and very playful boxer-bitch she'd agreed to mind for a couple of days for two absent friends, who lived in a terraced house in Bushey. Her *real* interest ought to have been that much clearer to me one starry night in Grosvenor Square, where as token partner I got myself up in evening dress, and having left her car with a footman 'escorted' her – a hand to the sequinned small of her back – to a private dinner, where what I remember most is a monocled raconteur who repeatedly tapped his wine glass with a cigar trimmer. The next morning I picked up the phone, then momentarily put it down, in an involuntary recollection of her eyes – a sparkle of liquefied hazel – just as her gaze had met mine (most probably an icy blue). This, over a first cocktail.

Eventually I did make my call, and explained that at the start of that previous evening, a subdued crystal of light slanting from the windows, I hadn't consciously registered that lackey I tossed her keys to, and who parked her car – although now knew him as someone who'd approached me between Corveau and Paris. Nor had I recognised our host, whose card I'd destroyed, and whose name I had not even attempted to memorise. He had been recently hospitalised – this I overheard as small-talk – and in consequence was grey, and had lost a tremendous amount of weight, but I was now more or less sure had once been the political aide to the cultural attaché.

"What's going on?" I asked, an abruptness that instantly killed the accustomed drool of her telephone voice. She told me there was no conspiracy, not anyway as far as she knew, that these things I referred to must be coincidence. She wanted to make up, she said, and show me there was no sleight of hand (in itself dubious), therefore could we hug and once more be friends, and why not on centre court, Wimbledon, for which she had two tickets…

Among others we watched a fourth-round match, on a day disrupted by rain, which forced us into embraces and sultry conversation under the protection of her umbrella. It gave us Rensburg, unable to repeat his success at Queen's, bowing out in four sets to an unfancied Pole. A few days later, I set off alone for my Bavarian retreat.

9

McGregor was inescapable. That's to say it was now impossible to isolate any open space – a town square or village green – before a team of overalled technicians laid and connected a cable to one of those gigantic screens. As a 'development', these were now never blank, since in moments of temporary pause – i.e., when no transmission had been purchased – some clever member of his board had suggested putting up McGregor's profile. At that time this was craggy and hawkish.

Is it worthy of note that had it stopped short of our peasantry, I might just have found a rolling hillside on whose dirt track the potential for passing trade had been ignored? I had my doubts when it came to other extremes, such as a fortnight paddling up an Amazonian swamp, or beating a path through the exotic flora of one last jungle, even a safari expedition into the diminished wilds of Africa. Or would McGregor's footsteps also lead to an innermost sand, burning under a desert sun?

10

I watched one of his sloppy movies – a tale of how the communications industry was won – on a flight from London to Ix, where to 'supplement' my year in the Bloomsbury breeze, in the bosom of an on-off affair, I was invited to a 'conference'. This was at a private house, under the afternoon shadow of Castle Martin. The house itself was an old merchant's dwelling, having stone facings and deeply stained timbers. It had been refurbished throughout with peach marble flooring, ineffably welcome to touch, after the radiance of Ix's sun.

I don't know how to describe the 'conference', which took place initially on the neatly clipped sward to the rear of the house, directly below the yellowing, lichened wall of that steeply banked castle, all among the scent of peach blossom (a chance match to those floors inside).

Apart from myself – anyway unable to take it seriously – there were two junior ministers, their ministry being Culture, and one senior officer from its labyrinth of supporting bureaux – in this case, the Bureau of Data Protection. Amazingly, this was a trio who shared (or perhaps interchanged) an identical forename, John – where II and I were from the ministry, and III was their technician. Did they also invest in the surname Frame? (Blank looks.)

II sported a billowy shirt, whose sun-faded blueness he tucked into a malnourished waist. John I seldom ventured past the frontiers of his sun specs, which were mauve and reflective. III said "Aw!" in response to any question he was ill-inclined or felt it too indelicate to answer. Our parody of concord went along following lines:

"Frankly, Anno, it's this man McGregor…"

"We shall soon see him, John, struck with our Eurodollar."

"John here made that same joke, before you arrived."

"Great minds, John."

"Here comes Andrea with iced lemonade."

"To be honest, Anno, we've been watching you for quite some time."

"In the end you bait me with a frigid divorcée!"

"Aw now Anno!"

"Just there on that table, Andrea."

"But McGregor…"

"You're fretting, John, because he owns practically everyone."

"Now I wouldn't go that far, Anno."

"Lemonade?"

"Thank you, John."

"Soon. He will *soon* own everyone."

"He doesn't own you, John."

"Quite right, Anno. That is how we want it to remain."

"This lemonade is delicious."

"Would you like me to call Andrea? Would you like another glass?"

"Would that get us any more quickly to the point, John? I *can* call you John?"

"Here, Anno, we're all friends."

"Andrea's a marvellous girl."

"There is a post, Anno, which has not yet been created, but which we think would suit you to a T."

"Please do elaborate."

"John, Anno, John. Anno. Perhaps we should step inside, out of this sun."

"First I must go to the John, John. Too much lemonade."

11

I can't claim to have greatly influenced – other than being the person I am – the rationale by which this monitor's office was conceived. Its blueprint existed several years in advance of that 'conference' event fully intended for the framing of my signature. That tangle of black ink had scarcely left its reverse impression on the blotter when the four of us shambled up the hill to Castle Martin, all masquerading as casual visitors to its international summer school. Commercially that meant a complex of workshops – arts and handicrafts – such as marionette-making, plus I recall a tall, shaven-headed Cossack, who constructed poems through the random selection of words from a computerised *Webster's*.

I did meet Aimé briefly and by accident, on an unauthorised walk with two of my triumvirs (Johns II and III). This was in a deep excavation several winding metres beyond the terraces of Emma's open-air theatre – a place drowsy with scent and bathed in a sweetness from the surrounding spits and rotisseries. Aimé was positioned weak-kneed to the lower grade of an escarpment, soil blooming with herbs, in the hurried action of re-zipping his fly. A big bronzy local half his age – I identified her, later, as a kitchen girl – now off her knees and back-to-back with her master, quietly expectorated, which left a green viscous slime glittering on an hibiscus leaf. They scuttled away – Martin to remoter shades – his succubus back to the twang of civilisation.

Johns the ministers placed the whole 'successful' day in joint perspective, Ix having been singled out as the perfect location for the sprawling limbs of the Bureau. Why Ix? Well, Anno, it has everything to do with size, and the scope it offers our se-. curity people, who like to dot every last i. As to procurement, inquiries had been made, but of course Emma regarded her little experiment as far too important culturally to sell-up now and start again. There was Florence, however – at this time a child of two or three – in whose future life certain 'influence' could be brought to bear. Until then I, Anno, last of the great sceptics, took up office in the Worldwide Communications Tower, newly built on the Isle of Dogs, and recently 'opened' by Herr Hahn, President – with scissors, a beaming smile, and lots of red tape.

A day in the life...

As to routine, having troubled Miss Ashley with suggestions for guidance, I don't now wish to show my indecision – or sheer bloody-mindedness – in binning the numbered list she has spent half the morning on. Yesterday's spectacular sunset, a pure heaven of orange flame, has slightly altered my frame of mind. I watched, cooling through my tall windows, the changing silk silhouette of Ix's mountain range, and now hark back to that as a counter-chime to the clatter of Miss Ashley's keypad. But. I like to smooth things over. We chatted about her imminent retirement, which is planned for a favourite shore – last things for her greatly to do with the salty smell and sound of the sea, the fortunes of brightly coloured pleasure craft, and all around that scene the raucous clamour of gulls. She looks forward to a cliff hotel, at one of whose windows I can see her writing postcards.

Nonetheless life shall go on at Ix, where the citrus dews of my mornings, the painted fires of my evening skies – in fact the zest and all the pleasures I associate with our detached mountain life – weigh in exact opposition to the pedantry I am trying to prevent, but which I now see engulfing the Bureau. There is an ancient office called Samples – still the first in-tray in the flow of information. Under its newly appointed chief – who happens to be my counterpart – Samples has puffed itself up to the full status of department, and is now not merely a data interception room. Codename Six, whose offspring Samples now is (that codename by the way he insists on), means well, I'm sure, but does not fully understand either his role or mine.

I have noticed he is easily made breathless. He wears a rumpled white suit. His five ashen strands of hair are swept back to the mottled dome of his crown. There are three downy folds of flesh to the nape of his neck. He perspires freely, and would, I think, be lost without his large white handkerchief, with which he dabs his frequently silvered brows. He tends to be impatient. It so happens I have an hour or two before my next meeting (he, too, will attend), which is just time to tell you more about him.

1

I had no involvement in the recruitment process, whose closing series of interviews took place over a cold but sunny weekend in a shuttered gîte south of Pontivy. 'Six' was the third and final candidate, proving his map-reading in a drive from the Roscoff ferry, without major mishap. Myself I find our routing and position systems never account for the mountain road that has only that morning crumbled into the sea, or an army road block, or *some* disaster somewhere, and when *I* drive, in the end without computer aids, or without navigation, I always miss the turn.

Nowadays I drive to Pontivy mainly for recreation – the quiet walks and bike rides. Others like the pool table. There is also ping-pong, in a draughty, ill-lit basement. My approach is from Bordeaux, where my mother, widowed a second time, spent the remaining years of her life, in a large, rambling house, which is now my private museum. It consists of family memorabilia. The problem I have, which Six did not, is identifying that correct turn-off south of Pontivy, which over the years has been variously landmarked: a water trough, a signpost drunkenly indicating a timber yard, a particular configuration of fence-posts, etc. Nevertheless, it is not until I see the aluminium glitter of a poultry farm that I know I have gone too far, and follow the signs back towards Baud.

When Six was introduced to me, his jowls were still pink from the vernal breezes sweeping over Brittany. This was on his first guided tour of Ix, a task undertaken by the Bureau's hospitality centre. His palm was damp when we shook hands. He was hot and agitated, having not yet acquired the light suits and short-sleeved shirts appropriate to the climate here at Ix, and which were certainly more sensible than the pinstripe he did wear. I saw him again, by chance, some hours later, in the cobbled town of Ix, where I sometimes take a three o'clock lunch – or 1500 to him – in the shady terrace of one of several street cafés. His shirt – that morning a dazzling white

– was an archipelago of dark perspiration, which he'd evidently worked up, inspecting our many offices tucked away in Castle Maqueda (that title restored). He bore his folded jacket over a tired arm, though hadn't loosened his tie. I fortunately had work papers, which I retreated into, so soon as I saw him emerge – head, shoulders, stumpy torso, stubby little legs – from the deep angular shadow of the ramparts. His escort was close behind him, a supple-limbed youth in shorts and a plain open shirt, wielding a clipboard.

Six, who found himself among Ix's first wave of tourists, swatted himself lethargically with a chequered blue hanky, appurtenance he then stuffed away in a trouser pocket, one of its four tails dangling. A genteel old lady in a long floral dress, a swarm of children in a zigzag at her feet, caught a thread to the seam of his shoulder in a twirl of spokes from her parasol. Six turned sharply, then trudged off stormily. He wasn't to blame either when a stall-holder, an elderly, happy-faced man, in the velvety garb of local tradition, clattered into him, practically head-on, and incapable of pessimism went on singing his varnished bric-à-brac. Theatrically Six dusted himself off, scowling.

I dared to glance round my icy carafe, which I had lifted, about to pour water, and through its distortions watched him search for that hanky, whose flower of blue checks he put to use, waving away a photographer. He began to walk, precariously, round a consort of Moorish street players, and in my direction. I looked away and back again, some moments later, and saw him step from the doorway of a souvenirs shop. Here he had picked out and weighed with approval a blackthorn walking stick, with a hook styled in ram's horn. His escort followed, checking his watch, fanning his face with his clipboard. After brief consultation, they walked off in the direction of the car park, by which time of course I knew that Six was the third and successful candidate.

2

Miss Ashley says I'm looking tired. I reply that my day-in-the-life is now no such thing, but an amalgam. This is my tacit indication that her list (for which thanks) is no longer of use. I can guess, because she has just tottered away with my memos file – which I know from its colour, a sugared strawberry – that there has been some unexpected news from the ministry.

The BDP relies for all its major strategies on its close connections with EuroSHart – the first real rival to McGregAir, and the one empire or organisation through which we can safely broadcast our own propaganda. I did once meet with Steven Hart, whose brainchild EuroSHart was and still is. I was even among the first to shake his hand, when it appeared finally that McGregor's market monopoly had been broken. However, that's all beside the point. Word we have from the ministry concerns that world-led celebrity, a man now in exile, and one-time doyen Craig Diamond – not these days a media star so much as a network owner himself. Twenty years ago he left the continent for good, declaring that Europe was dead. Diamond has since based himself on the west coast of America, and over the past two decades has reshaped his interests as shareholder, broker and policy-maker, through a range of US corporations. What naturally alarms us is a bid it seems Diamond has tabled, for a major share in EuroSHart. That, if successful, we would find, politically speaking, 'difficult'.

What I personally find irksome is the complications it's likely to bring – precisely what I can do *without*, in my own retirement year.

3

Six's office is visible from mine, a distant rank of lower-floor windows, whose end group of three (so to speak the dark glaze on his inner sanctum) is almost permanently hatched in a cross-shadow from the communications tower. Foolishly I tried to make him feel welcome, on the morning he and his trunk-loads of documents arrived for a first full day of work. I left a few friendly lines on his virtual scratchpad, which he returned to me some hours later, largely re-worked. His name he'd ferociously crossed through in red crayon, and replaced by his personal code, which is 6, or as he terms it, 'Six'. Two innocuous placenames he'd coded X and Y. He'd also modified my punctuation. Lastly the date – which in any case was electronically generated, and appeared with the footer information – he'd completely erased.

During his first month I saw that Six seldom ventured outside, which is not *my* working practice. I claim as now belonging to me a lacquered bench in Emma's old azalea dell, which today is in the shade of a flowering cherry, a spot I often retreat to with a file full of papers. Here in an almost perpetual pause for thought, I can remind myself of that prophetic era under the pale sagacity of both the Martins, in the handful of outdoor monuments that have survived our purge, and which the part-finished inventory shows to be their work. There's a saturnine Flora, whose pedestal has weathered to the same streaks of caramel and green in the bosky to her rear, and whose loosely apparelled figure I have seen sarcastically adorned with brackens and yellow flowers, come springtime. On a direct line to Six's crepuscular triptych of windows is a round-limbed, round-shouldered nude, reclining – 'to convey', as I have read in one of the catalogues, 'a sense of tranquillity'. Six, on one of his rare and laden excursions, was far from tranquil himself, in the pugnacious little strides that he made towards me – this was early one morning, over the pearls of dew filming the lawns. By then he had done away with his pinstripe, preferring the many creases and overlapping folds of his light linen suits, for which he had also bought a matching hat. He asked, did I not think this at all dangerous, and almost to prove his point a slight breeze tugged at my papers, detaching a single leaf from the rest, where they were lodged under a largish pebble. He scooped it up, and returning it advised me to take much better care. I later had Miss Ashley print off his CV, from which I learned – hardly a surprise – that although his background was military, he had never seen live action. He had however regularly co-ordinated manoeuvres and exercises in the Gulf of Finland, in that on-off entente with our Eastern friends. We'd got him apparently because of his nose for trouble.

That slightly peppered vane showed itself to be fallible in the first selection of papers *his* office passed to mine, via the outtrays of Samples, and through the intrays of my own half-dozen satellites. I can bemoan the fact that at its inception the Bureau relied too much on its agents in the field, men and women downloading TV programmes all day and all night long, and that the sprawl of mass entertainment – all that dross posted on the network – brings with it such an enormous pro-liferation of production companies, some of them minutely small. Our world of course is one of natural inequity, where all wise persons running things cannot fail to anticipate bloody revolution, and view as inevitable a call to arms via this most obvious medium. We wait anxiously, and there really is the rub – for here we find it so problematic. In all those acres of trash we take such a huge professional interest in, very little is remotely subversive – or so our reports seem to show. We must add to this that Six himself is wedded to the screen, and sug-gests, in the absence of any *political* rooting-out, that we exer-cise our *moral* authority. His obsessions seem to be, in approxi-mately this order:

1) Domestic pornography, which, in most of the examples he offered, involved a slightly overweight housewife, in bestial li-aison with either her whey-fleshed husband or some sunburnt gigolo. Aim seemed to be to create an impression with one of the large corporations, whose talent scouts were imagined to be stick-at-homes. He cited examples too of teenage acts of fel-lation.

2) The Spikenard Global News Service, on those frequent occa-sions when a team of technicians – whose only outward sign was a limpid reporter – had penetrated to the heart of a junta, under the cratered streets in some godforsaken republic, where a hapless dissident – that shrieking subject of blows, incisions, and the surgical removal of parts – as climax to a night's enter-tainment finally snitches on his friends.

3) Filmed confessions of serial paedophiles.

4) Ditto mass killers.

5) The testament of last hours, with close-ups of execution, of inmates on Death Row.

6) The tendency among naturalists to concentrate wholly on the reproductive cycle of their prey (silver-backed gorillas in a welter of anthropomorphous flatulence, plus copulation) – which as conclusion I was wrong in suspecting as levity on Six's part.

42

4

To be honest Six tended to make me absent-minded. It was only much later that I knew I had filed under 'S' papers indexed 'B', though on a first inkling dismissed any thought of this. It seemed no more than a first broken thread in a bureaucratic maze, and I was confident Miss Ashley would soon sort it out. To my wonder I found myself – having also rambled in deed – in the spooky half-light of Sir Oscar's musical theatre, a forgotten precinct that had now re-greened as savannah, host to things that munched on velvet. There were great engineering feats too in the number of spiders' webs.

Backstage I kicked at the tubular leg of a chair, which was still enmeshed in the barbed wire that formed, I imagine, a prop. Dust immediately rained from its canvas seat. Incredibly I found a conductor's score – Sir Ossie's *Nuptials Charade* – commissioned by one of his American patrons, an academic institution. This, according to an acknowledgements page, had been *premièred* at Tanglewood – though its natural home of course was Ix. I looked up and out through one of the pointed windows, to a deep blue sky, which in the course of my twilit odyssey had become streaked in mare's tails. By now I thought I knew what to do (about Six, I mean).

5

I asked Miss Ashley to revise and circulate the standard agenda re the department's policy meeting, which always took place at an oval table, in an oval room – but whose timing varied. Six had already been to his first of these, and had thrummed with his fat little fingers. My insertion was above the remedial AOB, and was a tactful *Let's now be informal…* Persons who knew me also through the cocktail lounge asked with a slight smirk if this was politic. I replied that I thought it imperative. In the same breath almost, and not without hope, I maundered through a thin catalogue of Sir Oscar's works, and there learned how *Charade* first twitched under the conductor's baton (quarkish in temperament), when Florence was about fourteen. I couldn't follow up on all the reviews, but did ring the first paragraph of one, which was gushing, and witty, and what Samples could sometimes do with in *its* reports. Could I lighten Six's mood with passing reference, I wonder...

6

NO! is the answer...

7

...followed by several hard hours together. These were in contemplation of Flora's chiton, which now that I've really studied it is a garment cut away at the waist, and draped, in a moulding of flutes, from a raised upper arm, all the way to a rounded hip. Means by which it catches the breeze.

Her finger, aloft to perch a sparrow.

8

Now... a review of Miss Ashley's minutes... here on my red-wood bench... some days after the event... when even so I have not appreciably cooled...

Six opened proceedings with his own 'insertion' – being that, imperilled as we all now must be (because of a new generation of remote listening devices), codenames, gentlemen, 'must' be observed. The chief becomes One (or is that atman?). I am Five (I am also sixes and sevens). Associate heads are the remaining factors Two through Nine.

Agenda item twelve (*Let's now be informal...*) was, I now think formally introduced by Five, who hinted gnomically that in keeping a close watch on the thousand and one production companies, our purpose was not to comment on programming integrity, a discipline well outside our brief. Five asked Six if, therefore, he could reconsider certain submissions that had been put to his, Five's, office earlier in the week. Six said, "What submissions?" Eight said, "Why are you hesitating?" Two said, "Six needs to know which way he's pointing. Spit it out." Five, or rather *I* thought: "Six knows very well what submissions."

44

Six said something like, "If what you mean is those TV snollygosters..."

I have since referred to the *Concise Oxford*, and uncover 'n. (sl.) shrewd unscrupulous person. [perh. f. snallygaster, a mythical creature]'. In the same trip I stumbled over 'snicker', apposite as something I'd managed to repress.

We suffered the litany. Those deeply engorged members, manoeuvred in all sorts of crab-like contortions into high or low waters. That gore-faced, earless dissident. Child-snatchers. Genocidal lunatics. Death Row's citizens, *in extremis*. Leafy, jungle coition, in all its nutritious manures.

Six by then had passed through his shades of lobster, and thumped the table (remember this was oval, and therefore partially democratic). His action produced surprised and puzzled looks. He accused me – as someone conniving at all this filth – of liberalism, to which I replied there were certain ways of doing things – none of them quite in *these* personal terms. At this he accused me also of being a snob (which to a certain extent is true), and from this point couldn't get through AOB without showing his impatience.

He left, in a hail of bluster, without collecting his action points (the enlarged directory of in-house etiquette, which Miss Ashley has subsequently mailed him). One and Two paused for a third cup of coffee after the meeting broke up (One, with his clipped moustache, Two, in the flash of his wedding ring), and asked me what I thought was troubling Six. "Me," I said. "Clash of personalities." Two told me to have those six submissions (those Six submissions) put on his desk, for him to peruse.

"I'll have Miss Ashley get on to it. When she's sent the minutes."

9

Miss Ashley, who puts up with my fatigue, but not my irritability, suggested one or two days in Bordeaux. There I keep spirits and such in an embellished cabinet my mother shipped from Elsinore, and having poured myself a glass it's a short walk to the rail of my balcony. Here I'm a man who

45

mostly looks down on the life around him, waiting only for the sun to slide away. This evening's was a fireball.

I cooled my hands round a tumbler of iced liquor, and later, under lamplight, opened the closet door on my hoard of sentimental objects, starting with a backgammon. This was a game that belonged to Capel, onto whose painted spears I spent an hour or so heaping my old photographs. Of Mum. Dad. Mum and Dad. Mum, Dad, on the banks of Lake Konstanz, with toddler and plastic, plum-coloured, water-filled boule ball. Various odd envelopes yielded an assortment of broken necklace chains. A blue plastic sachet, which I didn't think was mine, when I tipped it up disgorged itself of dozens of Japanese postage stamps. Finally I weighed in my palm, not the ball of the photograph, but its only surviving companion, in a grazed yellow. This I placed down in the ellipse of its own shadow, for paperweight.

10

Aimé, to commemorate his marriage, or looking forward to a first decade among the breezes and purplish mountains of Ix (or perhaps to celebrate both), erected an obelisk in a corner of the Maqueda camellia walk. It came with lapidary – an inscription he and his wife commissioned, on the news of another English newspaper winding up its operation. Its editor was a man known personally to Emma, who throughout his latter professional years adorned his society page with scurrilous rhymes, mostly politically motivated. Often these were Limericks – not the case however here with his *last* gesture. His pen for this – which invariably leaned to the Right – mustered what Emma saw as finely wrought rime royal, and the perfect foil for his patriotic views. All round us, he said, the wheels of European convergence crushed any last moiety of sovereign tradition.

Emma, when it was time to think about that inscription for her obelisk, as usual did her research, and finally lit on Dulot's *bouts-rimés* – an explanation of which is given in the section below, and is verse constructed using given rhymed ends. She decided her editor might appreciate a double list of these,

46

which in part she made straightforward ('nightingale', 'sing', 'tale', 'stirring', 'ring', 'stint', 'intent'), and in part not ('computerised', 'attic', 'bowdlerised', 'tooth-pick', 'stamp-lick', 'tower', 'sower'). Again this is something I glean from *Our Love Affair With Ix*, where her newspaper man is described, surprisingly, as a cottage dweller, and shabbily dressed, if orderly. We are to picture him scribing away at his cold wintry verse, to the soporific accompaniment of fireside symphony – the monotonous tock of his clock, and a woody crackle in a roaring grate. Emma remarks that the commission took a helluva while. This was because her man in the English counties – or 'cointies' – had immersed himself almost totally in a final lost cause. With the demise of his own, there was now only one British tabloid that remained independent of the McGregor machine. While it might have been impossible to join its payroll permanently, he did turn out hack work on a freelance basis – usually for the opinions column. So, when that tabloid too went phut, expiring with it was this and many other hortative gems: *Don't let the President / Make the people hesitant*. When, at last, he did turn to the Ix obelisk, it was with the same anti-federal bile:

No! I will not snare the bashéd nightingale,
Or put it in a strictly English cage to sing.
I'd rather pen a brand-new EU tale –
As federated birdies, stirring
To the plea of sovereignty, the ring
Of nationhood, and each to its nation's stint.
I say: defy Herr President's intent.

He says opinion is computerised,
With x-mit machines in every household attic.
I say the statutes have been bowdlerised –
Easy as removing plaque with a tooth-pick,
Or the sticking of official stamps with a stamp-lick.
Europa! Defy Herr Hahn in his ivory tower!
Don't be reapers, after him as sower.

Notes

1) X-mit – 'transmit' or 'transmitting' (this is old-fashioned computer jargon).

2) Plaque – which I suppose *could* be removed with a tooth-pick (consult your dentist).

3) Stamp-lick. Presumably the moist sponge of pre-automated office life, used for activating the gummed side of ordinary postage stamps. An image that does not logically follow from that of the preceding line, although there again I'm no editor.

4) A few thoughts in summary, because the era is interesting, in terms of what those old-style tabloids now had to compete with. McGregor had offered to practically every newspaper and journal on European soil – not to mention inroads east – any of three outlets through his satellite network. You as punter could produce in part or whole any chosen publication via the printing facilities linked to an ordinary TV screen, in all its palette of pixelated colour. Or you could download selectively onto that screen. Or, you could have the page read, in a range of digitised and human-sounding voices. The tabloid for whom the Martin chiseller blew his shire horn – and pale-cheeked, professionally died with – did not have the prescience to enter this exciting new market, an omission that led him, smug and resigned, to an Englishman's grave. By the way Miss Ashley thank you very much for bookmarking Emma and Aimé's memoir, for my insertion below…

11

…which I shall come to. First I point out that nowhere does Emma acknowledge that other noted pilgrim, Geoffrey Chaucer – not even in her bibliography. Compare that first verse above, with this, which is from *Troilus and Criseyde* (III, 177, 1233-39):

> And as the newe abaysshed nightingale,
> That stinteth first whan she biginneth singe,
> Whan that she hereth any herde tale,
> Or in the hegges any wight steringe,
> And after siker dooth hir voys out-ringe;
> Right so Criseyde, whan hir drede stente,
> Opned hir herte, and tolde him hir entente.

Where Emma acquired her second set of rhyme-ends *I* couldn't speculate, although on that subject generally it is worth reproducing her own footnote:

> *Bouts-rimés*, meaning, literally, 'rhymed ends', name applied in all literatures to the form of verse that Addison described as a list of words that rhyme, drawn up by someone other than the writer, and to be used in the order given. The odder the rhymes are, the greater the ingenuity required. Invention of *bouts-rimés* is attributed to the seventeenth-century French poet, Dulot, who is known for little else. It is said that one day in 1648, Dulot complained he'd been robbed of valuable papers, which included three hundred sonnets. Naturally his friends were astonished he'd written so many, at which point he explained that really these sonnets were 'blank sonnets' – meaning, he had settled on the rhymes and nothing more. Amusement all round, as one might imagine. However, the idea caught on and became the fashion. The elder Dumas, in 1864, even went to the extreme of inviting all French poets to parade their skills by versifying to rhymes selected by Joseph Méry (himself a poet). Over three hundred writers responded.
>
> The Rossettis composed sonnets to *bouts-rimés*, with, it is said, Dante passing one off in roughly five to eight minutes [which marks the end of our poetry class].

Bouts-rimés or no, a quaint old stonemason, with a gnomish-looking smile, was finally tracked down, under a windswept hill in the skirt of Hardy's Wessex, where he worked on the obelisk in the weeks before it was shipped to Ix.

12

This brings me back to codenames, and Two's slight jest that had the commission been entirely down to Aimé, it might have been an odalisque, whereas in fact his propensity for handmaidens here gives way to hand *tools*. Two's theory incidentally of the Martin throb – irrepressible monster of Aimé's bored and boring life – is that it took to the explosive friction of servile hands (was positively volcanic when it came to soft palates and labial caresses) because of an exaggerated, almost neurotic terror of that great twentieth-century ghoul, whose acronym is AIDS. Or what is more likely, very loud, public repercussions should he infect his clean, healthy, American wife.

I had chosen this moment with Two, because Two too likes the gardens. He groaned on that closing couplet (to Emma's chosen ends, her tower/sower), just as that stone bodkin pointed out a dreamier heaven – a milky whip of tangerine, a cloud in an otherwise cloudless azure – which as I stated to Mal is a paradise purer than any plain architect had planned for in the hills and valleys of Ix.

Two told me: "I have passed Six's submissions to One, who I am sure will think as I do."

"How, Two, do you think?"

"Well of course I share Six's moral outrage, but you're right – he misses the point. Did you enjoy your break in Bordeaux?"

"Immensely. While I was there, Two, I placed a spy in Six's camp."

"A spy! Is that necessary? I mean there are moves afoot to have Six sidelined to Security, on which he's already been asked to advise. By the way did you see his memo?"

"The one insisting on codenames?"

"Yes, codenames."

"Why do you think, Mal, I keep calling you "Two"?"

"It's because, Anno, you've a penchant for farce. How are those handover notes?"

"Much broader in scope than I'd planned. Plus I have to keep revising them. Though Miss Ashley – I mean One Eight Six – is a great help."

"One Eight Six! Are there really that many staff?"

"It depends on which point in the scale you're looking from, and in which direction. Look. That tangerine cloud is now in the shape of a basilisk."

13

That spy, whose codename I care not to utter, and whose pseudonym shall be Luis, has cost me a doubt or two. I am not permitted to name his provenance, a vibrant, southerly commercial centre, whose Moorish ruins are infested with damp, and lie in the shadow of a later conurbation. That's a rather distant monotony of sun-bleached office blocks, a solar gleam of window panes, with a ripple of diluted silver – all coastally situated. This is where Luis taught himself the language of federated Europe, thereby enlarging his opportunities for work, and gaining a skill that finally laid his escape from a life of bruising sodomy. That had gone on under makeshift lights, but always through the lens of a camera, the scene rigged up with rugs and silks off an uncle's back room (all for eventual posting on the network). This the authorities found it impossible to find, when I asked them to, a mere dot in the sprawling, disease-ridden shanty town, in the hem of that sunny white city, where as envoy of the BDP I had delivered a triad of lectures.

I was able to help only because I out-bid a kerb-crawler, a man now obliged to look elsewhere. His shoulders and upper arms remained partly hatched in the shade of a railway bridge, as I watched him recede. I looked to the boy Luis, whose large brown eyes flickered with fire and sadness. His pimp ran my credit card, with its flash of holographic light, through an old-fashioned swipe box clipped to his waistband. With the receipt, he also gave me a disc – "Gratis!" The other, or rival, hopped in to his open-top car, whose crimson tail lights lit up under the arch of the bridge. 'You back here by five,' I was told, although by that time Luis was trying on his new clothes, just as I had dialled Europol. Incidentally they did nothing at all, aside from confiscate that disc, whose peep show featured a younger Luis, more baby-faced than now.

I have put him to work in Data Archives, where he has added IT skills to that second language of his. This at the moment regularly takes him into Samples, right under Six's nose, where he knows to look out for papers destined for the shredders. I have slight reservations about this (there is only so much one alone can do, this tragic flotsam washed round our ankles). My worst fear is that under interrogation, he is bound to confess everything to Six – and I mean *everything*. Fortunately, Luis has found something – a few crumpled memos rescued from a bin, addressed to Six, and regarded by him as unimportant. I shall pass them to Two. When I next see Two, he will tell me he's passed them to One. Then I shall, without fuss, reinstate my dark-eyed angel to his labyrinth, known within these castle walls as Archives.

14

Unusually a quiet moment. This gives me time to review my last batch of dictations, which Miss Ashley printed several days ago, and left in my in-tray. I see from her pencilled notes, which end with three exclamation points, or 'shrieks' (as she calls them), that she liked my little joke with Two (odalisque, obelisk, basilisk). Two takes these things in good part, and himself chose one other amusing location – that's to say Emma's former study, a place without ears – to confirm that One still put his faith in me. All that's now left of Emma's private chamber – perhaps even then a monkish scriptorium – is a hard wooden bench on a cold stone floor. Light, despite the southerly windows, is a powdery grey.

According to Two, who stood with his back to me, One was certainly alarmed at Six's submissions, but as ever was sanguine. One pointed out that only some mishap would see those papers land on the minister's desk. More important, he connived at my methods, with the coded declaration that the two intercepted memos warranted further investigation. The first was an agenda for Diamond's first meeting on his proposed EuroSHart bid, with curiously the department's own Natsuki designated as chairperson. Natsuki had once worked for Craig, many years ago, but would not I'd have thought – in her time here since at Ix – kept that contact up.

Two also wanted me to take a look at Ryder Twill – man whose rumblings we were bound to hear more of – since with no sign of revolution at the *fringes* of society, perhaps it would come from within, and if we only looked would find disobedience eating away at the larger corporations – McGregor's included. Twill had upset things with what for him was eccentric programming.

I joined Two at Emma's window, where he looked out and across, and I suspect didn't see the encircling mountains of Ix, whose crags and fissures just then were a hazy purple, touched with charcoal and fringed with a palish blue.

"Good," I said. "I'll put someone on to that."

Two replied: "Six as you know is surveying Security, but it's not proving easy to get him transferred."

"That, Two, is unfortunate."

"It means we shall need your source to remain in place."

"That's quite impossible!"

"Anonymity respected."

"No."

"Look, this Twill's probably harmless, but Diamond definitely isn't. You know the climate. All this mutual suspicion. Personally, I find it almost claustrophobic."

"Mal!"

"Orders, Anno."

"In that case I insist on certain guarantees, foremost that my plant, whatever the outcome, shall be fully rehabilitated to his former position – by which I mean lowly."

"How lowly?"

"Insignificantly so."

Two touched his chin, and looked down thoughtfully into Emma's old azalea dell. "Leave that with me, Anno."

Six of course was stolid, though managed not to ignite his brimstone, when at the next policy meeting One thanked him warmly for the points he'd raised, but did not wish to trouble the minister. Six dabbed his temples. This I watched through the slits of my eyes (I find certain ocular contractions unavoidable in situations like this). Seven, or 007 (as One Eight Six intriguingly transcribes it), having been coached by me beforehand, was able to tell us that Ryder Twill, a jaded TV chat show host, was now known to question his own *raison d'être*, and in recent broadcasts had made certain disrespectful comments regarding his position, or 'function', as cog in the McGregor empire. He poured water from a jug. Six waved his blue-black hanky – perhaps irritation at an air-borne pest – then folded it to a rabbit's ear, which he pocketed with a flourish. He commented, not without justification – were the world organised as he perceived it – that what was important got ignored, while what seemed trivial the ministry was likely to get in a flap

53

about. (My belated news for him is, the ministry was in a flap.) Roll on Six's move to Security – under the codename Twelve I understand (half the job, twice the title). I asked him what evidence there was of these remote listening devices he had warned us of, to which he replied 'None – that is their strength'.

I behold the faded image of a grey shaft of sunshine dampening one patch of cold floor in Emma's sub-intellectual sanctum. I fear for Luis. That is because I behold also the salty wastes of a Western-style Siberia, which I don't doubt exists.

The communications centre

More correctly the communications 'tower'. This is one of those Disneyfied constructions (or reconstructions), circular in section, with crenellations two-thirds to the summit, from which emerges a narrower tower, itself capped in a cone of slates, which in its turn is speared with a flag pole.

Internally, there have been a great many modifications, in the twelve years or so since purchase from Florence Martin, who I see from a recent press release is unwilling to authorise use of certain family papers. This is in respect of a new television biography. The sad part of Florence's legacy was – and these are museum pieces now – its heaps of halberds and helmets – some, I recall, still crested – for which the tower became a dumping ground. This has metamorphosed to a warren of raised floors and suspended ceilings, all accessible centrally via a glassy elevator, which, as you might guess, is of American design, albeit German manufacture. The lower floors and basement areas are inhabited by white-coated boffins, all wielding shiny screwdrivers, and it is they who form the fraternity I recently introduced the angel-eyed Luis to.

Security, Networks and Information are the main arteries threading the various platters above. Under an earlier sampling system, all information for the monitor (me, or one day soon, you) was gathered to the tower and collated, before sifting took place and the results passed to my office. I do not propose to describe in any great detail how our many men and women in the field, weary people clamped in headphones, or glued baggy-eyed to TV or computer screens, listened and watched incessantly for anything vaguely provocative. If there *is* something, it will now pass through Samples before it comes to me – an arrangement I have already shown *one* result of. I mention this because Six's sweeping analysis of all that goes on, brings with it some equally sudden reforms – or proposed reforms. Let us take a look at the most important of these.

Security Six, with that nose of his for bad odours, sniffed out and ensnared a quite harmless technician – a Dr Thornden, a man whose unruly coiffure gave way almost overnight first to a tonsure, then to complete baldness. Spectacles he searched pockets for. Thornden explained to Six, long before I got to him myself (and told him to close ranks), our limited use of the datascope. Its function isn't hard to grasp. It's a little box of magic lights, or maroon fizz of sky rockets. It remains connected here at Ix to a computer screen, and ethereally to the world's data networks. You use it by selecting any given network ID, at which it faithfully reproduces all data traffic to and from that address. The implications are obvious.

In its early utilisation, way back in those heady millennial days – long before my student life – its targets were journalists and politicians, and sometimes civil servants. Before that, a prototype was put through its paces in two key areas. The first of these was a television impressionist, in email conversation with his script writers, well known for the sharpness of their satire. The other was an electronic bulletin board, owned and serviced by a fashion magnate, whose empire was global. This had evolved to a trans-continental discussion group, whose conversation touched on practically everything: the privatisation of national utilities, Third World debt, the West's two-tier health and education systems, tabloid and television propaganda, the Swiss banking system, terrorism, the international arms industry, a prickly geo-political triangle called Dublin-London-Belfast, the rising powers of the East, and just occasionally the silky red wonder that *was* Manchester United (the Busby-Ferguson axis) – because let's get this in perspective.

Nowadays we like to monitor only those members of the intelligentsia likely to cause embarrassment – those handful of media personalities who against all our best efforts (in-service training, etc.) still show signs of independent thought. Six is keen to extend the facility, in order to scrutinise practically every public person dwelling on planet Earth. Thornden, then as an upward escalation his line-manager Schmidt, point out that Ix is already touching capacity. Schmidt states too, with the endorsement of his development chief, a Monsieur Barbier, that even current hardware upgrades, which arrive with the whirr of helicopter rotors, won't be enough to meet the increased demand. It has to be pointed out too that there are few people clumsy enough to transmit digitised data in unencrypted form. Six's reply to that will be, I know, to expand our decryption lab – meaning more of those pebble-eyed boffins.

Nor could Six quite accept the innocence of Ix's Library of Culture, which amounts to virtual reality representations of every global landmark, both historic and present. I showed him round this facility myself – with a stroll in the Via di Stabia, Pompeii, where we lost our way, and called in for directions at number five (the Casa del Citarista, or House of the Citharist). The accompanying sound was a voice-over, delivered by a computerised tenor, which as a touch too nasal for me I soon switched off. The citharist was Apollo, under a bronze statue of whom a waggish engineer had placed himself, cross-legged and trite, strumming a contemporary guitar with a contemporary piece of tortoise shell.

Should you be curious, 5 Via di Stabia is an aristocratic dwelling dated to the Roman period, and combines two adjacent houses – simple fact indicated by a double atrium and three peristyles. Once we'd got out of there, and Six was let loose on his own, I had to call a halt, Six testing in ever louder terms the acoustics in a rebuilt amphitheatre – that place a blaze of marigold under a particularly bright blue sky. But I digress. My purpose in revealing this is that Six – a man known to click his heels in certain reverberative passageways – stoutly recommends barring all public access to Ix's Library of Culture, and severely restricting *authorised* access.

What is his rationale? Well. His latent fear, like mine, is of terrorism, yet unlike me he thinks it's only a matter of time before bomb-makers somewhere start to meander (in virtual space of course) through the nooks and crannies of the European Central Bank (for example), or the Europa Trade Centre (that unassailable glass tower, with its panoramic views of the Rhineland), or odd little satellites, such as a certain address in Threadneedle St. Six wants further to tighten up Ix itself (no more tourists allowed to touch the damp stone base of the castle), and between departments, stricter use of voice-, pupil- and finger-print recognition. And that elevator I mentioned, which is transparent… he wants it tinted.

Networks Excuse terseness. The most I feel I can do is enumerate Six's paragraphs – or paragraphets – in imitation of his own laconicisms. He wants to see:

a) no real distinction between the world-wide network (which is open), and those innumerable private set-ups (which are closed) – which would mean indiscriminate use of the datascope;

b) simplified access to all $network_IDs, with linked lists to associated information (name, address, marital status, occupation, bank details, political affiliations, parental and educational background, memberships, etc.);

c) a gigastream link to the Pentagon;

d) ditto our 'friends' in Moscow;

e) controlled access to all prison records over the last seventy-five years;

f) ditto medical records;

g) a highlight on all private (not corporate) share dealings;

h) ditto all sackings and resignations;

i) permanent updates on Church attendance;

j) ditto all UFO 'sightings';

k) one-page synopses on all new films, soap operas, sitcoms, books and ebooks;

l) the introduction of more wide-ranging push-button opinion polls;

m) details of all property purchase;

n) school, college, workplace and other statistics, as are relevant to social and ethnic groupings;

o) dietary and longevity statistics in respect of all family groups;

p) permanent updates on the population count in all areas defined as 'shanty' [of the kind that spawned Luis];

q) more 'imagination', and a wider range of 'alternatives', in decoding public statements, such as those issued by company directors and/or their PR specialists;

r) more sophisticated 'obfuscation tactics', or the release of disinformation, for the consumption of our trade competitors;

s) the denial of all public access to the digitised libraries of Paris, London and Rome, in the case of such works as Machiavelli's *The Prince* and V Nabokov's *Bend Sinister* [these are his 'notables' – Six continues to pester me for an 'exhaustive' list];

t) ditto certain specialist works in the dead disciplines of philosophy;

u) ditto historical accounts of all lawsuits involving ministers;

v) revised tariffs (downwardly revised) in respect of programmes and hire games;

w) a simpler sales strategy re trips to the moon;

x) public declaration of the incomes and properties of Europe's 'successes';

y) sanitised accounts, and the removal of all statistical data, that relate to mental disease;

z) a block on research data in the area of eugenics and genetic hybridisation;

a1) [because Six had anticipated no more than twenty-six shots from his hip gun] data tags on all youngsters brought up under bizarre conjugal arrangements [meaning lesbian or homosexual marriages, which the Minister for Domestic Rights tells us now outnumber 'conventional' matrimony];

b1) wackier route guides for the motorist, in something other than the present brass or ochre background;

c1) more Chinese recipes, cuisine as a bridge between superpowers;

d1) no unguarded hint that China is a superpower…

We shall doubtless unravel some, if not all of these.

Information Or quality of information. Six, in the salvos set serenely off in the sinister pyrotechnics of that extra-alphabet above – perhaps because its inception was through a fountain pen, and the reverse side of an envelope – remains unclear on one important demarcation, which I have divined for myself, from the skeletal notes he makes under this, our present heading. For what, we ask, is the difference (though I grant in some cases it's obvious) between publicly available propaganda, and the kind of data that only designated officers of Ix should be allowed to process? Let us take that list again, with that fine line engraved:

A) Closed, or private networks. Myself I cannot conceive that for Six there is any sense in which the doings of the intelligentsia – however banal those doings have become – can be closed – or more accurately, closed to him. Why should he want the datascope?

B) Simplified access to all $network_IDs. What Six means by this is a directory, jealously guarded here at Ix, of all network nodes, either symbolic, named, or numbered. The associated lists are not of course for public consumption (this information, though not fully linked in the way Six envisions, we do already gather).

C) Gigastream link to the Pentagon. Yet the US is a closed system.

D) Ditto our 'friends' in Moscow.

E) Prison records, for the last seventy-five years – for Six's private gratification, and not the public domain.

F) Medical records – are much as **E)** above.

G) Private share dealings. Six would like these secretly recorded, since any spectacular success, which is not on behalf of a corporation, imparts dangerous knowledge.

H) Sackings and resignations. Who is, who isn't socially adjusted?

I) Church attendance. As **H)**.

J) UFO 'sightings'. Cranks are both a menace and useful to the state. Six later proposes that a 'special interest' team, with wide-ranging brief, and not necessarily based at Ix, is unofficially formed.

K) One-page synopses. I hardly need say, these are *not* consumer guides.

L) Push-button opinion polls. Already widely used, of course, to gauge anything from the popularity of soap brands to the perceived *bonhomie* of senior politicians. Six would like to identify areas where more effective presentation seems to be called for.

M) Property purchase. Does anyone need to know who is buying what?

N) School, college, workplace and other statistics. A brief glance at Six's CV shows us a man of modest social origin.

O) Dietary/longevity statistics. Six needs to know to what order of being that succulent-looking burger, under a fresh tomato relish, in a seeded bap – so important to the amiable cosmetology of TV and poster campaigns – is aimed.

P) The rising population of our shanty towns, or 'scourge' of the developed world. Six has good reason to fear these growing numbers. Allow me, calmly, to predict, that one day they will rise up.

Q) Public sentiments by or on behalf of company directors. Let us not deceive ourselves. Commerce is the determining factor for cabinet policy, and not vice versa.

R) Misleading our trade competitors. This means also misleading our own 'man in the street', since what I think Six has in mind is open access to histograms and pie charts, in an attractive polychrome, in a disseminated, highly subjective view of our economy.

S) Denial of public access to the libraries of Paris, London, Rome (and one in High Wycombe, which I know still bothers with an annotated Orwell). Hatred of intelligent literature is one of those viruses gorging itself via high-ranking hosts in the military and police. What surprises me is Six's awareness of particular authors' names, and how all of these coincidentally are ones that Craig Diamond, one-time doyen of the media, has at one time or another declared dead or defunct. That 'exhaustive' list that Six is still pressing for, shall include the name Diamond.

T) Ditto specialist works in the dead disciplines of philosophy. Six, had he really looked into this, might applaud the free availability of Kant, say (whom many find unreadable), but insist on the quiet removal of a Russell (who reveals Kant in no-nonsense language).

U) Lawsuits involving ministers. It is quite impossible to keep the best of them down, or out of the courts. Six likes to see dirty linen in private.

V) Cheaper hire games. Pointless entertainment is the best device yet in keeping a lid on the masses.

W) Trips to the moon – an adjunct of **V)**.

X) Public parade of Europe's 'success stories'. I think I hear the ad man: 'You, too, can be like me…' (only be obedient, and work hard).

Y) Mental disease – or I should say, there is no mental disease.

Z) Eugenics, genetic control, genetic hybridisation. No responsible administration can admit to these aims.

A1) Our mixed sons and daughters. Unfortunately the minister's is also less than a total purview, and is focused through Six's shared, and darkened lens.

B1) Aids for the motorist. Put in I imagine in a spirit of magnanimity

– to show me Six's human side. I include this point in corresponding good spirit, not in any way wishing to present a bias.

C1) More Chinese recipes, or statecraft reduced to a cookery book…

D1)…but without saying why.

Ryder Twill

Perhaps I was tenth or so in Six's circulation process, and had less time than One – who was lean and had bony digits – to study or consider these proposed security arrangements. There was a loose moment by my window, the sky a holy magenta – in a criss-cross of crumbling jet trails – when One entered my office. That is to say, he did not call me to his.

Huge words fell from his lips, as I turned to face him. There were two to three microscopic specks of fluff, which he flicked from his lapel. He referred, with a thin-lipped smile, to the dangers of talking openly (Six and his remote eavesdroppers), and for that reason asked me to a private exhibition. This was of Europe's most complete postmodern collection. Doubtless you know – this is a period enjoying a small revival. Clean, healthy, golden age.

1

The canvases, which represented just a small fraction of the collection, belonged to a man named Kuhn, whose background was banking. His other passion was the sea, which explained the beefy tan of his jowls – two mottled sacks that shook with each syllable he uttered. His dwelling, currently doubling as showing space, was, curiously, subterranean – the first of three excavations in a thinning, red-leaved woodland, only a few kilometres inland. One, who arrived in a separate car, and who waited at the map reference privately agreed on, led me through the configuration of glassy domes studding the woodland floor, then down into Herr Kuhn's surprisingly airy labyrinth.

I did not meet the great man until well after the last tray of cocktail gherkins had been passed around among the guests, a protocol that in fact left me clutching the empty salver (for a short while only, until I signalled a steward). Kuhn was every bit as gushing as I expected – as far as you judge at a distance – vigorously shaking my hand, rattling off a long series of questions, to which he did not expect an answer. One in the meantime advanced to the cross-lights and conic shadows in one of several passages. Here I watched him exchange one or two words with Frau Kuhn – all plump curves and bursting *décolletage* – before stepping up to one of the exhibits. This was a primitive depiction of fire, a black circle enclosing red flames edged with yellow. I joined him, and opened my catalogue. We discussed, not this hanging, but the next – which was a collage of sun-dried tomatoes. He adjusted his cuffs then rolled his own catalogue into a tube, before casting out on the subject of Six:

"There are certain shall we say difficulties in moving him to Security."

I replied: "Not least his report."

"Gracious no…"

"Do you take that seriously?"

"Serious, Anno, is not the right word. Certain recommendations are interesting."

"Does he not want the job?"

"He hasn't been asked. Frankly my problem's Two, whose brainchild the new-style Samples is, and whose preferred candidate always was Six."

"Does that also affect the appointment of my successor?"

"You should know better than that, Anno. It's not really Six – for whom a solution *will* be found – or indeed you that I wanted to talk about." It was Twill he wanted to talk about.

Bypassing Samples – or at least its official methods – he told me was again how he wished to approach this. In this instance, a 'friend of a friend' – someone not unconnected with the present exhibition – had made certain 'observations' concerning Ryder Twill.

"Do you know him, Anno?"

"When you say 'observations', do you mean beyond what we discussed at the policy meeting?"

"Do you *know* him, Anno?"

"I know of him."

"Good! I shall have my man pass you relevant papers from time to time." This was hardly exciting, though I supposed it *would* fill time till my retirement…

64

The last of Kuhn's exhibits was a phosphorescent stairway spiralling vine-like round a tree trunk, connecting a yellow plain and a graduated turquoise heaven. In the background haze was a shadowy range of hills. To the foreground was a freshly made corpse, in a burnt orange toga.

2

My informant – courtesy One's fragile, if golden thread through society – shall be called Mitrovich, which as an incognito is either an approximation, or the inverse of his actual identity. I personally can't stand this cloak-and-dagger stuff. Muscovite Mitrovich – to pepper further that false trail – had researched and knew the subject Twill, whose name is faintly ludicrous. This took him back thirty years or so, to a long and unresolved career, when Twill was first a provincial journalist (somewhere in a Sussex vale), then a small-town editor. This latter post was on the Medway. I am therefore not myself surprised that 'Twill the Quill' – epithet identifying his editorials – plunged foot-first into an underworld of pessimism, from which, stubbornly, he hasn't quite emerged. He moved into radio, and learned to modulate his tone, his natural gravity increasingly interspersed with just those hoots of enthusiasm broadcasters endlessly rehearse.

Mitrovich asks, can I conceive how difficult such a role can be, when in his county-wide waves as conversationalist, our Twill extracted his pearls, all from a journalistic oyster bed of local celebrity. Twill's were everyday tales: the likes of Billy Butcher, veteran of the Gulf; or in her distant youth a moonish nude, who'd streaked across the turf at Twickenham, yet nowadays, as writer of confetti, had set some very dependable plot – lots of bedtime writhing, culminating in murder – in Twill's very own town. Gasp!

3

Now I quote Mitrovich verbatim: '…till finally Twill escaped, to that heady ether greater mortals breathed in McGregor's central studio.' (Mitrovich, an unsung poet.)

Mitrovich in fact is a junior, or a senior, or no, an *ad hoc* consultant, on Ryder's programme planning team – but that's to run on (and on). Let us first take a look at that central studio, in many ways the hub of McGregor's chatty empire, rooted as it is in rebuilt Berlin (a few blocks only from that disrupted Europlaz where twelve floral tributes were laid, and later a thirteenth). All sorts of circus performers have crossed its floor – only recently fire-eating, ululating, finely balanced unicyclists. This of course was all part of McGregor's Eurofest, staple entertainment for the world's second economic empire, good clean family fun from every fireside TV/PC/HomeManager.

Twill's regular slot according to Mitrovich was always shot in the daytime. This was before an invited, lunch-time audience, in an ambiance suggesting midnight. Twill's was the inquisitor's seat, drawn up in opposition to two plush sofas, which were squarish, and in shade a brickish orange. This under the twinkle of studio lights. The show began with a sudsy band, all soupy strings and saxophones, on whose opening chord Twill trotted down an ivory staircase. He reached its foot under the full brassy hail of his signature tune, and a thunder of applause.

His smile was broad but his gloom laconic. He sat down, gabbled, then under a swirl of lights reeled in that succession of chat show guests whose natural sojourn was his sofas. These were exhausted athletes, whose autobiographies were even now in preparation. Or comediennes. Or chart musicians. Or newly retired politicians, whose memoirs we all looked forward to. Twill had a penchant too for movie stars, and a fascination for lottery zillionaires. Once he invited an education theorist, who was followed by a steeplejack.

After a decade of this, Twill began to tire, and in quitting the lens took himself off to the relative peace of his dairy farm. Incredibly, now that he's silver-haired, the show has been revived, and has run, to date, for eighteen months. There is a new breed of guest, more earthy, more pointedly stupid, more extravagant with its hair-dos.

"Or does it mean," a fatigued Twill asked his team, "that I'm simply getting old?"

Mitrovich thinks he might be getting wise, and I don't need to say that that is also dangerous.

4

A first sign of Twill's grand old sagacity was his open defiance of the planning and research team, rejecting a transsexual cleric, whose self-confession – from the pulpit that was also a McGregor tabloid – only compounded the scoop. Attractive as such a goop might be, Twill at this time favoured a quiet, pipe-smoking cove he'd found among the dampish spires of Oxford – in fact one of its college's elderly historians. This was a man in brown tweeds and carpet slippers who had dared to write a treatise on McGregor himself. Not many people remembered – or so rambled this owlish academician – that McGregor, with all the new zeal of his nativity, had worked hard to establish his media monopoly, not, at first, in Europe, but in Great Britain – which was not, as the professor pointed out, the United Kingdom.

McGregor, as alien and parvenu, banked his chips with the then Labour leader – a youthful gadabout – and engineered the immediate shift of his two English newspapers, a tabloid and a broadsheet, left towards the centre. The Left papered over its splits, and showed itself 'fully committed' to the 'idea' of Europe – a policy dilute enough to help it get elected. That, according to Twill's quite genial historian, necessarily spawned all sorts of McGregor-like monopolies, ostensibly 'competing' in a world market.

Twill's research team watched their ratings plummet, and no doubt shook heads resignedly. McGregor's heirs probably smiled into their tea cups. Then it was discovered that Twill, who belonged to the old school of broadcasters, did not, un-like his TV colleagues, go in for regular therapy, therefore one possible solution (to that ratings problem) was to urge and persuade him to do so.

I instructed Mitrovich to have all such therapists' reports copied to my office.

5

Twill's next leading guest should have been a brunette called Lila, who with partner Babiro planned, initially clad in leopard skins, not the *first*, but to now the most intimate broadcast record of sisterly cunnilingus (cameras implanted heaven knew where). Allow me, please, a first hearty handshake (and no hidden eye), as clearly I would wish them God's speed and good luck. Not that I intend by this to undermine Twill, who by now had had too many intimate moments of his own, among the fleecy meadows of his dairy farm, with its sonic rills and the gentle roar of hillside winds – so to say the numinous breath of angels in his ear. Thus borne aloft – a pastoral cloud after so much city exhaust – Childe Ryder painfully conceived (yet failed to graduate, philosophically, beyond the woolly bourne of his kindergarten) that the intense inner life of humanity projected itself as signs, symbols and artefacts onto that colourist's vellum, the world – which was vast and external. He argued the purpose of these analogies, a kind of lantern show, in sub-religious jingles – for example 'know thyself' – meaning, get to grips with interior things, and we surely transform what's contingent around us. Someone remarked how thoroughly Lila knew *herself* (for that matter Babiro, who wanted to show-off some recent plastic surgery). Twill overcame that little dig, producing yet another professor (also unwisely Oxbridge) – this one a specialist in cross culture. This was a man who gabbed, and was permanently foamed in spittle to each corner of his mouth. His argument ran something like this:

The masses get bored. That boredom is assuaged through a constant drip of soaps, gameshows, Lila-types. This is all harmless entertainment, performing a necessary social function, yet carries with it the potential for at least one lethal side-effect. Which is? urges Twill. Which is, Mr Twill, the full range (or rather its lack) of those 'projections', as you yourself term them, as you yourself place them in a model, ergo…

"Ergo," interrupts Twill (an exchange I downloaded, one late night with my cocoa), "ergo, the masses are bound by convention. In short, we lose our capacity to question."

Well bravo, Ryder Twill!

6

Twill's third professor – and here I personally wouldn't wish to go beyond that trio – preferred a script, a half-dozen rehearsals, and plenty of make-up – mainly as cover for a slight disfigurement to his cheek bone. In fact he refused to appear unless these conditions were met. His name was von Recht, and even Twill considered him a liability. After a great deal of thought, four minutes and twenty-two seconds were as much as he would allocate.

7

Studio One, McGregAir

Scene, Studio One, night, or really day. Ringmaster's chair. One square sofa, shade a brickish orange. Lights go up. The Twill show signature (saxophone and strings). Twill, bearing papers, trots on balls of feet down gleaming staircase. Applause. Music fades out. Twill in spotlight, "My first guest tonight, etc.," in slightly nasal tone. Drumroll, von Recht down staircase, applause, fade-outs. Host, guest, shake hands. Both men sit. Introductory chat, not too contentious, then:

TWILL I know you have spent many years looking into this, this question of programme integrity, a theme my viewers have become familiar with over the last few weeks.

VON RECHT Ja, ja…

TWILL I shall be accused – and perhaps my accusers are right – of biting the hand that feeds me, but much of your research, over the last decade or so, has centred on the McGregor corporation, whose hospitality we share.

VON RECHT Ja, McGregor, thad iss korrect.

TWILL In particular, I know you've examined certain

areas of McGregAir's – or MGA's – huge media output, in relation to what you call *balance* in our society.

VON RECHT High ard belongs to MGA's kommercials. [Chuckles.]

TWILL Now I know that's not the frivolous comment it seems. Perhaps you could talk us around that.

[Director in control room already anticipating edit process. For now holds head in hands.]

VON RECHT Firsd I vanded do say id is no form off kridicism on dhe McGregors or dheir granddaddy. It does nod madder to dhese people, thad is kommercially, vhedder dhe mass vonts Berg or dhe Bilge Boyz. For dhe minisder in goffernment id is a liddle bid komplicaded.

TWILL Could you explain that…

VON RECHT Off course Berg or Barb belongs in dhat school vhere dhe people are ask do dhink – vhich MGA vould kader vor, if dhe people vont. Dhat for goffernment's a liddle problemadic, since vot is an edoocation if nod a preparation for dhe rigour off kommerce/intustry – no I dhink Alban must lead dhem away from dhis – dhat iss dhe danger.

TWILL Though that isn't, you think, how the case is presented…

VON RECHT Ach nein! Your afferage media presender/kommendador I dhink can predend a selecd or élide holts dhe svay…

TWILL Holds sway.

VON RECHT Ja, ja.

TWILL But is that really so?

VON RECHT Id is nod. [Difficult pause.]

TWILL So, um. Could we perhaps summarise the position so…There may well be an 'élite', but an élite only in name – in other words exercising no power of influence on the mass.

VON RECHT Ja.

TWILL The mass, which still thinks of itself as shackled by, and would like to rebel against, an élite, is in fact already very well spoken for.

VON RECHT Ja, ja.

TWILL Could there be certain advantages in maintaining this situation?

VON RECHT Ja, ja – jusd so…Egonomic.

TWILL Well on that subject, my next guest…

VON RECHT Feneffer vee see a represendadiff off dhe mass, who hass komm indo dhe konzert –

TWILL Professor…

VON RECHT I vill say Oscar –

TWILL Professor von…

VON RECHT He vill ask: "Heff vee still nod eradicaded dhis?"

TWILL Herr Professor von Recht, how eloquently you have made those interesting points. No, please, don't go away! Stay! [Turns to camera two, forced smile, muted applause] My next guest…

8

Imagine my concern when Mitrovich – who had large, close-set eyes, was youngish and wore his hair long – when Mitrovich got himself seconded to another team (briefly I grant). Too abruptly for my plans, I found he had flown to the English Riviera – more precisely to a palm-strewn hotel in Torquay – for a deputising role in MGA's coverage of this year's trade conference. This as you know is entirely geared to the business community, in all its grey opulence, and is never averse to odd words of advice transatlantic-style. The attraction was a dusting of star orators, all from Capitol Hill. I did not venture into that Colosseo, and instead lodged at the Golden Barb – black beams, brasses and local beer – which was hidden in a veil of windswept elms, some yards off a track going NNW out of Slapton. On my first foggy morning, after a night of mulled brandy and bedwarmers, I met up with Mitrovich on Slapton Sands (or actually shingle). Mitrovich wore a long grey coat, onto whose epaulettes his mousy ringlets – uniformly darkened in the sea air – contracted themselves damply and dejectedly. Fountains of spume crashed to the edge of the bay, and dissolved. The sea's horizon, a steely blue arc, was distant and dewy. Mitrovich said that Twill was now under control. This, not because of the ratings – a blasphemy Twill dismissed, with irritated gestures – but because his argument was self-defeating. That is to say, one may challenge the god Mediocrity – in full panoply as necessary – in only one way. That was, as denizen in the god's own country. Those hapless crocks of Oxenford – who represented quite another strain of banality – merely united the enemy. I said I therefore looked forward to the warm pinkish swathes of Lila's interiors.

9

A memo to One. In essence, we can't see a problem with Twill. One replies with an invitation, which I accept. This means: a few pleasant hours with sherry, sandwiches, and a private tour of his eighteenth-century aquarelles. Excellent. And what a place he's got.

Bitstream

Here I have the benefit of hindsight, which I hope to pass on to you, once you have read these memos, because Diamond – I hope against only *geographic* hope – must one day declare a final destination to the maze of his world-wide travel. His journeys I find so meticulously singled out in the coloured tissues he drops in my path as bait ('scuse me while I just blow my trumpet on this peach-tinctured sample I have found in my boudoir). I am running on. However, allow me to tell you that wittily he has chosen the casket of McGregor's nativity as the place where he wants us to meet, where I'm told to expect a frame house miles up a dirt track. It means that almost the last duty Miss Ashley performs for the BDP – or Bureau of Data Protection, after years of service – is a flight booked under the plump signature of my alias, for of all places Auckland. In anticipation I have packed my toothbrush. I'm ready to go. I still submit to her vetoes nevertheless, which rest today in the pile of electronic memos I made her print and sift, a whole mountain of lettrure I later thought better of, and tell her to bin. Her reply is *Certainly not!*

"But I don't think, honestly, Miss Ashley, they're suitable for the handover file…"

"On the contrary. They are so extremely illuminating. Apart from which I spent a whole morning…"

"Okay – "

Miss Ashley is well travelled. That in part explains why her face is so full of English character, and lined. I by the way am glum. Therefore she means to tell me how the New Zealand air is bound to be good for the wheeze of my European lungs – all spiced with the scent of gum or eucalyptus (NZ a paradise of woodsmoke and overnight stoves).

"Okay," I say. "Put those memos in the handover file. Though I reserve the right to edit. Annotate…" You see, I cannot allow electric pens in others' hands to undermine my tyrannies. "…though it looks as if," I say to Miss Ashley, "I'm after all to miss your retirement bash."

74

Subject: Samples   **Date:** 14/4/51
To: JohnFrame@BDP (Private_net)
From: Anno@BDP (Private_net)

John – Miss Ashley remains stalwart, even in the throes
of impending retirement (eterne knows when that happy
vacation shall also be mine). She passed me those
thickly rubber-stamped recruitment papers, which I have
now examined, notwithstanding the treacly blurs of ink
picked up somewhere between your desk and mine.
Personally I'm glad not to have been involved in the
process, given those prickly breezes apt to blow through
your gîte (I call it yours since it's no one else's preference) – that is once all its shutters are open. Pontivy,
so unassuming (you say).

I see your third and final candidate is a man of military
distinction (knows how to wire a bomb or two). Does
that also mean he set compass and calipers to a well
rehearsed road map, all spread out on his passenger
seat, driving solo from the ferry at Roscoff – which after
a lifetime of wrong turns and sudden reversals I should
begin to consider myself… Did he enjoy the quiet walks,
the bike rides? Does he play pool?

Best, Anno

Subject: Re: Samples   **Date:** 17/4/51
To: Anno@BDP (Private_net)
From: JohnFrame@BDP (Private_net)

Anno – He's a Blimp and a man of action, but not so far
as I know keen on sports or recreation. Mal did the social bit, so why not ask him… He's got good ministerial
references.

Can't stop, John

Subject: Blimp   **Date:** 17/4/51
To: MalDeFak@BDP (Private_net)
From: Anno@BDP (Private_net)

Mal – From what JF says, it looks as though we're going to get the above named. I know you took a look at him, up Pontivy way. What's he like?

Anno

PS: Bletsoe I *would* defend, if only because so many of his reprints adorned so much of my mother's kitchen space. Back then it wasn't *all* formaldehyde, silkscreen repros and corporal laceration. If we ever get to an exhibition, I'd like to talk to you about some new ideas I've got for Archives. No doubt we'll come back to this. Adieu

Subject: Revival   **Date:** 17/4/51
To: Anno@BDP (Private_net)
From: MalDeFak@BDP (Private_net)

Anno – No doubt we *have* come back to this. The past I think is out of bounds, at least that part of it we remember, simply because it speaks out by abstention, not absorption. It tells us the time of day from a timeless shade.

Blimp unlike you I don't think would see this as having any relevance to the network, whose culture of decisions follows linear paths – could never submit itself to the relative structures of the network's sub-relative nodes. Nevertheless I think he'll be useful. Perhaps what we really want here is someone free of our nodal swamps.

Yours etc., Mal

Subject: Blimp   **Date:** 18/4/51
To: JohnFrame@BDP (Private_net)
From: Anno@BDP (Private_net)

John – Any chance I might have a word with this Blimp before he's appointed? You know, second, third opinions…

Anno

Subject: Blimp   **Date:** 20/4/51
To: Anno@BDP (Private_net)
From: JohnFrame@BDP (Private_net)

Anno – It isn't by any means certain that we *will* recruit him. There might even be late applications, which I for one would want to look at. I will speak to you.

John

To my best recollection, John, or One, did not touch on this subject again until Six's inauguration – all under the hot golden oils of Ix's unremitting sun, with Six himself in tetchy mood. If he looked anonymous, *I* especially knew, at a first chance glimpse, exactly who he was (ludicrously ill-apparelled in a pinstripe suit, his jowls still pink from the vernal breezes sweeping over Brittany). By the nose nearly, I watched him led round the cobbled streets of Ix by one in a team of deodorised youths, who were nowadays permanently employed at the Bureau's hospitality centre. Later, when we shook hands, his palm was damp. He was hot and agitated.

I saw him again under the town's awnings, at three o'clock still desperate to find shade from Ix's fiery sol. His shirt was damp with perspiration. Under the walls of Castle Maqueda, I watched him take out his kerchief and mop his brow, his jacket by now removed and borne limply over a weary arm (stiff upper Six hadn't loosened his tie). I had work papers, into which I retreated, at my café table, so soon as I saw him emerge – head, shoulders, stumpy torso, stubby little legs – from the deep angular shadow of the ramparts, his escort close behind him, clipboard permanently poised.

I couldn't help but observe, as Six swatted himself with a chequered blue hanky, impatient with the many tourists, most of whom were German. Then somehow he pinned himself to an elderly lady wearing an old-fashioned floral dress, whose grandchildren buzzed at her feet, and whose sun shade caught itself briefly in a loose thread to the stitching at Six's shoulder. Six disappeared, into the bourne of Ix's marketplace, where as haplessly he ran into a stall-holder, then a photographer, then a troupe of Moorish street players. When I caught sight of him again, he had stepped from the doorway of a souvenirs shop, dark, airless cavern in whose umbral depths he had bought a blackthorn walking stick, an article crowned with a stylish hook in ram's horn. His escort followed, checking his watch, fanning his face with his clipboard. After brief consultation, they walked off in the direction of the car park, by which time of course I knew that John and Mal had no intention of holding out for late candidates.

Pity.

Subject: Craig Diamond   **Date:** 28/4/51
To: Anno@BDP (Private_net)
From: JohnFrame@BDP (Private_net)

Anno – Word we have from the ministry concerns the world-famous Craig Diamond, who I thought had disappeared long ago (didn't he quit our fair continent in very bad odour?). It seems he's made a spectacular bid for a major shareholding in EuroSHart – and I don't have to tell you what *that* means…

Needless to say, we must all keep a careful eye on what develops.

John

I didn't in fact read this memo until 1st May, when Miss Ashley, noting how tired and puffy round the eyes I looked, placed it on my desk. That's the degree of trust, Miss Ashley set free with my notepad and password. She was there long enough for me to tell her how the retirement process, what with handing over to the *figment* of my successor, had taken its toll. Queyntly she tottered off with the file (you remember the one, its tinct a sugared strawberry) whose bulge and detailed history, expressed in a thousand other memos, went a long way back.

Diamond, himself having played no small role in the re-commodification of an earlier epoch – which today looked to me like a miles-long meander of fence pieces – if he could now give up his pleasure beach in Malibu, I reasoned must be bored. Could that fantastic line in indoor swimwear you'd think of him in, or the daily trek into the glassy dome of his studio, workplace all kitted out with electronic media paints – could it all have suddenly lost its attraction?

I couldn't at this stage say whether or not he was bound for Europe, even when the out trays of Samples were still being sifted into the intrays of my own demesne, with its many satellites – a scheme soon to be swept away by Six. Did I resent Six? He after all as a new appointee operated slightly behind my back, and already seemed likely to storm the paper summit of the sampling department, thing spawned in a reluctant, not to say unwieldy process of fission from my own...

I could reflect that Six seemed very determined to re-invent his new department, one afternoon as I gazed down at the three lower-floor windows of his office. Just then Frame crossed my threshold, a man newly troubled by the minister, and having to realign his chain of command. Could I now report directly to De Fak?

Why yes:

Subject: Media goop   **Date:** 3/5/51
To: MalDeFak@BDP (Private_net)
From: Anno@BDP (Private_net)

Mal – JF asks me to keep you posted on the Diamond case. Also I hate to tell you this, but I don't think I've made exactly the best start with our man of action, Alexander the Blimp. I did try to make him feel welcome those few mornings ago – slightly overcast, all for the great man's benefit – when he and his trunk-loads of documents arrived for a first full day of work. You know I left a few friendly lines on his notepad, which he redirected several hours later, completely re-worked (my own text comes back to me, and looks like a runestone littered with hieroglyphs). His name he replaced by his personal code, which as you know is 6, or as he terms it 'Six'. Two innocuous placenames end up as X and Y (not Exe and Wye). Document date – in any case electronically generated, and as a footnote – he sees fit to excise completely (probably because it also bears a document name, in whose watermark 'CastMaq' is a component).

Let me ask you this. Are you entirely sure about this man?

Anno

Subject: Re: Media goop   **Date:** 5/5/51
To: Anno@BDP (Private_net)
From: MalDeFak@BDP (Private_net)

Anno – Does seem a bit excessive, since this *is* a private network. Still. Just might be some whizzo bit of firmware *he* knows about that we don't. Who can say what the military has secret access to!

Thanks by the way for that note on Diamond. Can't say I've followed his career that closely, though I do remember that drama-doc of his, *Stand Up For Europe!* Was that his classical period?

Yours etc., Mal

Subject: Goops in general   **Date:** 7/5/51
To: MalDeFak@BDP (Private_net)
From: Anno@BDP (Private_net)

Mal – It was his blue/depressed/depressing, ironic period, but the height nevertheless of his media starburst – that staged fantasia with gold and purple sky rockets, all fizzing up in a TV sky. I try not to be irascible, but Six in his general incommunicado doesn't much help. He never seems to venture outside – his office, let alone the building. I forget what he looks like...

Best, Anno

Subject: Re: Goops in general   **Date:** 8/5/51
To: Anno@BDP (Private_net)
From: MalDeFak@BDP (Private_net)

Anno – I'm out for the next week (ABC conference), but will I promise speak with Six.

Yours etc., Mal

Subject: Out of office hours   **Date:** 13/5/51
To: One (Private_net)
From: Six (Private_net)

Cc: Two, Three, Four, Five, Seven, Eight, Nine, Ten (Private_net)

Gentlemen – I note that some or all of you think it perfectly acceptable to re-route internal office mail to home receiving equipment on those occasions when time away from your desks is anticipated. This is a security breach and as a practice must stop.

Six

Subject: Networks   **Date:** 13/5/51
To: One (Private_net)
From: Six (Private_net)

Cc: Two, Three, Four, Five, Seven, Eight, Nine, Ten (Private_net)

And how private is the Private_net? Does anyone know?

Six

That, according to Two, earned an angry rebuke from Three, Eight and Nine, who are all women. (It's slightly unsettling to see that Six works on a Saturday – Saturday 13th May.)

Subject: Security   **Date:** 17/5/51
To: Anno@BDP (Private_net)
From: MalDeFak@BDP (Private_net)

Anno – This might amuse you. Natsuki, Charlotte and Anne-Marie [Three, Eight and Nine] are up in arms over Six's sexism, all on the strength of a memo. As an issue it's overshadowed the one the memo has raised, re security. Do you have a view?

Mal

Subject: Sex's sixism   **Date:** 18/5/51
To: MalDeFak@BDP (Private_net)
From: Anno@BDP (Private_net)

Mal – I have personally encountered Natsuki's outrage, who over a canteen salad discoursed with passion and an icy splash of watercress on **a)** the backlash against women, and **b)** the more recent Jeta Olsen (d. 2032) (whose position is wholly political, and therefore compromised – though you'd have to check this out, being Natsuki's specialism, not mine). In respect of security, I think you'll find our bone-missived Bonaparte isn't particularly interested in *my* view, or indeed anyone else's. According to Hany [Procurement], Six has already inquired as to budgets and hardware upgrades, with particular regard to a brand-new generation of datascopes (scopophilia seems to be Six's disease).

Isn't all this getting out of hand?

Anno (apprehensive)

Subject: Re: Sex's sixism   **Date:** 19/5/51
To: Anno@BDP (Private_net)
From: MalDeFak@BDP (Private_net)

Anno (apprehensive) – Don't worry, I shall speak to Six.

Mal

Subject: Anno (apprehensive)   **Date:** 25/5/51
To: MalDeFak@BDP (Private_net)
From: Anno@BDP (Private_net)

Mal – Then do that soon! Yesterday he at last ventured outside, and found me on my lacquered bench in Emma's old azalea dell, point as you know I often retreat to under the load of my papers. It's here that, in an almost constant pause for thought, I can think back over that part-finished inventory and handful of outdoor monuments, and satisfy myself that nothing shall survive our purge. There remains that round-limbed, round-shouldered nude, on a direct line to Six's triad of windows, reclining in a period sense of tranquillity. Six – laborious – was far from tranquil himself, in the pugnacious little strides that he made towards me, over the pearls of dew filming the lawns. Glad to see him in a light linen suit and matching sun hat, though there all reasonable commerce ended. He asked, did I not think it at all dangerous working outside, when just then a slight breeze tugged at my papers, detaching a single leaf from the rest, where I had lodged them under a pebble. He scooped it up and advised me to take better care.

Incidentally I later had Miss Ashley print off his curriculum vitae, from which I learn – hardly a surprise – that although his background is military, he has never seen live action – bar regular manoeuvres and exercises in the Gulf of Finland, in that on-off ambiguity with our Eastern allies. We've got him, have we, because of his nose for trouble?

Please tell me something positive about him...

Anno

To which Mal did not reply. Instead during the last operatic death throes of the old and trusted sampling system, the only mail I received over the next few days was from Six's department, Six now fully controlling Samples. Efforts he made – and which I cannot condemn him for – bore that moral shade of his, and weren't entirely political. With Mal, and perhaps also with John (and on a lesser timescale probably with the minister too), this in itself could not be considered serious, since the assumption was that Six would eventually fit the role. On the other hand, this may have been only a prelude to the plans Six had for target organisations and a range of individuals, where plunging his moral litmus offered valuable insight as to their political sensibilities. That the problem was compounded by his evident personality clash with me was immaterial, since Anno (I don't mind telling you how much joy I feel at this, and how light-headed too) was about to retire, in which case my successor might well enjoy a healthy rapport with Six where I emphatically don't (never mind the problems in recruiting one). As I have already said, Six's studious gaze into McGregor's and other networks at this time told us more of his own obsessions than of anything else.

I did think that I could patch things up with Six, though in mulling this over filed under 'S' papers indexed 'B', a slight mishap I am sure Miss Ashley will some day remedy. I took cold showers and regular strolls, and in one instance found myself lost in the ghoulish twilight of Oscar Barb's cathedral – or actually his theatre – which these days was all grey walls and stalactites. Here I found a sodden conductor's score, chewed at the corners and badly discoloured at the spine – his *Nuptials Charade* (piece *premièred* under its creator's baton at Tanglewood). I looked up and out through one of the pointed windows, to a deep blue sky, which as I stood there gradually streaked itself in mare's tails.

I had an idea of how best to approach Six in a sense of conciliation.

Subject: Monthly progress meeting **Date:** 30/5/51
To: One@1009 (Private_net)
From: 186@1009 (for Five@1009) (Private_net)

Cc: Two, Three, Four, Six, Seven, Eight, Nine, Ten {@1009} (Private_net)

All note – Revised agenda (attached)... Section 'Let's now be informal...' inserted above 'AOB'.

Natsuki commented. Then Mal, with a smirk and a first daiquiri, asked if really this was such a good idea, scepticism fully justified when, some days later, and at the close of the meeting – when I had placed a much over-cooked review of Sir Oscar's *Charade* under Six's volcanic gaze – that latter twitched then stoked himself up under a brooding smokestack (with what a fulsome dynamite!). Actually no – Six did not find it in any way remarkable that right here, under the loping shadows of Castle Maqueda's sun-oranged towers, the last clamped twitches of twentieth-century idealism, a constrained plop and trickle of art, had found spiritual expression in the naïve conflations of an Englishman's dramatic little musiquette.

What did I do? I looked again at Flora's chiton (that bench, that azalea dell). Looked gravely at that garment cut away at the waist, and draped in a moulding of flutes from a raised upper arm all the way to a rounded hip. Looked at her finger, aloft to perch an ostrich.

Subject: Ah well!   **Date:** 2/6/51
To: Natsuki@BDP (Private_net)
From: Anno@BDP (Private_net)

Natsuki – It looks as though we're *all* going to have to put up with Six, and his solid planes of discourse, for some time to come. For myself I'm off to Bordeaux (how well do we recall its showers of fairy dust), in just a few days from now. There is, Natsuki, nothing I'd like more than to see you there again.

Anno

Subject: Re: Ah well!　　　**Date:** 2/6/51
To: Anno@BDP (Private_net)
From: Natsuki@BDP (Private_net)

Anno – Nice idea! Sadly I've heaps to do…

Natsuki

Subject: Re: Ah well!　　　**Date:** 2/6/51
To: Natsuki@BDP (Private_net)
From: Anno@BDP (Private_net)

Natsuki – Then what about at least the open awnings of
a restaurant – tonight, or tomorrow night – which we
can drive to – long lazy headlights mooching all over
the pine-blue of Ix's mountains… What do you say…

Anno

[Not that I will tell you what she said.]

Subject: Diary　　　**Date:** 5/6/51
To: JohnFrame@BDP (Private_net)
From: Anno@BDP (Private_net)

Cc: MalDeFak@BDP (Private_net)

John – I shall be out for the next three or four days. If
there's anything urgent, tell Miss Ashley to get in touch,
who knows how to reach me (I shall be in Bordeaux
then London).

Anno

In Bordeaux I cooled my grip round a tumbler of iced liquor,
then having emptied a blue plastic sachet of Japanese postage
stamps (Natsuki's) I made several conference calls over the
BDP's private network – nothing more secure, one might have
thought. Finally I weighed in my palm a water-filled boule
ball, its shade a grazed yellow, which I placed down and left
in the ellipse of its shadow. I meanwhile pressed on for the
Manche, and for Dr Ducane's damp London practice, where
Ryder Twill was having his fortnightly therapy sessions.

On my return, this:

Subject: Security   **Date:** 5/6/51
To: One@1009 (Private_net)
From: Six@1009 (Private_net)

Cc: Two, Three, Four, Five, Seven, Eight, Nine, Ten
{@1009}(Private_net)

Gentleman – It is imperative we use code names not just over the network (private or no), but in person too. Laxity will cost.

Six

(Still that suspension of Three, Eight and Nine, on which topic, or related topic, the one-time scholar Mal De Fak made certain observations, all derived from economic theory – not that I myself am qualified to comment. Therefore I shan't comment.) But enough, these dual asides (sheathe my flashing blade)…

Subject: Ducane   **Date:** 9/6/51
To: MalDeFak@BDP (Private_net)
From: Anno@BDP (Private_net)

Mal – Plonked myself down in those wetlands at the foothills of Dr Ducane's Therapy Centre, by which I mean a park bench in the square outside his office. Appositely, that is Other Pater Square – you locate it as a short walk from the more famous Kenford Square. A bronze cast centring the latter has that Euro PM (extinct breed) as a St George, overseeing his last horseman's thrust into a writhing House of Luds (dead peers, dead bishops, dead loss). All this (I'm tempted to say propaganda) takes place under a brown London sky, pendulous with fog and smog, and for all I know frogs. But don't forget this was once my country.

Ducane did appear briefly, in a hurry with his document case, a chubby-faced cherub, off to some meeting a ghastly tube-ride away. Techies back at base (the beautiful Castle Maqueda, which I adore above all under a setting southern sun) confirmed that Ducane's wasn't an organisation to which it was planned – at least in the short term – to connect a datascope. I asked them to change that and fork all output to my portable. Result, following report:

Our quack's clientele isn't at first that exciting. Notables consist of a prize-winning author – the inherent deceptions in *that* kind of charade do cry out for therapy, I agree; a grey banker of Bank; an anchor man I imagine on the same moulded shoreline as Ryder Twill (because aren't they all!); a ragbag of other minor media pundits; also one English blue-blood, who in pre-FRE days might probably count himself nth in line for the throne (very big n, very doomed throne). But here's the shock, for not only has Diamond suddenly enrolled *himself* at the Ducane Centre, he is even now in London!

I didn't chance to meet him, though I did learn that what he wants from Ducane (or what he *says* he wants) is recovery therapy, because he's trying to remember the one college buddy who lurked in the shadows, and whose name however much he strains his neurons remains a blank. Soon we shall see a media jamboree in celebration of his sixtieth birthday, and for this Craig wants to round up all his Benbrook coevals, the closest of whom he wants on his top table, so to speak.

I ask you!

Anno

Old King Craig had forged his early career on the thorny tail of student subversiveness, yet since the height of his success (in practically all media) had been docile and house-trained. At sixty, did he gnaw on that same old bone, for a last jibe and hurrah at Establishment Europa?

Subject: Diamond   **Date:** 12/6/51
To: Anno@BDP (Private_net)
From: MalDeFak@BDP (Private_net)

Anno – I think we need to talk.

Mal

88

We talked about names, Two scything in benignly with asides on the Martin obelisk – which, had it been entirely down to Aimé, might have been instead an odalisque (that, I tell him, is witty). I had chosen this moment with Two, once again in and around Emma's azalea dell, because Two too likes the gardens. Her stone bodkin skewered my dreaming heaven – a milky whip of tangerine, its one cloud in an otherwise cloudless azure – which, as I stated it to Mal, is a paradise purer than any plain architect had planned for in the hills and valleys of Ix. Two told me:

"I have passed Six's submissions to One, who I am sure will think as I do."

"How, Two, do you think?"

"Well of course I share Six's moral outrage, but you're right – he's missed the point. Did you enjoy your break in Bordeaux?"

"Immensely. While I was there, Two, I placed a spy in Six's camp."

"A spy! Is that necessary? I mean there are moves afoot to have Six sidelined to Security, where he's already been asked to advise. By the way did you see his memo?"

"The one insisting on codenames?"

"Yes, codenames."

"Why do you think, Mal, I keep calling you "Two"?"

"It's because, Anno, you've a penchant for farce. How are those handover notes?"

"Much broader in scope than I'd planned. Plus I have to keep revising them. Miss Ashley though – I mean One Eight Six – is a great help."

"One Eight Six! Are there really that many staff?"

"It depends on which point in the scale you're looking from, and in which direction. Look. That tangerine cloud is now in the shape of a basilisk."

Subject: Ducane   **Date:** 15/6/51
To: MalDeFak@BDP (Private_net)
From: Anno@BDP (Private_net)

Mal – Our Sweeney Ducane, butcher whose psychic hands bear psychic blood in a daub of symbolic ordures – Ducane ain't such a mug. This is because that first electric trickle of kilobytes drip-fed via the datascope into my various tiptops (pockettop, palmtop, laptop, and latterly my desktop) – all traffic here hath biblically ended. As well I placed codename Luis under codename Six's proboscis, lithe boy from the damp igneous shadow of a distant ruin *somewhere* (Moorish). Lightfinger Luis has learned the language of federated Europe, and having escaped his disease-ridden home – a shanty town – now thrives on the sicknesses of Ix. I find I share in its paranoias. All this time he attends to the shredders of Data Protection, and particularly those of Samples. Alas, there is only so much one can do, among all this tragic flotsam washed up round our feet. My worst fear is an inquisition military-style, knowing how, in that ingenuous way of his, he is bound to confess everything to Six – and I mean *everything*. I would reproduce here a few crumpled memos rescued from a bin, and addressed to Six, and regarded by him as unimportant, though I prefer to pass them on by hand (that paranoia I talked about). No doubt you will pass them to One. Then, without fuss, I intend to return my dark-eyed angel to his labyrinth in Archives.

All beset, Anno

One of those memos was a proposed agenda concerning Craig's first meeting with the board of EuroSHart, where curiously Natsuki was listed as chairperson. This prompted Mal to meet me again on Friday afternoon, after a breeze, and a rising wind – then finally a cloudburst followed by an hour or so of warmish, diamond-coloured rain. Those creeping paranoias first mentioned in my last memo had now also wrinkled Mal's otherwise smooth limpid brows, who suggested, then went on to insist that we rendezvous high

90

above the vacant boards of Aimé's – or was it Emma's, or was it Sir Ossie's? – miniature Bayreuth. This in its piquancy represented a precarious five minutes gently at sea, slung up among the rolling catwalks, ropes, ladders and lighting rigs, attempting above all else progress, and the prosaic business of everyday censorship, which in its quiet moments held itself suspended over the moving crags and quakes of Ix's dramatic void. One whole season of farewell performances had seen Barb's programmatic *Mount Volcano* develop from its initial, merely discordant tableaux – its geometric scheme a triangulation of grass-skirted, South Pacific islanders – to the full-blown stridency of political innuendo, where any solid artist of that time paddled in the streams of Third World ethnography, bearing hooks for our public conscience, and somewhere discreetly an antiseptic lint for those individual acts of reflection indulged in safe within the mirrored walls of our privacy. Mal firmed his grip. Papers were passed. I said if this was industrially safe, structurally it wasn't, whereon sympathetically a slight dusting of grey fungus cascaded from the loose plank my uncertain foot forward had made more insecure, a minor hail coming to ground with the faintest patter among that empty space some ways beneath us. Mal did attempt to assuage this and other fears, making the point especially that Six had now been briefed as to our interest in Diamond – politically a clever operator during the social climb of his early manhood – such that no missive on that subject, passed to Six, and however minor, should find itself destined for Luis's intervening hand, an incurious Blimp having had it jettisoned among boxloads of who knows what other flotsam, to suffer instantaneous death in the jaws of the shredder. "I'm glad to hear that, Mal," I said.

On the following Monday morning, an astonished and out-raged Hany (Procurement), in the comfort of knowing I for one would understand his pique (my eyes did roll towards Ix's indistinct mountain ridges), showed me this, a memo whose transmission should have been lackey-to-lackey:

Subject: Paperless office (so-called)
Date: 18/6/51
To: Ten@1009 (Private_net)
From: Six@1009 (Private_net)

Attention Ten – Please note the tendency in all departments to generate excessive paperwork. Please order
for <u>this</u> department two fast-feed shredders.

Six

A look at your calendar (mine for June shows the empurpled
wintered vertebrae of the Coromandel) will tell you the
eighteenth was a Sunday.

Subject: Surveillance   **Date:** 22/6/51
To: MalDeFak@BDP (Private_net)
From: Anno@BDP (Private_net)

Mal – Think Ducane has rumbled my datascope (nothing but line noise grating through my portable). Can
hope he's uncertain as to why it's connected. In the
meantime I've arranged for the cleaning contractor
blessed with several clients including Ducane to sub-
contract all its Other Pater Square accounts to a smaller,
more efficient, and wholly fictitious firm, 'employing' a
Jack of all Jakes, who is also in the espionage biz. He,
when not emptying square-cut glass ashtrays, will forward on to Samples even the least sparkle of Diamantine
plunder.

All beast, Anno

A good-natured Mal, all nuptial smiles and the studded flash
of his newly engraved wedding ring, had chosen one other
amusing location – that's to say Emma's former study – in
order to confirm that One agreed thus far with me, that Six's
choice of samples wasn't so far suitable for the minister's over-
burdened desk. All that's now left, incidentally, of Emma's
private chamber – perhaps even in her day a monkish
scriptorium – is a hard wooden pew on a cold stone floor.
Light, despite the southerly windows, is a powdery grey. More

important than this were One and Two, who connived at my methods, with the coded declaration that my findings shared as much importance in themselves as the means by which I'd obtained them. I joined Two, or Mal, at Emma's window, where Mal looked out and across and I suspect didn't see the encircling mountains of Ix, whose crags and fissures just then were a hazy purple, touched with charcoal and fringed with a palish blue. Two said:

"Six as you know is surveying Security, but it's not proving easy to get him transferred."

"That, Two, is unfortunate."

"It means we shall need your source to remain in place."

"That's quite impossible!"

"Anonymity respected."

"No."

"Look, this Twill's probably harmless, but Diamond definitely isn't. You know the climate. All this mutual suspicion. Personally, I find it almost claustrophobic."

"Mal!"

"Orders, Anno."

"In that case I insist on certain guarantees, foremost that my plant, whatever the outcome, shall be fully rehabilitated to his former, lowly position."

"How lowly?"

"Insignificantly so."

Two touched his chin, and looked down thoughtfully into Emma's old azalea dell. "Leave that with me, Anno."

Six of course, at the next policy meeting, was as usual stolid when the Twill case came to be discussed. I asked him what evidence there was of these remote listening devices he had warned us of, to which he replied "None – that is their strength".

I behold the crusted image of a grey shaft of sunshine dampening one patch of cold floor in Emma's sack-cloth under-sanctum. I fear for Luis. That is because I behold, fear or imagine the salty wastes of a Westernised Siberia, which I don't doubt exists.

93

Subject: Paperless office (so-called)
Date: 24/6/51
To: One@1009 (Private_net)
From: Six@1009 (Private_net)
Cc: Two, Three, Four, Five, Seven, Eight, Nine, Ten {@1009} (Private_net)

Attention all – Far too much potentially hazardous information is committed to scraps of paper here and there. This must stop.

Six

Subject: Surveillance   **Date:** 30/6/51
To: MalDeFak@BDP (Private_net)
From: Anno@BDP (Private_net)

Mal – Don't wish to be alarmist, but... Our Jack of all Japes, as handy with a secret camera as with all those thickly coloured rinses for the toilet flush, can count among his domestic honours a carefully photographed transcript of Diamond's weekly therapy session – or should we now say clay, crafted in those bloody hands of Dr Jacques Ducane. The world according to Craig is a symbiotic order, where a bleakly conceptualised mass (of men, women and apes), to widen its life and world experience, seeks nourishment (and gets a chewy pap) from people like him (people like Diamond). These, the thirteenth tribe, unlike the rest of us don't swim against the tide (our metaphysical gruel one suddenly sees as pea-green and viscous), for theirs is a network of stellar proportions, whose frontier or canopy of starshine is coldly incandescent. Through it much of this mysterious abstract knowledge – and doubtless other assorted bric-à-brac – is relayed.

The good doctor (did he nod politely? did he count himself one of that thirteenth tribe?) made negligible progress on all other fronts, including that recovery of names (or I should say one name in particular) from Diamond's bad old student days. Would Diamond be semi-conscious, do you think, and chanting as a mantra

94

the few bits of detritus that did come out? Do I have the correct fixed mania when I intone, so, the fragmented lyric of something or other Craig is certain he penned in his last year at Benbrook:

O amber light [gap]
all my celluloid heavens [gap]
man, bird, beast, fish or herb or greenwood tree [gap]
clapper-board eternities [gap]
steamy *scenes* of love [gap]
instigate my cutting-room amours [gap]
after one of your seraphic smiles [gap]
Gee loves Exe and Exe loves Wye [gap]
wriggles up the weir [gap]
make-up brush benignity [gap]

I have no idea what this was intended to mean. I don't even know if it was anticipated that the desired name should eventually replace one of those many gaps, since nor Gee nor Exe nor Wye was evidently the magic appellation sought by the doctor's client. Worse than all this has been the bullish resolve with which Six swept it from his desk, on receiving his own copy, which I arranged to be sent to him, having myself studied that gibberish above (Six's frightening levels of inattention). Six sent it to be shredded – a flutter of incriminating paper that has fallen into the waiting arms of reliable, well paid Luis.

Thought you said Six had now been briefed...

All best, Anno

Subject: Re: Surveillance   **Date:** 30/6/51
To: Anno@BDP (Private_net)
From: MalDeFak@BDP (Private_net)

Anno – Six *has* been briefed. Don't gloat.

Mal

Six however had other things to consider:

Subject: Library access   **Date:** 30/6/51
To: Five@1009 (Private_net)
From: Six@1009 (Private_net)

Five – As you know, in the current review of security, denial of all public access to certain digitised libraries, in particular those of Paris, London and Rome is recommended. Machiavelli's *The Prince* is an obvious target for censorship. Can't agree with you that this V Nabokov is also a jolt to the popular mind. His *Bend Sinister* I've just struggled through, and found almost completely impenetrable. Please send me exhaustive list of other such books, authors, etc.

Six

Ra. Six in the fogs of Six's rudimentary critique spares one in our canon the barred gloom and cold stone floors of martyrdom and exile. Mal on the other hand fondled quite another ball and chain:

Subject: Diamond/Twill/security   **Date:** 3/7/51
To: Anno@BDP (Private_net)
From: MalDeFak@BDP (Private_net)

Anno – Six I think neatly recedes to a corner through that very long shortlist of proposed new security measures he so recently circulated – copy of which even the minister perused. This is our chance to concentrate on Diamond and Twill without Six's intervention.

John tells me you and he are off to view a private collection. Enjoy.

Mal

Subject: Re: Diamond/Twill/security
Date: 3/7/51
To: MalDeFak@BDP (Private_net)
From: Anno@BDP (Private_net)

Mal – Seems I'm a distant orb in Six's newly adopted linear circulation process, so I haven't had much time to consider his security document. That private view's tomorrow.

Anno

Subject: Library access   **Date:** 4/7/51
To: Five@1009 (Private_net)
From: Six@1009 (Private_net)

Five – I've looked at your list (you took a risk, jotting it on paper). This James Gould Couzzens, heading it – how dangerous in your mind is he?

Six

Oh, Six, a crazed pistolaire…

Subject: Golden age   **Date:** 6/7/51
To: MalDeFak@BDP (Private_net)
From: Anno@BDP (Private_net)

Mal – John's intriguing social set numbers the German banker Kuhn, whose collection of postmodern artefacts is claimed to be Europe's most complete. Showing ranged from Cubist cut-and-paste, to Surrealist dreamscape, to 3D VP exhibit, which the charming Frau Kuhn, in a flush of pomo enthusiasm, treated me to privately, in a distant chamber, long after most other guests had gone home. Her simple, heartfelt, bosom-heaving joy – not to say the alluring arch of her eye-brows – at so 'seminal' a period, now enjoying its first small revival, she attributed (she said) to the golden glow and healthy clean pursuit of 'liberated' art. She drew my attention to a piece whose faded cardboard plaque proclaimed its creator's name – a Cram Pollo, I think – and the title, *Seeing, de Grey, Zero*. These had

97

been applied in furry black marker pen – a dead hand scrawled on an emerald background. Piece itself was the glass dome of a fish bowl, newly filled with tapwater, whose curved blue-green surface is scattered with translucent Cyrillic characters. These with a haze of refracted sunlight stencil their mobile watermark onto a surrounding wedge of floor space. 'Marvellous...' I said. Frau Kuhn lamented our relative paucity today, which to the sods and clods of her cave-dweller consciousness (did John tell you about their house, which is underground) consists of no better pastime than blow-up dollies and virtual headsets, Europe's perennial rutting season having been reduced to probes, erogenous props and computer simulations. A *coitus dejectus*, without the complication of other persons involved. Why Pollo's or Bollo's or even Bordello's *Degree Zero* was clean, healthy and liberated wasn't so much aesthetics as a vagary of power, Frau Kuhn congratulating any form of public expression that had freed itself of a controlling institution or institutional cognoscenti (meaning books, books, books). Frau Kuhn hoped her and her husband's courageous little revival, bright bubble of civilisation, might do its bit to restore community faith in an art not wedded to *today's* legitimising power (that death ray of binary digits coupled to our 3D screens). "Fortunately," I said, "not all of us lag behind with the avant-garde" – these words a lost moonlit symphony, gentle plash of paradise besprinkling her pearl-garnered ears.

Herr Kuhn I think suspected nothing, now that I'd reached that alarming point where, with his rose-hued *hausfrau* – large, fluttering soprano, who led me by the hand – I returned to the hub of his Wonderland lair. Here one or two late whiskey-drinkers, including John Frame (that scent of anaesthetic on his breath), still propped themselves up alertly before those canvases. Politely I extricated myself. Politely I interested myself in the volcanic sky, whose mauve streaks graded to zinc, thence to the mauve lead of a molten sea, in the canvas Frame had paused at. He adjusted his cuffs then rolled his catalogue into a tube, before casting out on the subject of Six. Attractive though the proposition seemed, there

98

were certain difficulties in moving him to Security. Was that to do with his report? Gracious no, that was the least of it… Did Frame take that report seriously? "Serious, Anno, is not the right word. Certain recommendations are interesting." "Does he not want that job?" "Hasn't been asked. But it's not really Six I wanted to talk about." It was Twill he wanted to talk about, in respect of whom he wished to bypass Samples and Six again. "I shall have one of my men pass you relevant papers from time to time. I don't want this Twill thing to get out of hand…"

The last of Kuhn's exhibits was a phosphorescent stairway spiralling vine-like round the trunk of a tree, connecting a yellow plain and a graduated turquoise heaven. In the background haze, a dun range of hills. To the foreground, a freshly made corpse, in a burnt orange toga.

Good showing. Anno

Subject: Twill   **Date:** 7/7/51
To: Anno@BDP (Private_net)
From: MalDeFak@BDP (Private_net)

Anno – Twill's show until recently was listed among the top tiers of download catalogues. Now that he's turned pedagogic, he's been moved to the middle tiers. It's easier to find him through the search engines. I warn you he's smug.

Mal

Subject: Re: Twill   **Date:** 7/7/51
To: MalDeFak@BDP (Private_net)
From: Anno@BDP (Private_net)

Mal – Smug, I know… I downloaded, and watched, in the early hours one morning.

All bruised, Anno

And in fact, courtesy Mitrovich, a young, large-framed man of Swiss Alpine stock, I'd got plenty of research papers on Twill's thirty-year career, from his days as a provincial journalist tucked away discreetly in a tree-dappled Sussex High Street, to his current cold climate among the white sterile porcelain of McGregAir's Berlin studio. Mitrovich, himself a talented quill, I rely on unreservedly, having been either permanent or *ad hoc* consultant to Twill's programme planners for one or two or fifteen years (Mitrovich, incognito). In Mitrovich's view, screen host Twill is at last getting wise, perhaps through all those vacant hours spent in a drizzle of English weather, the red soil and windswept blackthorn of his dairy farm. Wisdom I don't need to advise is a dangerous acquisition, particularly as it relates to the careful displacements in a world run by media chiefs.

Subject: Numbing Sunday   **Date:** 10/7/51
To: MalDeFak@BDP (Private_net)
From: Anno@BDP (Private_net)

Mal – Am all bleary-eyed this morwen, having witnessed another Twill show. Have you seen this one? Guest, a pipe-sucking Clerk of Oxenford, wheeled out from all those dreaming spires – *no tyme for to studien here* – chosen, according to Mitrovich, in preference to a transsexual cleric, who in the frays of his Romish priesthood has decided to sell his story to a McGregor tabloid. Fifty-minute chat. For goddes sake!

Anno

Subject: Re: Numbing Sunday   **Date:** 12/7/51
To: Anno@BDP (Private_net)
From: MalDeFak@BDP (Private_net)

Anno – Regret lights out in conjugal household is 11 p.m., 11.30 Sundays – and no TV in our boudoir. Do tell me more.

Mal

100

Subject: Clerk of Oxenford   **Date:** 13/7/51
To: MalDeFak@BDP (Private_net)
From: Anno@BDP (Private_net)

Mal – You sure about this? 'More' is a man fitted to the ears in English brown tweeds, who says only that he wants to set the record straight, having written a tract or treatise on McGregor. It sounds like a biography, tracing, sensationally, McGregor's early years as an Oxford man himself, who at seventeen sputtered up Auckland's Southern Motorway, in a world-weary Nissan. McG and his rust-dotted Bluebird left almost terminally the sunny white gloss of small-town, clapboard frame-houses (his town was Paeroa, should you have a map; his bungalow was under Primrose Hill, should that map be ordnance). Not many people know (or even care) that McGregor – or Red Robbie in his Oxford days – adopted as debating stance a sentimentalised Leninism, or that his North Island community zeal, well-tempered by clement Pacific zephyrs, led to a first contract with one of the then plethora of UK phone companies. Great business idea was this: a conference chat line (no TV, no radio), with smooth-talking glazing specialist as anchor-man. McGregor, who throughout his life remained lean and acquisitive, thereafter soon established his media monopoly. The rest, as they say, is history.

Anno

Subject: Re: Clerk of Oxenford   **Date:** 17/7/51
To: Anno@BDP (Private_net)
From: MalDeFak@BDP (Private_net)

Anno – All good clean fun. Am surprised Professor Tweed didn't babble on about quantum leap in convergent technology, great part of which McGregor money gave rise to during that period.

Mal

Subject: Convergent technology   **Date:** 20/7/51
To: MalDeFak@BDP (Private_net)
From: Anno@BDP (Private_net)

Mal – Perhaps more correctly, convergent *ide*ology. Had Mitrovich held the casting vote, we might have looked forward to just such an analyst, man looking back to the workday world of the commercial academy, its gowned and flat-hatted gurus still at pains to control an expanding universe called hypertext. Their revelation seemed to be that conceptual systems, once founded on centres, hierarchies, margins and linearity, must now be abandoned and replaced by nodes, links, networks – in fact every kind of *multi*linearity. Their pet misconception saw all this multivectoredness as a revolution in human thought, while all along it must have been known that human thought is synaptic. Soon then, the TV broadcast followed in the hollow steps of cyberspace – with the consumer now seen as just another network link. As we all know, the frontiers of any broadcast are never clear-cut, since each screening is imprecisely bound by a chain of references to others of its kind (the same actors, directors, storylines cropping up here, there and everywhere). Any one programme downloaded to any one viewer's screen is in other words just a nodal incident. Here already we begin to identify those endless layers, that whole universe of other constellations superposed on a pinpoint known as the TV transmission.

Most alarmingly (for my money anyway, which in the high office I enjoy is golden doubloons), is the great potential our expanding networks have in confirming what linear deliveries established long ago, in the shape of all that detective, romance and 'human interest' type viewing, under which any odd enclave of slightly more sentient programming found itself oppressed. That was a tyranny taken to new levels of sophistication by the McGregor and other broadcasting empires – whose controls we ensure from the safety of our castle walls here at Ix. I therefore cannot agree that the technology is wonderfully democratising, and as such points the way to a decentralised, more liberated kind of existence – though of course that's the propaganda. Our purveyors of all this ubiquitous trash see only endless scope for proliferation.

This whole issue of the network is not so much one of irradiation (*where* I happen to be happens also to be the hub of the universe, and the nodal links are my access to any point in it) – it is one of utilisation. Twill in a way knows this, but is so subsumed by its culture that his efforts to resist it will always be clumsy.

Transmission ends. Anno

Mal I met next under the blare of Ix's medieval clock tower. In the shadow of its beaten gongs he recommended, mouthing at high noon, my 'convergent ideology' as the basis of polite coaching, aimed at Six.

"No," I said, "and anyway it's all down to Mitrovich, who knows just how to put his hands on all this museum information…"

"What's he got for us next?"

"Twill's show was set to feature a stunner called Lila – brassy brunette – who with partner Babiro planned, both of them wrapped in leopard skins, intimate tongue-and-grooving, with camera implants."

"But not now…"

"No. Childe Ryder's had too much time on his hands. Intense inner life on a three-cornered stool seems to have brought him to an ideal of humanity as projecting itself through signs, symbols and artefacts, onto a no longer bald canvas called the world. Therefore knowing ourselves is only really a question of reinterpreting the world we've created."

"I see. What world is he looking at?"

"World of culture. Rather he's investing in more of those Clerks of Oxenford to do it for him."

"Keep me posted, Anno. Any more news of Diamond?"

"I'll get on to Luis."

"And how are those handover notes? It's amazing, really, to think your job has never been written down, or – you know – specified…"

"That, Mal, is because I *am* the job."

"Well, yes – that's precisely it."

Subject: Twill, Mitrovich   **Date:** 21/7/51
To: MalDeFak@BDP (Private_net)
From: Anno@BDP (Private_net)

Mal – Can see why John chose Mitrovich, who sends word that Childe Ryder's soot-filled Aladdin's cave, his do-or-die metaphysics, with its stone echoes, Christian jingle, *know thyself* – this is just one more imperfect concentration of all that tacky mysticism left over from the last century – all somehow shop-window and artificial. Mitrovich, a blue-eyed inhabitant of Sark, medium build, sandalled, leather-thonged, deeply tanned, bearing an alpenstock, asks this of Master Twill: 'Does he perceive, in our general conspiracy of media imaging, a system that precedes us all, one whether we like it or not we are born into? That is, a surrounding flicker that is by definition outside the individual, that the individual can never create or modify by himself, or instead is compelled to get in among, in a contract passively signed-up for by all other members of his community…"

That is I think the idea of McGregAir et al, eh, Mal…

Best. Anno

Subject: Twill, McGregAir et al   **Date:** 1/8/51
To: Anno@BDP (Private_net)
From: MalDeFak@BDP (Private_net)

Anno – As if Twill didn't know, that *is* the idea, yes…

Mal

Subject: Twill   **Date:** 2/8/51
To: MalDeFak@BDP (Private_net)
From: Anno@BDP (Private_net)

Mal – Mitrovich, whom I finally reveal as a pale New Yorker, shows us a different Twill, a man confined in his fairy-tale tower – gold locks, an oaken door bolted by his evil keeper, the tangled forests of ancient Europe a wild bracken in every direction. From there he is able to profess himself undaunted at the drop in ratings, though perhaps regrets that it was, finally, a Clerk of Oxenford who beat a path to his gaol. Their conversation, whose grammatic structures throb with much the same pulse as digital empires everywhere, amounts to just one more among our many indefinite sets of social activity, each serving a different purpose. Specific examples aren't hard to think up: daily drip of soaps, Twill's own chat show even from twenty years ago (nostalgic, particularly when a guest of that era has recently died) – even Molly Bloom in Microcolor. The prevailing significations, which he obsesses himself with now, won't change until our prevailing purpose does – and Twill is as 'free' to initiate that change as anyone (though what I wonder would happen should he try!).

Anno

Mitrovich, one henna-burnt afternoon, drove into Ix, to carry out some business he'd got with Frame – all to do with the French Revolution. I watched those grey-black curls of his advanced age and sagacity, swirling in a speed-induced vortex, as, young at heart, he clattered round the cobbled bends of Ix, turning the wheel from wall to turreted wall, a manchild gleeful in his loose, lilac, fast-coloured convertible (did I say convertible!). He spared me some time, in the deep cross-shadow of Castle Maqueda's little Buddhist temple, where we both looked out over the meticulously raked, dove-grey pebbles of Emma's Japanese garden.

"Now tell me," I asked, "do I really need to fret about Twill?"

He told me yes and no, Twill now having got to the real conspiracy – by which he meant that the world constructed in the cutting room was the world that pre-existed our citizens. To enter into it was to enter the broadcast schedule, and to know, implicitly, its grammar. Yes, I should fret because of this; no, because Twill on his own wouldn't make the connection between innate linguistic competence and the punch-bag of media manipulation planted in our human mental processes. It was, ultimately, the 'word' that had spawned its many broadcast adjuncts, as a natural efficient tool.

"It does beg," said Mitrovich, "an amusing question…"

"Which is?"

"If, as Twill thinks, what is organically within us is directly applied to our exterior constructs, and given that the social world changes, does our interior life increase its potential in a re-absorption of external manifestations, or are all possible realities already inherent in it?"

"Given that Twill wants to change things, he must believe in at least a *range* of possibilities, all locked up there inside us."

"Yet, Anno, can a fully paid-up media man find the key?"

"I suppose we shall find that out."

Subject: Entertainment biz   **Date:** 3/8/51
To: MalDeFak@BDP (Private_net)
From: Anno@BDP (Private_net)

Mal – No further news as yet re Diamond. Meanwhile Twill's next expert witness has been another professor (also unwisely Oxbridge), a specialist in cross culture, and a man who gabbled, and was permanently foamed in spittle to each corner of his mouth. His observation seemed to be this: that the masses get bored (condition not considered dangerous until you understand that what they're bored with is their lives). That boredom is carefully tissue-wrapped in a permanent swaddle of entertainment, which is all harmless until you detect in its simplifications potential for self-negation. How so? urges Twill. Well, Mr Twill, by the very fact of its self-referential process. Herein is its meaning. Therefore once its conventions have been penetrated, so has the artificial structure of human society. This never happens, ergo…

"Ergo," interrupts Twill (this, a screening in whose bilious glow I nursed my cocoa), "ergo, the masses are bound by convention. In short, we're conditioned by our amusements."

Bravo, Ryder Twill!

Anno

Subject: Re: Entertainment biz   **Date:** 3/8/51
To: Anno@BDP (Private_net)
From: MalDeFak@BDP (Private_net)

Anno – *Means* of entertainment becoming ever more sophisticated, which is where you feel our Twill has already missed the boat. Don't honestly think we need worry.

Mal

Nevertheless I did sign up dutifully for Twill's third professor, who couldn't work, according to Mitrovich, without a script, and even then required half a dozen rehearsals. His name was von Recht – who even Twill considered problematic, were he to offer more than the four minutes and twenty-two seconds he eventually allocated. Von Recht's thesis was this – that all our purveyors of highly polished trash maintained a permanent state of resuscitation in that long-dead war Popular *vs* High Culture, not because they'd failed to notice that the latter bled on the ropes, exhausted and defeated, but because any last sign of life remained a threat educationally (elevation of Berg over the Bilge Boyz – which was *his* example – was in the end inimical to a media-based mass culture).

I think my disappointment must have been twofold when Mitrovich – who had large, close-set eyes, was youngish and wore his hair long – found himself briefly seconded to another team (I had enjoyed his company, and I had come to depend on the quality of his information). He did leave word with Miss Ashley that he had taken a short domestic flight to the English Riviera, where in a hill-top, palm-strewn, Atlantic-lashed hotel in Torquay, he and other deputy members carefully assessed both on-floor and behind-the-scenes doings and deals at the MGA's, or McGregAir's, annual trade conference. This, being almost wholly geared to the business community, whose dreary grey opulence I have long lived without, I wouldn't normally take much interest in, particularly as its night sky was brightly plugged by a ploughful of star orators from Capitol Hill. I did though decide to sound out Mitrovich one more time, and flew out there myself – not to the verdant hilltops of

107

Hotel Torquay, but to the humbler Golden Barb – black beams, brasses and local beer – which was hidden in a veil of wind-swept elms, some yards off a track going NNW out of a rain-blurred crag called Slapton. On my first foggy morning, after a night of mulled brandy and lukewarm heating accessories, I met up with Mitrovich on Slapton Sands (actually shingle, 'Sands' is a tourist enticement, though the crunch of it under-foot might well be abraded to finer particles given a few bil-lion years). Mitrovich wore a long grey coat, onto whose ep-aulettes his mousy ringlets – uniformly darkened in the sea air – had damply contracted themselves. Huge fountains of spume crashed to the edge of the bay, and dissolved. Mitrovich, until then teetotal, now offered me his hip flask. I declined, then suddenly changed my mind. Twill, he said, was now un-der control. This had nothing to do with ratings – one of those old-fashioned blasphemies the new Twill angrily dismissed – but because his argument was self-defeating. You may chal-lenge the god Mediocrity – in a steel suit as necessary – in only one way – and that was as denizen in the god's own country. Those hapless crocks of Oxenford – who represented quite other strains of banality – merely united the enemy.

In essence I said as much to Two, who advised me to memo One (Twill problem solved, I told him). Frame replied with an invitation, which I accepted. This meant a few pleasant hours with sherry, sandwiches, and a private tour of his eighteenth-century aquarelles. Good and entertaining. And wow! What a place he's got! "Built," Frame told me, "as an Omani fortifica-tion" – all crenellated towers and tapering stone stairways, points vanishing as architect's makeshift lines into the untrou-bled depths of Ix's topaz-flamed sky. Dotted slits below the battlements minutely reproduced those found, Frame said, by researchers in the Sultanate, and were designed originally (and here decoratively) as a gesture of repulsion to any coming en-emy (soon likely to savour the golden sweets of boiling honey poured from that Mideast heaven).

"Impressive," I said.

"Defence has been the special preserve of Omani rulers for over a thousand years," Frame added. "Next time you come

I'll show you my escape routes" – these a crystal honeycomb of secret passages and interconnecting tunnels.

"When as you say there's time. I do need though John to get out of this heat."

Frame took me – step on weary step – to the closed shade of the gun tower, from whose reticulated window arch – iron frets barred across its open air – was an unbroken view of Ix's surrounding mountain range, a sloping pine-wood blue, dissolving at its ridge to black ink, and there melding with a paper-thin skyline. Appropriately here among the firearms Frame got onto the subject of Six.

"Problem," I replied, "isn't so much that Six wants to use network facilities to monitor products in the planning stage…"

"…or in fact prevent certain kinds of programme ever being made…"

"It's that Six still thinks it's all to do with the moral fibre of the viewing public."

"Has he met Twill!"

"One thinks he should."

"Well there is, Anno, one other problem. Ix's Library of Culture offers any world_net visitor open access to a wide range of virtual cataloguing, which includes certain buildings of public interest – information not likely to be lost on anyone planning a bombing campaign."

"As you know, John, to me that remains a sensitive subject. And yet. I don't feel my own information is faulty here. Do you *really* think we're entering a new era of terrorism? Hasn't McGregAir done its job, and numbed everyone!"

"The fact is, Anno, it really doesn't matter what *I* think. The minister's impressed with Six's report, and in some areas wants to see immediate implementation. Feasibility studies for practically everything else. You'll have another glass, won't you, before you go."

"Iced."

"In theory that ought to keep Six out of your hair."

"Why only in theory? These steps seem darker going down."

"Well. Six says he won't go to Security unless he heads it up…"

"That's a big step from what he's doing – and not doing very well…"

"Incredibly the minister's not against it, though she can't as yet work out what to do with Schmidt, or indeed Thornden."

"John. I see your point. We'd better have that other glass. Wonderful aquarelles, by the way."

"Glad you liked them. I'm contributing to an exhibition – art of the French Revolution. I'll let you know the venue nearer the time. By the way that cleaning firm you sent mop-handed into Other Pater Square…"

"Go on –"

"Ducane fired them."

Subject: Information   **Date:** 7/8/51
To: Mitrovich@MGA (Private_net)
From: Anno@BDP (Private_net)

Mittie – Don't know to what extent you can help me regarding one other real-life soap opera, whose iridescent snowflake dissolves in the lashes of my lashes, long before I can identify any sort of pattern – that unique crystal, its little microscopic ferns, its tiny world of frost. For reasons I can't disclose, BDP finds itself chasing false hanky trails in pursuit of Craig or Iago Diamond (that mega-buck'd mega-star), a client recently contracted to the quicks and quacks of Prudean therapy – with Dr Ducane, of Other Pater Square, central London (all acid fogs and disintegrating pavements). Ducane's psychic thermometer, once pressed to the client's outraging organ, almost busts its zeal in an anguish of ruby, and represents a severe test to its silvered calibrations. This produces readouts Ducane construes as a first index to a world of psychic contractions. Don't know who's kidding whom, because what Diamond says he wants – a far cry from Ducane's cosmic gynaecology – is a name from the past, one deeply silted over in the muddy stream bed of his memory. All I have is some intercepted gobbledegook, fruit of one session (crab apple, methinks), which Ducane dutifully passed on to the ITC (International Therapy Centre), governing body of

110

Ducane's profession, whose mammoth archive (in *many* ways pre-historic) is managed for research purposes.

All best, Anno

Subject: Re: Information   **Date:** 13/8/51
To: Anno@BDP (Private_net)
From: Mitrovich@MGA (Private_net)

Anno – Am sending a Faststop courier, whose ID (though not his *ego*, *ergo*, or *raison d'être*), I want you to scrutinise *carefully*.

Mitrovich

[So Mitrovich too works Sundays...]

Subject: Diamond   **Date:** 15/8/51
To: Anno@BDP (Private_net)
From: MalDeFak@BDP (Private_net)

Anno – Natsuki tells me her old boss [Diamond] got in touch with her through her old production company [NatKnotNite Productions], proposing that she chair his EuroSHart meeting. She said she refused, and so can't understand how that memo came about and why her name is on it. No end to the Ducane blackout, I take it...

Mal

Subject: Re: Diamond   **Date:** 16/8/51
To: MalDeFak@BDP (Private_net)
From: Anno@BDP (Private_net)

Mal – No news, you're right, via implants or networks. However. John's man in the MGA, codename Mitrovich – stocky, cropped red hair, complexion a bowl full of tulip petals – sent a long and detailed report via Faststop. Checked over the courier carefully (green hotel livery edged with dirty black trim; a sloping smile; an ID card whose biometric encodings agreed with all natural engravings – eye colour, vocal timbre, fingerprints). Had

111

the gall to suggest it wouldn't have been possible to progress even to the reception centre had all or just one of these things *not* been in order (therefore why was I checking them again?). 'One couldn't be too careful' – is all I said, though even then he wouldn't be escorted back to the motor park (his a powerful Japanese bike, its twinned tubas for exhaust, or nowadays are they rocket launchers) until I had tipped him EU$40.

Mitrovich did somehow tap in to the video conferencing system that Diamond's hotel – the Sheraton – has proudly extended, gossamer-like, into the floating, star-kissed haven of all its suites. This I'm afraid revealed no more than Diamond in an afternoon session sodomising his latex dolly, appropriately wired (his crowing cock, his coccyx and balls), and donned in his helmet and cyber visor (can't guess – can *you* guess – at dumb toyboy's virtual identity). Mitrovich then it seems spent a morning in Other Pater Square, chipping away at the rutted encrustations in the frost-bejewelled sidewalks, first with his steel toe, then with his steel heel, then with his steel bayonet [scrub that out], before stomping off in an outline of shivers to a pancake bar. No sign anywhere of Diamond. Nor for that matter Ducane. Only a post girl, who walked to an ancient poppy-coloured pillar-box, with mail.

With what electronic aids, sensors, whatnot, I don't know (we are in, Mal, an asymmetrical world), but our man for all costumes, got up lavishly in silky black hose and a turtle-neck, later retrieved from that old rustic maw – that maw for mawkish mail – a padded handibag bound for the ITC. I can and do admit to one dizzying moment – a floating double crown tangentially free of a sunshaded occiput – when even I suspected even Ducane of nursing a sense of humour. That handibag endured a double life – as what it empirically was, and as repository for a computer disc, which in its layered encryptions posited, or underposited, Ducane's theoretical mistrust of the electric nerves of our universe – its nets and notted nand gates. For that reason he had plumped for old analogue transports in reporting his daily doses to the ITC.

112

Mitrovich, by now an aging, sallow-faced technician, with a faint lisp in that trace of Eastern European – his a calm, and measured dialect – M had no trouble at all reproducing that disc verbatim (handibag was therefore carefully re-sealed, and returned to the mail, in the full bulge of its cargo). I find I am now all ready to behold him, in the powdery glow of an overhead lamp, that lamp with a gently swinging chain, a diamond-cutter's spectacles perched to the tip of his thinly pinched nose, our Mitrovich here meticulously engaged with slab-shaped encyclopædias all bursting with decryption algorithms in a litter on his workbench. Therefore with what patient counterfeits, and all the cunning of his sixty-five years, and in the saturated glow of an English dawn, has Mitrovich at last unlocked that dormitory of bedtime apologies.

We find surprisingly, Mal, that even Ducane expresses doubts and suspicions as to the true purpose of Diamond's weekly appointments, which so far have all ended either deadlocked or deadly embraced. Diamond you'll recall came with his picnic hamper and spread out from that a checked cloth, then planted down a gold-plated champagne bucket, all under Mnemosyne's olive tree – in the hopes of disentangling some very particular name from the poisoned vipers of his memory. It's not a name we get. Merely crass extensions to that verbiage quoted above [my memo to Mal, 30/6 – in June they seemed such heady days]. Now in mid-August, what we have is this:

O amber light, whose beams have ravaged my empyrean!
Johnny or Joe's fair son… O praise to that face…
In all my celluloid heavens, on land and in my salty sea…
whatever I think I'd script or emulate…
could be man, bird, beast, fish or herb or greenwood tree.
You fill my living moments with clapper-board eternities…
in our picture world no cinematic creature can live
without the steamy *scenes* of love.
Johnny or Joe's fair fruit, fill my filmic glade…
And grant my work-day screen hams a life in your golden light.
Come you, come, and instigate my cutting-room amours…
Turn leaden mortal boys, whatever the tease,

113

into love's delight, to love's adultery…
I'll bet your courtesies rejuvenate and make benign
both high- and low-born, after one of your seraphic smiles.
Our joy is in the power you radiate. Your producer's wonder's
all those superficial qualities for which you're fond
of finding so many handy adjectives, when he can't fathom
how it comes about that Gee loves Exe and Exe loves Wye,
and why this fish, and not this other species
wriggles up the weir. Full bright in make-up brush benignity,
revered by all who'll come to serve you, your singing scribe I am…
You in my trembling heart have infused such a passion…
O how our movie buffs need, nay crave you!
We of the studio floor, O heed us!

Now I can't help hearing echoes, Mal, of certain
Chaucerianisms (*Troilus and Criseyde*, see Book III, Introduction):

O blisfil light, of whiche the bemes clere
Adorneth al the thridde hevene faire!

for example, or –

In hevene and helle, in erthe and salte see
Is felt thy might…
or

As man, bird, best, fish, herbe and greene tree
Thee fele in tymes with vapour eterne
or

Ye fierse Mars apeysen of his ire,
And, as yow list, ye maken hertes digne
or

Ye knowe al thilke covered qualitee
Of thinges which that folk on wondren so,
Whan they can not construe how it may jo,
She loveth him, or why he loveth here;
As why this fish, and nought that, cometh to were
or

Ye in my naked herte sentement
Inhelde, and so do me shewe of thy swetnesse

– wherefore Ducane is only right to be suspicious. Nonetheless Diamond still insists that with his sixtieth birthday
only a few months away, all he wants from Ducane is that
one innocent blank on his guest list at last inked over with

114

one innocent name. Now I wonder what name he has (or hasn't) in mind…

I think, Mal, I'm going to send Diamond a nice muscular rent boy, all a burnt brown-lemon beach hue, if only to save Diamond all that strapping up, all that mess with latex and lubricants.

Anno

The one-to-one specialist I made contact with was one I chose for the video logotype, which was scarlet flames in an outline of liquid blue, these the petrol exhalations of two intertwining green dragons, boisterously rearing up through a volcano of torn macadam – locality, a slate-grey street somewhere near Soho Square. Manning the phones that day was a *belle* from Hamburg, not quite as hardened as the gum she chewed, who misunderstood. (No, I am not checking in to the Park Lane Sheraton. This was an early birthday gift for a great lonely, great appetent, great panda of a man already there. Giggles.) She blew a pink bubble. She pressed buttons and downloaded the very latest from Gay Town Catwalk, honey-dew boys in a parade of vibrant codpieces (mink, tortoiseshell, leopard, the rainbow of an old English Union Flag or Jack or Flaganapes). I rejected practically all – one for an atavistic mouth, another for his gloomy chin, a third for the distant glaze of his eyes – yet another for the surplus of lard filming his pectorals. Here my Hamburger bombshell doused the transmission in its closing logotype, now a lather and sweat in the gobbets of fiery magma exuding from those two necking lizards.

"That all you got?" I said.

Didn't I understand? This was high season – just weren't that many boys available.

"Okay. I'll take the tortoiseshell. My secretary runs a hospitality account, I'll pass you to her…"

She understood, discretion the watchword.

Not a few days after Diamond's first romp (with what turned out to be a snake-belted boy, square-faced, hair cropped, eyebrows blond), a slim-waisted beauty less than half my age shared a late-afternoon table among the parasols fronting my habitual café in Ix. She was a tourist, she said, and ordered patisserie with a lime-juice fizz, and if I wanted I could call her Morwena (Morwena, whose hair was cut pageboy; whose polished hazel eyes were the sheen of Celtic mystery). She had studied music and media, and although an EU School graduate – in fact Poulenc College, or Poulenc Gothic, whose campuses are Paris and Prague – all she had done since was promotional work for Taittinger (which meant champagne) and Perrett (which meant of course diamonds). Only classics she had ever liked were *Mozart's Greatest Hits*, which she thought might all be down to a rare broadcast she had heard while still only a girl, by a then ailing Viennese orchestra – and now defunct – whose conductor was Schmitt or Schmidt or Schmitters or something. Just lately she had taken to line and country dancing, craze sweeping both the European Republic *and* the United States, and with this spare ticket (shoulder bag open), to a private function, in the refreshing cool airs high up in a mountain barn, could I be seduced?

"Who sent you?"

"Excuse me?"

"Where in Ix are you staying?"

Subject: Diamond/Mitrovich   **Date:** 22/8/51
To: Anno@BDP (Private_net)
From: MalDeFak@BDP (Private_net)

Anno – John tells me how keen you are on his French Revolution exhibits, and expects to see you at the viewing, which as you may or may not know takes place early next month at Champs-le-Vent, at a venue I'll have Fräulein Buxt pass to Miss Ashley. I shall be present myself, as will the minister. There are things, Anno, I don't want to have to tell either John or Mrs Quinn – she widely tipped for Health in the last re-shuffle, but alas still at Culture. I don't for that matter wish to tell *anyone* of our dependency. That I mean is on Mitrovich, with his twilit scrimmages, among the pillars of an antiquated mail system, all for high-level intelligence. What other plans have we got?

Mal

Subject: Re: Diamond/Mitrovich   **Date:** 24/8/51
To: MalDeFak@BDP (Private_net)
From: Anno@BDP (Private_net)

Mal – Re Champs-le-Vent, attachments received, so please convey a hearty thanks to the freckled, fulsome, formidable Fräulein Buxt, who also passed me a ten-gallon hat. Into that bottomless shaft she has begun to gather currency of all kinds – ingots, costume jewels, bonds, pledges, pounds of flesh – intending to organise a festive farewell for the retiring Miss Ashley. I wince and am disappointed that my own escape looks ever less imminent.

Now I do think, Mal, that Diamond, though he might *plan* a takeover of EuroSHart, isn't likely to reveal much of this through Ducane. Do you think at some point we shall have to confront him? Or do the plummets and flutters of fallen angels, pink-and-satin-cheeked, bear also in the strain of all those tenuous wingbeats, paper missiles destined for yours but never troubling the polished depths of *my* desk?

All best, Anno

Subject: Re: Diamond/Mitrovich   **Date:** 25/8/51
To: Anno@BDP (Private_net)
From: MalDeFak@BDP (Private_net)

Anno – Point taken. What are our contingency plans?

Mal

PS Fräulein Buxt suggests cleaning, re-decorating, and hosting the soirée in parts of your fellow-Englishman's New Bayreuth, for Miss Ashley's farewell. Apparently she loves the Elgar violin concerto, which we wouldn't be able to stage, but indicates she would settle for a string quintet and Schubert. What do you think?

Subject: Re: Diamond/Mitrovich/postscript
Date: 28/8/51
To: MalDeFak@BDP (Private_net)
From: Anno@BDP (Private_net)

Mal – In answer to question two, reasons abound as to why you can't call me an Englishman (firstly). This you should know. Secondly, isn't it the irony of Ix that a genteel English spinster, whose frail hands are mottled, whose hair is a moonlit grey, who in the pleasures of that incognito has operated for so long here among the naked raw nerves of Planet Media... Is not Miss Ashley – not our Twills and our Diamonds – the *real* subversive? Unbent that reed is, despite these lifelong, coercive serenades of TV Digital – magic programme sleeping draft even the hardiest insomniac can't easily turn off. Schubert and Elgar – two of Old Europe's poison-pointed rapiers – tell us I think we should have Miss Ashley clapped in gaol, in an iron mask, on subsistence rations...

As to 'contingency' (and I am only sorry you here adopt the cold-wall lingo of Old Europe's institutional communiqué), well... do I need to restate that I personally have had to suck a disgusting desert air, swirls and eddies and acrid vapours, in order to satisfy Craig Diamond's appetites... That chunk or hunk charged with domestic duty, tweaking Master's pillows, dispatching each seed-stained undersheet to the hotel laundry, adopting I don't know how many contortions of the flesh, contumelies of the brain (and go ahead, call me reactionary)... That boy, man, man-childe I shouldn't have to say (I shouldn't have to say this to you, Mal) is already in the pay of our inscrutable Mitrovich. Mitrovich, that broad-hatted, gaberdine'd sleuth, who can be seen sometimes striking a match on the Sheraton's perimeter wall, lighting his pipe in the drizzle of an English summer, each vortex of damp tobacco smoke softly enwrapping the granite textures of his face, his whole upper body in a cross-slide of shadows. In return I am given, all gift-wrapped and besprinkled in dewy *eau de Klee*, a low priestess from the mists and liquorice peat of Druid Isle, whose getups are various. There has been a red-check cheesecloth shirt, cowboy hat, knee-length boots (without spurs, except in her boudoir, at playtime), as, distantly, I happened to take stock one recent balmy night. That was my Morwena – for that is my lass's delicate *nom de guerre* – sitting out *Strip the Willow* on a hay bale. Did you know, Mal, there is country dancing here in Ix? She cradles my enormity, even as I drive her round Ix's rockiest corniche, headlights a sweeping torch, the precipice almost sheer. She is expert, Mal, in what prudish America legally termed – oh, decades ago – a lewd act, and is equipped on most starlit nights with a gloopy green mouthwash, whose stinging chemic cancels any projected aftertaste. She can be less rustic. For example, some nights ago in Bistro PhoenIx, while I sat there bored with my *aperitif*, waiting, and waiting – oh endlessly waiting – she did eventually show. Interpret that literally, by which I mean my gold-prospecting Morwena had got herself dolled and glammed in black diaphanous lace, with a great many trims. One was a Swiss neck-coil, whose pendant gold globe was studded at its equator with a dusting of tiny diamonds (Etienne Perrett). Her bedtime allure was a black, or very black, washable, lash-doubling, clump- and glob-free mascara, hypoallergenic and no trouble at all to wearers of contact lenses. Her scent was *Eau de parfum*. Her snogger bore frosty pink lip gloss, with vitamin E and anti-oxidants, whose flavour I well recall as a sickly cherry vanilla. I later discovered a clip-on/clip-off test-tube hip spray (fully tested, I assure). Then there was body glitter, applied as a sky-blue gel. And a nail polish, designed to the clockwork prism of every change of mood, whose range registered a blue scale of boredom, a plash and pout of pink, a rebellious ache of violet. She chose no *hors d'oeuvre*, and instead quaffed several glasses of Merlot, orphan of an exclusive reserve, and one the sophisticated management had taken in from the private bins of Hawke's Bay [I know it very well]. Her dinner was tuna confit, overwhelmingly

119

steeped in fennel seeds and lemon zest. For dessert, a grilled nectarine. For recreation, a long night drive to the beach, where Morwena dispatched her lace to the shadows at her feet, a black rumpled pool in a desert of tufted dunes. She daunced, in and out at the crescendos of foaming surf, then on her haunches finally, when she straddled my loosened thighs, I watched and breathed with the firmament, which momentarily throbbed above her glazed limbs and rhythmic head, in a blaze of cobalt and carmine stars. She exhausted other possibilities – once in those spurs I mentioned. There was another occasion too, after she had hastily applied her kerving-toles to an incriminating envelope, which she had not so secretly removed from the ornately padded pockets of my jacket. That jacket she had so carefully carelessly slung on a chair, in the louvred half-light slanting in through her hotel window. Did that document tell her what she wished to know, or had been charged to find out? No, I think no. "You must continue to call me Anno," I said, and poured her one more brandy, she filling the bathroom spa with steam. Yet I believe and trust she is no more ungracious than her counterpart trawling the depths of Craig Diamond's split-level suite, far to the north, among the cloudbursts and blusters of London's agitated skies. For Diamond, evil befall. Though as for Morwena, long may we ride with her charhors!

All blest, Anno

Subject: Morwena   **Date:** 29/8/51
To: Anno@BDP (Private_net)
From: MalDeFak@BDP (Private_net)

Anno – Sounds quite a gal!

Mal

Subject: Remote listening   **Date:** 29/8/51
To: Six@1009 (Private_net)
From: Five@1009 (Private_net)

Six – As to these new, more powerful, more easily concealed, ever more remote audio devices – how can I get hold of one?

Five

Subject: Re: Remote listening   **Date:** 29/8/51
To: Five@1009 (Private_net)
From: Six@1009 (Private_net)

Five – You need contact either with the military or with the Ministry of Defence.

Six

Subject: Re: Remote listening   **Date:** 29/8/51
To: Six@1009 (Private_net)
From: Five@1009 (Private_net)

Six – I'd like to use your connections with the military.

Five

Subject: Re: Remote listening   **Date:** 31/8/51
To: Five@1009 (Private_net)
From: Six@1009 (Private_net)

Five – You'll have to put that request in writing, via form S/Z-1009-1967a. You will need one top-ranking signature.

Six

"Miss Ashley. Please could you obtain form S/Z-1009-1967a, from Dr Thornden's secretary. Thank you so much. I hear there are plans afoot for a live performance of Schubert's *Trout Quintet*, which is a rarity these days. Just in this past week an innocent, peach-complexioned lass, from one of the remotest, wind-lashed crags in Christendom, has whistled me snatches of *Eine Kleine*, though imperfectly, being tone deaf. Oh, and here's the itinerary you say for Champs-le-Vent. Well, I'll take that away, peruse…"

§

John Frame's contribution to the French Revolution wasn't in fact that great, at least in its revived form here in reedy Champs-le-Vent, a festival of tainted deals plus all that curdled gore. Thing took place in a reconstructed château, along the whole long length of a single high-ceilinged chamber (opposite flank was all windows, north-facing), John's one or two or 'handful' of incomplete Davids (all sketches) occupying a cold spooky corner next to an over-done yet beautifully hand-crafted calendar (it ran Vendémiaire to Fructidor). The floor, I noticed, parts of which must have been original, was adorned haphazardly with rush mats. Mal, after spectacles of indecision, *had* brought his young bride – she looking virginal, because of her gold braids, and a pale blush, and her sumptuous waves of muslin. As a matter of fact both found themselves dizzily transfixed at the extravagant inlay of Marie-Antoinette's secretaire, the one from Versailles, a 3D exhibit placed under the strictest placard, with the added interdict of a cranberry-coloured cordon. He did introduce me, after I had discreetly tapped his shoulder – my pleasure to meet, and all that – that uncertain blush now flecked with the thorny rose of dawn. Mal then ushered me confidentially, one firm hand to my elbow, into the splintered light of a mirror, whose frame was gilded, where in not quite approving undertones he revealed that Six had got suddenly precipitous concerning that proposed move to Security. Well, I couldn't guess why, I said (and kept a straight, and reflected face). "Frankly there are problems with that," said Two, who went on to tell me how Samples always had been John Frame's brainchild, and Six his preferred candidate. "That," I said, "is news to me. Look at that porcelain figurine." Catalogue said, Parisian *sans-culotte*.

All John Frame, under a high shuttered window, top man

fleetingly chalked in a shaft of pine-blue dust, I noticed eyed a David not his own. This was a riot of raised hands and hats in the air – the 'Tennis Court Oath', as he later explained – which under his icy collector's glare, and an irritated tension to his brows, to him was evidently more an object of possession than revolution. Immediately, John unclasped hands, which, until I had grazed his purview, I noted were clenched and red behind his back. "Mal," I said, "(such a pretty young wife) seems to share your concerns over Six's move to Security" – a gambit that didn't wrong-foot him. "Exceedingly pretty," is how he replied. "I believe, Anno, she's Danish. Have you seen my sketches?" I told him I had. He lectured me: "David, you know, can become an obsession." Threats I perceived, as dramas and fated gestures when he, the very last of all those John Frames, ushered me to David's martyrdom of Marat. "How, Anno, are those handover notes?" "Fairly rambling, John, without an audience." "Ah, now look out of that window…"

Mitrovich, in accustomed garb – knee-length boots, trousers tucked in, a three-quarter tunic a dull olive green, a peaked cap, and a blaze of brassy buttons – had just reversed Mrs Quinn's long black limousine, whose windows were a tinctured indigo, into the shade of an acacia tree. He got out and opened the two rear doors – one for the fawning Monsieur Pasquale, junior minister, who on stepping out dusted down his jacket. The other was for Mrs Quinn herself, plump-faced and slightly overweight, in one of her off-duty floral dresses, a pair of sandals, and a white, broad-brimmed sun hat, whose edges curled in that slightly salty breeze that always stroked the poplars of Champs-le-Vent. A great many old-world Gallic gestures on Pasquale's part, and an almost purple grin, preceded his gambols as he partnered Mrs Quinn up the steps, where four fantastic urns, lichened and powdered white, collectively adorned the foot and stair head. John Frame, his shoulders and lapels spattered in coloured dew – or the glass of a shattered rainbow – or the movement of coloured ribbons off a chandelier – or how to describe it, really – was down immediately to greet them, his large open hands at the ready for hearty shakes. He led them to his Davids.

Mitrovich meanwhile had planted the shiny seat of his wrapped-up pantaloons on the warm bonnet of Mrs Quinn's official car, one of those booted feet wedged firmly to the sun-dazzled bumper. I'd seen him smoke a pipe. Today he'd brought rolling tobacco, a French brand in a blue sachet, which he smoothed and carefully licked into a rectangle of liquorice paper. He lit with an antique Zippo (resulting miasma a quaint amalgam of petrol, roasted tobacco, liquorice gum). "I've ordered some hardware," I said, "which might help us eavesdrop on Ducane." He removed his cap momentarily and scratched his head. "Ducane's as puzzled as we are," he said. "Does this mean, Mitrovich, there is something I should know?" "There's quite a lot you should know. Now isn't the right time." "Or the right place." "Exactly. By the way don't call me Mitrovich. Today I'm Rivière, and a chauffeur." "I'm sorry, driver Pierre. Mail me. Enjoy your smoke. Nice-looking car."

Subject: Diamond jamboree   **Date:** 19/9/51
To: MalDeFak@BDP (Private_net)
From: Anno@BDP (Private_net)

Mal – Soft-footed Mitrovich, in a haze of anonymity, and a costume to match, his stamp of innocence unusual in an age like ours, has at last succeeded in pinning one of Six's magic antennae to the under-edge of Professor Ducane's consulting-room door. Therefore I formally request Luis's release. Spinoffs you know Mal involve the voyeuristic contemplation of a whole host of Ducane's clients, so here I go with inconsequential things (this is today; doubtless tomorrow I will cite someone else). Did you know there's a wretched curator still hanging on at the Imperial War Museum? This is a man who much admires the womb-like velvet of Ducane's waiting-room wallpaper, yet cannot satisfy the rampaging lusts of his marriage bed, *without* accompanying portraits of his mother – which I can't help deduce, given Ducane's slightly over-detached response, fills this latter with disgust. I'd like to move Luis back to Archives.

We get when Diamond himself sits in the patient's chair

that same insistence on a name, which he still can't find. For the record, here are the least absurd our good Pater has sifted from the African desert of Craig's unconscious: MW Clae Trope; the hybrid McWeto La Pré; the blue-eyed babe William Clear Poet. All these however were greeted with solemn headshakes and disappointed sighs. Professionally, Ducane is hesitant to link these names – the frozen nuggets of his client's amnesia – with that fractured student text, which I have twice reproduced (though why he assumes 'student' I am not too sure). Diamond, who is momentously nearing sixty, now ceases to reveal further workings of that text – at least so far as Ducane is concerned.

Surprisingly that solid of bronze flesh, sent to tickle Diamond's dreary afternoons, now finds himself a helpless dupe, caught between the slippages of desire and the defiles of Mitrovich's payroll. Our dumb Mr Hunk Chunk, when not manicuring toe nails, rifles through Diamond's papers much as that delicious, dirty cow Morwena rifles through mine. (Yesterday, wearing only a lilac-coloured anklet, she concealed – you may guess where – a note torn from my telephone jotter. I tell tourist Morwena this is turning out to be a very long vacation.) Craig Diamond, in the long dead-ends and the fruitless fogs of his London by night, I know to have filled several notebooks with surgical incisions – stab on blood-stained stab at Mnemosyne's secret arteries, those gore-clogged gates of the mind. You can surely understand, that Luis placed as he is, can fulfil no further useful function. Incidentally all Ducane has said of this – I mean this splinter of ancient text – so to speak as verbal shrug of the shoulders – is this, loath as I am to quote: it's possibly a syntactic displacement, raised to the power of narrative. This I believe is a technical term, and means: what superficially might seem gibberish, is linguistically connected to the name a nostalgic Diamond seeks (*ray, Monsieur le Professeur!*). Ducane's best advice for Diamond has been to list members of that Benbrook circle he *can* remember, with who knew what concealed trigger... Given that all are persons well known in the public eye for the last thirty-five years or so, it's hardly likely (and Diamond himself points this out) that they'd ever been forgotten – therefore what cloaked surprises in the twilit vales of Diamond's personal history could they bear? Just I think to humour the perplexed Ducane, here are the five names Diamond pulled from a hat, the sixth not yet a tantalising solid – still only a tiny spot of claret – on the tip of his tongue. Lisbeth Fatuaiii, film-maker (and in that capacity also a board member of several production companies, including NatKnotNite) – famously outspoken on a range of public issues. Gavin Smayle, broadcaster, whose reputation is today indis-solubly glued to the bruising nature of his interview tech-nique, exercised under a battery of studio lights, usu-ally on lavender-scented politicians – all good news, and a shared bouquet of smiles – who as we know only *conspire* to effect a pounding, Gavin's portfolio of ques-tions having been carefully pasteurised beforehand. Lorenzo Constant, socialite and art critic. Dondie Millar, sculptor. She, if you didn't know, Mal, has been the crea-tor of so many of our modern civic landmarks, often welded together from found materials. A piece I have personally witnessed is her reconstructed Anderson air raid shelter, in Rye. Finally Chelsea de la Mare, per-former. Have to say there is no sign yet of invitations to these, or to anyone – nor are there preparations, so far as I can see, for Diamond's birthday celebration. I want Luis out of all this.

Anno

Subject: Re: Diamond jamboree   **Date:** 21/9/51
To: Anno@BDP (Private_net)
From: MalDeFak@BDP (Private_net)

Anno – So glad to see you and Six co-operating so successfully. Line into Ducane's should I'd have thought prove extremely useful.

Mal

Subject: Re: Diamond jamboree   **Date:** 21/9/51
To: MalDeFak@BDP (Private_net)
From: Anno@BDP (Private_net)

Mal – Co-operation isn't exactly it, I'm afraid. The device Mitrovich has been able to use isn't the best available, and certainly isn't of the kind described by Six at our policy meeting back in June. That, as I understand it, doesn't require anything like close proximity to the target. Can Six not be made to understand that the last time Diamond spent appreciable time on European soil, was as a very bad-tempered student?

Anno

Subject: Miss Ashley's retirement **Date:** 25/9/51
To: Anno@BDP (Private_net)
From: CBuxt@BDP (Private_net)

Anno – As of course you're aware, Miss Ashley retires soon, after a long and unsung career. It has been suggested that we clean and re-decorate a part of that area of Castle Maqueda known as New Bayreuth. Here the Bureau agrees to host a soirée both in honour of Miss Ashley and for her farewell. Could you perhaps make some time in the coming few days? I'd like you to take a look at/advise on what we've done so far, and also think about a few parting words. Many thanks.

Christa Buxt

What Fräulein Buxt and her team had so far achieved was a plain timber platform, so to speak electrically charged, looking every inch a newly made extension into the auditorium's fourth wall. This practically any playgoer knew as a structure of open circuitry, in whose eddies and turbulence of human electricity something more than the claws of theatrical lightning snatched or snapped shut. Fräulein Buxt, from her inner furnace or too human warmth, had plucked out the simple idea – all in a pristine radiance of fire – of removing any last vestige of seating in the stalls, so making way for her

127

pier. I arrived just at the point where two bare-armed carpet fitters tacked on to it a sumptuous pile (as a match for the one and only remaining curtain). I looked up and casually roved round Emma's once gilded balconies. Here in a concealed plush, in a post-something era, those cigar-sucking stooges of Aimé's, for whatever reason deemed worthy of Emma's various pacts, had gathered (pale ghosts of themselves) onto the bent perspectives and the fantasticated world of Sir Ossie's stage. His was a masquerade of life set off to the tumble of understated trumpets and a tinkle of triangles. Hers, Buxt's, a *post*-post-something, was a weave of balloons, in an intertwine of helixes – one mauve, and one a headachy cream. These she'd suspended as swags, all round the balconies. Buntings were planned (a forest in autumn leaf). Also a banner: HAPPY RETIREMENT MISS ASHLEY (most striking colour scheme to date was a gold spray on unassuming jet).

Fräulein Buxt I knew vaguely from various committees. She was tall and all through her life fortyish. Her limbs were long and awkward. Her marine-blue eyes were awash in the violet aquarium glass of her spectacles, whose frames were large and square. An impious Muse at my elbow was quick to point out that Chris as she liked to be called (oh do call me) had recently changed her hair, from a can't-do-much straw-coloured bob, to a masculine crop, which on our next meeting I found transformed to a waltz of banana-yellow, but today was a battleship-grey. Under certain fragments of light this turned to a powdered gun metal. Her nose was slightly empurpled. She cornered me under the tooled scrolls of the proscenium, waving her clipboard, brandishing a dreary hello, explaining urgently that this afternoon (or as things now stood tomorrow morning) should see delivery of half a dozen sturdy round tables. In the cadence of that news she staked out on her mires of new carpet an efficient co-ordinate for each. Hard to imagine, she agreed (and so imagined it for me), those tables heavy with embroidered white linen, in every case hubbed with a slim-line flute, three-quarter filled with tap water and topped with the crimson satin of a rose (this to do with Miss Ashley's Englishness). Each guest was to receive advance notice of his or her table number. There would be a serrated card embossed with a name at each place mat. For the menu Chris or Christa toyed with foiled trout in a sea of cucumber.

"To go with the Schubert," I said.

"I'm sorry?"

"'Trout' Quintet."

"Ah. Yes. Trout quintet will be positioned there, behind the curtain…"

"You mean string quintet."

"…positioned there, behind the curtain. This I will open once your speech is over."

"I happen to know she prefers Elgar (perhaps to do with her Englishness)."

"Now that's a thought. Does she like trout?"

"I have no idea."

Subject: Lost papers   **Date:** 28/9/51
To: MissAshley@BDP (Private_net)
From: Anno@BDP (Private_net)

Dear Miss Ashley – I think this must have been at some point towards the end of May, and certainly during that period when issues of security generally were beginning to be discussed, then *seriously* discussed. I recall vividly anyway a series of cool evenings at my balcony, under the magic airs of Ix, sketching out my plan for a new facility in Data Archives. Increasingly archive material is subject to review, often through a wide range of key information or data tags. How broad that implementation is, is often in the hands of a hard-pressed technician working in Archives (and almost as often results in an umbral chasm into which a great deal of material is irretrievably lost). As a remedy to this, my blueprint minutely maps out an Archive beta site. The strategy behind this is the concept of control – exhaustive tests, exhaustive dry runs against all possible combinations of keys and/or data tags. Incidentally my preferred bistro tucked away in the shady blue depths of the La Colina district – you've surely passed through it, on the southeast side of Ix – is this week serving a rudely delicious trout, baked in foil and served on a sward of cucumber. I can heartily recommend it. Unfortunately I have some-how mislaid the four or five sheets setting out this plan. I felt sure I'd filed them under 'B' (for 'Beta Site, Ar-chives'), though of course may have filed them under 'A' (for 'Archives, Beta Site'). Shall you, do you think, try the trout? I'd be very pleased, as one of your last duties here, if you could hunt through the filing cabinets and find my lost papers. Recommend as side dish lightly buttered Devon potatoes, with a sprinkling of paprika.

Anno

Subject: Re: Lost papers   **Date:** 28/9/51
To: Five@1009 (Private_net)
From: 186@1009 (Private_net)

Will begin at 'A' and work through the cabinets alpha-betically. Trout sounds wonderful.

Yours, One Eight Six

Subject: Miss Ashley's retirement **Date:** 29/9/51
To: Anno@BDP (Private_net)
From: CBuxt@BDP (Private_net)

Anno – Date set for Miss Ashley's departure is 30th No-vember. That should give us plenty of time in the thea-tre, where tables have arrived. Any more thoughts on that trout?

Christa

Subject: Re: Miss Ashley's retirement
Date: 29/9/51
To: CBuxt@BDP (Private_net)
From: Anno@BDP (Private_net)

Christa – It's inevitable I suppose that so retiring a man as Schubert, who once sat in the same Viennese cof-fee house as the much more forceful Beethoven, but dared not introduce himself, could have dreamed up that string piece for five trout. How on earth did he expect to teach them to play?

Anno

Subject: Trout/Schubert/strings   **Date:** 29/9/51
To: Anno@BDP (Private_net)
From: CBuxt@BDP (Private_net)

Anno – I don't quite follow...

Chris

Subject: Re: Trout/Schubert/strings
Date: 29/9/51
To: CBuxt@BDP (Private_net)
From: Anno@BDP (Private_net)

Chris – Miss Ashley will be fine, with both trout and Schubert.

Anno

After one day's search, there was no sign of my papers, under whose late-night labours I had rendered up, in a confident blue crayon, a numbered series of elucidating diagrams. These as I remind myself consisted of solitary little satellites, rotating in a glazed ether of office information. OI, or *oi!* (to poke fits and peeks into our world of acronyms), is one of those abstractions that – anyway since Six's arrival – I had begun to think of as a troubled dark yonder, at unlikely moments apt to explode in a starburst of irradiated data bits.

These are subject, as the teacher of infants teaches, to who knows what cartwheels of translation – into text, sound, images, or as Six has come to fear into four navigational dimensions. He imagines bombers. He imagines bombers with aplomb.

I cannot begin to know how unbearably cold a life, an unnamed life, can be, there among those coloured dots of light. On cloudless nights, under certain atmospheric conditions, you can, Luis, pick out a distant flame of sapphire, or sometimes the flimsiest autumn leaf burnt to the darker shades of sienna. Shall I explain, in leaden trails (or should I choose perhaps the hottest human vapours), exactly why in my paper designs there is one gloved hand, with its index finger pointing? I have placed this as an article I am careful to set gravitationally free, to represent you, Luis, I *had* hoped anonymous, not a man or a boy but a distant constellation, unseen among all these floating archives. I suspect only now I have failed – for they show me no mercy, these daggers of hindsight. A gigantic Samoan, for whom casual wear is a rugby shirt, stands with an outstretched thumb on the edge of McGregor's trail. I zoom out and leave him hitching, there on the outskirts of Paeroa (*Paeroa farewells you*), and head for the ruts and twines of the Southern Highway. King Diamond has played his trumps.

Am all over the place.

Subject: Paper chase   **Date:** 3/10/51
To: MalDeFak@BDP (Private_net)
From: Anno@BDP (Private_net)

Mal – Something rotten in the state. I worked all last night, under the plugged dome of Ix's brightly burning stars. Only when that had turned to this morning's laden skies, did I arrive home, much exhausted much as usual. My Celt Morwena, who lives and lies with her clay-coloured feet always to terra firma, says I am hers, through and through. To play her little game, I have given her a house key. Also I opened up the old-fashioned marquetry adorning my cocktail cabinet, to the whims of her happy hours. I even make available the waves of warmth among all the cold molecules of my airing cupboard, for the dampness of her smalls. Sweet home too is where my private papers are, in compact wodges bound with twine, all packed tightly in the lacquered drawers of my escritoire. On to that, with its metallic scrapes crossing each keyhole (to date all unyielding), I frequently heap a pile of false papers. These I know her to have skimmed through, searching for clues. This morning though I found a trail of coloured tissues – the time

132

was six a.m. – that led from the bathroom (mirror a tropic of steam), then back and forth and through my middle rooms. With it was a patter of petered out footsteps, the soles of Morwena's feet having eventually dried. What can I say – dropped in my path as bait? ('Scuse me while I just blow my trumpet on this peach-tinctured sample I have found in my boudoir.)

I found on my balcony, in blued silhouette – against the purple hills of Ix – my ivory-skinned Morwena, wrapped in a fiercely orange sarong, and wearing over her shoulder a gun belt and holster. She turned abruptly, drawing out an ivory-handled six-shooter. Its silver barrel glinted under that hard brightness of dawn. Her eyes, a bullish red, after a long lonely night of iced firewater, told me that all that previous day she had failed to get through to me over the videophone.

"Oh now Morwena, stop!"

Far too late, she said, and pressed me to the door frame, her cocky trigger cocked, her silver pistol in the slightly trembling grip of both her hands. I stumbled awkwardly on one of her many discarded shoes, partly regaining balance just as a first faint breeze lifted those raven locks. For a moment, her thin, palely lit shoulders were exposed. A second stream unfolded the tuck of her sarong, which now unwrapped itself flimsily (Morwena, my one-breasted Amazon). In part it remained attached, under the pressure of that holster – a reddish leather stitched with pearls. I stumbled again, this time falling supine on our bed, where with one swift hand she unbuckled all the flaccidity of my weary middle manhood. With her other, and the gun, she pointed there.

With what borderline pressure of her index finger – all so hackneyed, I know – that trigger resisted less and less, a script performed under the furnace of her eyes. With a wooden twang, and a cushioned explosion, a melodramatic old trickshot disgorged itself as a brightly patterned flag on a stick, a mirthful BANG! bordered with red and yellow dynamite.

Via a memo from Mitrovich, to which I shall not reply, it

133

seems Mr Hunk Chunk performed some similarly lurid pantomime, his with an imitation knife, having pinioned his newly douched victim at the neck and the backs of his knees, and thrusting with its springy rubber blade repeatedly. Here all parallelisms end, since unlike Morwena that blond beach-loving boy did manage to raid his master's private papers, coming out before he was fired with photographs – of five lavishly printed invitations, *and* the draft of a poem (its fullness still unrevealed to a head-scratching Ducane). Those five invitations were for: Lisbeth Fatualli, film-maker; Gavin Smayle, broadcaster; Lorenzo Constant, socialite and art critic; Dondie Millar, sculptor; finally Chelsea de la Mare, performer. What is surprising, Mal, is that the birthday celebration isn't precisely his own, but will toast McGregor on his ninetieth. Venue, the newly renovated Raffles Hotel, Singapore. Date, next April (it's Diamond's birthday on the sixteenth, conveniently McGregor's on the twenty-ninth). I haven't seen Morwena since – all bags packed and fled. I seem to have lost my sense of humour.

Anno

Subject: Re: Paper chase   **Date:** 5/10/51
To: Anno@BDP (Private_net)
From: MalDeFak@BDP (Private_net)

Anno – Having talked this over with John, could there possibly be anything encoded in that poem (or I should say recovered memory)? It's hard to see how this might be connected with shares in EuroSHart, but I suppose if we're doing our job, we must look at absolutely everything. I assume you have a copy, photograph, whatever...

Mal

Subject: Recovered memory   **Date:** 9/10/51
To: MalDeFak@BDP (Private_net)
From: Anno@BDP (Private_net)

Mal – It's not honestly where I should have looked for any clue to Diamond's intentions, *if* we're reading this right (and am beginning to have my doubts). But since you mention it, here is his poem, courtesy Ducane and rent boy –

O amber light, whose cloistral beams
Have ravaged my empyrean!
Darling of the spheres, Johnny or Joe's fair son,
My tissue of love, my sweet, my debonair,
O won't you find in our pulsing breast your domicile!   5
Boon of all my health and gladness –
O praise to that face, that grace, that fabulous race!

In all my celluloid heavens, on land and in my salty sea,
I feel your silver breeze, whatever I think I'd script or emulate:
Could be man, bird, beast, fish or herb or greenwood tree.   10
You fill my living moments with clapper-board eternities.
You're a movie god – and a god that loves (*Take three!)* refuses nothing.
You see, in our picture world, no cinematic creature
Can live without the steamy *scenes* of love.

O you, Johnny or Joe's fair fruit, fill my filmic glade,   15
And grant my work-day screen hams a life in your golden light.
Come you, come, and instigate my cutting-room amours,
Turn leaden mortal boys, whatever the tease,
Into love's delight, to love's adultery,
And in your thousand gorgeous forms, bear for me   20
On story-boarded earth, your storey-bordered cumulus of light.

I'll bet on that mountain where you read, Mars is appeased,
And every soul around you fills up with pride.
I'll bet in every way, all those you set on fire
Aren't able to bear the smallest shame, and live a spotless life.25
I'll bet your courtesies rejuvenate and make benign
Both high- and low-born, after one of your seraphic smiles.
Our joy is in the power you radiate.

Imagine a majestic film-star reign, Hollywood's house in unity,
Your very honesty its cause of hospitality.   30
Your producer's wonder's all those superficial qualities
For which you're fond of finding so many handy adjectives,
When *he* can't fathom how it comes about
That Gee loves Exe and Exe loves Wye,
And why this fish, and not this other species wriggles up the weir. 35

Good honest film folk will, I wager, learn your universal laws,
And soon will swoon as I and lovers swoon
(Who quarrels with this will get the worst of it!).
Full bright in make-up brush benignity,
Revered by all who'll come to serve you,   40
Your singing scribe I am, so teach me to devise
Some script to place all preened and polished in your service.

You in my trembling heart have infused
Such a passion, therefore show me those stagy moves,
Allow me to hear your dulcet voice   45
(O how our movie buffs need, nay crave you!),
And how I must talk up this madness or gladness
To Venus, to Venus, to Venus!
We of the studio floor, O heed us!

amber light, turn green!   50

Do let me know, Mal, if there's anything I've missed.

Anno

Between them, did Mal and John tease out, in an overly
complex layering of word plays (traces across, down,
diagonally) their suspected matrices of verbal intent? Myself
I can't do much better than 'O Al, I am celluloid' [which is to
juggle a bit with the opening lines of the first two stanzas], or
'empyrean dots' [similarly the poem's lines two and three].
Whatever the outcome, Mal did not reply. In passing he did
wonder how a corrupt Chaucerian prologue was expected to
help in the task of recovering that sixth, and elusive name.
"Can't really say," I said, though I knew very well the name
that Diamond sought.

Subject: Paeroa   **Date:** 20/10/51
To: MalDeFak@BDP (Private_net)
From: Anno@BDP (Private_net)

Mal – How to counter the loss, when a genteel English spinster, with an innocent regard for the passions and torments of Elgar, is just two pay cheques from retirement... Miss Ashley points out that for several days now the all-smiling Craig has made certain intentions clear, having posted onto the world_net – all in a wash of media sugarstick (coloured stripes, rotating satellites, elephantine point sizes) – advance notice of our tiny globe's largest ever media extravaganza. This shall come to pass with world-wide link-ups, hosted and anchored by Craig himself, effortlessly tanned, and trussed in an English bowtie. An all-live, all-day, all-nation show, whose high purpose is the gratulate celebration of McGregor's over-stuffed empire (that's to say a powdered termite hill, with its news/sport/current affairs/ entertainment). Hub of this enterprise is the ancient McGregor household, a colonial clapboard framehouse in Paeroa, now the property of World Museums (should like to rename Mausoleum). You did read that, Mal, I did say Paeroa, which is, Mal, south of the Coromandel Peninsula, a range, Mal, of rimu-covered mountains toeing the Pacific. Plans include doting talk on the old days, with McGregor himself wheeled into the spotlight, his two inept grandsons (surf-loving, born-lucky shareholders) off camera but quietly in attendance. We shall hear, listening carefully, Diamond's own script team scribing away in a licensed motel.

It just occurs to me that any gerrymandering Craig is keeping under wraps – well... what more public opportunity to disclose...

Anno

Not quite your last duty, Miss Ashley, is to confirm my booking, flight NZ001, arriving Auckland 1st November (a Wednesday), 5.30 a.m. Don't know, till I've seen what is what, when I shall return. Think, Miss Ashley, I shall take those

137

handover notes, if you could just bundle them together. Might be something I can add. Might be things I can intersperse in retrospect. If I don't get back for the retirement bash, farewell…

Benbrook Height College
for the Performing Arts

First, that rubric above would not have splashed onto my canvas, had not Miss Ashley called me to her carrel on the eve of my flight. Instead I think I would have settled for the rubric below, 'Marua', and just not bothered with Diamond the media student. Miss Ashley pointed out that with no clear plan, I was likely to spend a great deal of time at the foot of the Coromandels, with not very much to do. She asked me was I likely, as an airborne Prospero, to spend my hippo days foaming myself in surf or sweating salt and bile among the hot waters of holiday commerce (these, Prosp, you find at a place called Miranda, spas and springs an hour from Auckland). There are long gravel tracks all over the Hauraki Plains. "Well, no," I said. "Tourism isn't of course the aim."

I put it down to the heady attractions of her own holiday vistas, a glimpse forward into a future devoid of Ix, that for the first time (to my knowledge anyway) Miss Ashley refers the faintest trace of cherry gloss, via the stamp of her warm lower lip, to the thin china of her tea cups. (Miss Ashley in her tea cups.) She had a ghostly knack of knowing exactly what I the Englishman, Anno of Ix – in every other sense patient, and even flexible – would find a sensitive issue. Failure's a thing I admit to only privately, over the swollen glass bubble of a brandy glass, and I therefore cannot publicly accept – with a clear head and dry eyes – that the Diamond case won't be wrapped up, and all his deadly mentations laid bare, before the appointment of my successor, whoever, pale reader, you eventually turn out to be. So for Miss Ashley I do this (while I wink). I shuffle this rubric above (worn out playing cards, think you), only to pass the time. Only to keep my balding head from the ferocity of New Zealand's late spring sun. Only to avoid these hard dry winds.

Lights. Camera. Clapperboard.

1

'Lights' is what I don't have (dammit there's a praying mantis on my wall), attempting to scrutinise King Craig's early vapours, not at Benbrook Height, but at Exe University. Now I go way back (our human time can sometimes run that way), to those occluded, repaid days, back among the windswept chestnut trees in Capel. To Le Pac belongs a personal history all greened with lichen, and a rocky kitchen table at whose half-century of incisions I was likely to read practically *anything*. Mostly this meant a fabric of half-truths – our obsessions were political and economic – all seamlessly summed up, with a home thought on what it all meant now, or rather then. This also entailed a kind of unscrubbed sub jub literature (claws that snatch), a baton passed on irretrievably into the calloused hands of a half-dozen brandname authors, who the moment they saw a camera either smiled or frowned. Theirs, I have to add, was a material emanating from my mother's book club – and books I read only through boredom. On the whole they're a waste of time.

So. I owe my charcoaled window onto the life of Exe to the memoirs of one of its professors. Through him one might have predicted the blandness of our times, for this was Professor Andrew Glaze, a man not content with his canopy of pillows, prinked and plumped and so thoughtfully arranged throughout his rooms. I am talking about his final haven, place tuned to the dawn twitters, and to the whole cosmic range of Kentish sunsets, where Glaze tragically hanged himself, an age ago now, back in the 1990s. He died not without hope, careful to do so only having exhaled, into the cold corridors of his sanitarium (with its surrounding hop fields, and apple orchards), the pale mists of his last thoughts on life and the world. These his estranged wife Samantha discovered in manuscript form among his private papers on her last visit of all from the bedlam of New York – property she auctioned, so stretching his five-minute fame to ten. I can't remember too much about that memoir now, though I vividly recall by what tactless means my mother's book club constructed its sale, in published form. Professor Glaze, beacon of a century we had all, thankfully, ushered out. Mentor to one of our masters, a man called Marshall Zob (whose fame I vaguely recall). Tragic death. Memoir a revealing insight. Well, yeah, y' nar wot I mean (gob, sniff)…

Post-Glaze, a new bird – our own Craig Canary, all drab and disports, and a velveteen plumage as yet unruffled – sauntered in on that world so fulsomely set out in the dead professor's memoir. That parfit old-world world – it went on, and on, and on… Exe a sometime eternal city, then as now with its stone and timber streets and market trade, useless handcrafts, junk like keyrings, air cankered with sour-smelling pasties, ancient quads in the lee of all those rain-dark towers, whose wag and woe of bells were a call to the lectern. Craig got there in just the same flourish as his plum-sucking seniors, yet something, the hue of his hose, or the side parting – sometimes to the left, at other times not – attracted only mute approbation. Craig wised up. Took his penny pomes, plus gobbets of half-chewed prose, into the caffs and cyber shoppes, where many a wine-rouged proprietor crashed about on the tail of all things 'new'. Craig or Cray or Crag shook his old sentences into those beautifully textured cigarette skins, which at that time – ah but that time *I* don't know… Carefully, these he gummed and rolled. Not to make too long his nights, into whose distant yards any transiting audience had the option to fade, and having passed from ash to grey ash, Craig fitfully spat out whole hexagons (whole lexicons) of neo-syllabic butts, all just slightly damp. You ask what it means. I say only I report what is garbled mythology. Some new line in cabaret. Nor are those electrifying epistles it's said he fired off over the then Internet, verifiable. These, I have read somewhere, were his fisher's hooks, the idea being that participating recipients added their own expositions, to make of our *Once upon a time* a pirouette of multiple infrastructures, and a teleology of very remote ends. Don't ask me to explain. In New Zealand I find it is no small matter, keeping the old continent clearly, neatly focused. There's this battery of crickets (green) and piped music (black), everywhere you go.

141

2

Come June, what with its rain and its sudden sunburst, Prince Craig had at last thinkingly underscored certain idle formulas committed to his notepad, an action whose penstrokes I cannot help view as decisive. These, Craig, were brave algebraic propositions, foremost of which was a favourite of yours: *let Exe equal ex*. Though please bear in mind that I quote, that I don't invent. Two sad semesters sat strewn at his feet (from these his hatful of unexciting marks). Particularly agonised had been all those tutorials, though in fact not the half dozen that, under a studio light, under the powder puffs from the makeup bench, he later, angelically, recalled. Had this student really understood the symbolic importance of, for example, disguise as a Shakespearean device, all those journeys into exile, whole litanies of mistaken identity, or the final costume change and reconciliation – uh, Craig, had you? Or why Lord Byron chose *ottava rima*? When Craig looked back, he did look back, an assertion he liked to inflate with his own special tucket or trumpet call, denoting no addiction at all to the syrups of sentimentality. Those inconclusive semesters were two dun islands, pinpoints on a complicated map, twinned hillocks lacking regular sanitation, and marooned in a cold leaden sea of academic backchat. Mean t' say, dead poets were dead poets, hey (a ho, a hey nonino)…

Personally *my* only visit to Exe was in the nature of a death throe, a last gasp to many months of fruitless toil, all in pursuit of a goddam book (I am irritable only because I nurse mosquito bites). This I had now tracked down and finally located among the walnut shadows of Modern College library. Book was, incidentally, a Chaucer *Complete* (whose editor was Skeat), and the library a purgatory of half-formed spots of sunshine, all in a mesh of refracted maroons on its old stone walls. A bust – this had pinched brows, taut lips, and a blind gaze – oversaw all, from an elevation of ten to fifteen metres, and for all I remember might well have been that of a canonised Andrew Glaze, academic who died an untimely, if heroic death, way back when I was a babe or boy.

In the years since, our Craig has assured an unbelieving world that to arrive there – all shepherd-like, Modern College library a windy crag of erudition – you are obliged to traverse one other plateau in Pluto's twisted chasms, a nether world treacly with subterranean runnels. Put less fantastyk, this is Modern's quad, whose topography is weeds and disintegrating flagstones, and against whose spring zephyrs one turns a collar to the freights of swirling leaves. To this I can testify.

Craig gathered what credits his one year at Exe had flowered, and were internationally transferable. So to speak he tucked them in his money belt. Our next scene's a night scene, under the swinging lantern light of a now dead dive (it was a parts shop, for hip replacements, the last time I looked), called Cyber Cellar Nought – venue of riotous entertainments, with scrubbed whitewash plus a collection of church pews. I speak no evil. Here our beleaguered prince filled a newly sheened graduate, not of Exe, but of Benbrook, with cupfuls of barley wine. Just how common is it, says Craig, for the acclaimed media school, at such a dizzy cliff edge, to take in disaffected sophomores, especially from the watered graves of Academe?

"That depends."

"Depends on what?"

"On what you say at the interview."

"I know what to say."

"*And* on the entrance test."

"Oh. There's an entrance test."

3

Actually that interview he thought didn't go at all well. The course he wanted to enrol for was Editing, Performance, Media, which seemed an ever receding target, after several tedious rounds of letter-writing, and a series of intimidating phone calls. Its course director, who did finally summon him to her office – this was one cold and windy afternoon, in an otherwise flaming June – like Craig thought of life as just about serious. At no point in their two years scrapping out their respective positions, did either guess at *why* that was so.

Ms Zinine kept everything tidy. This was as true for the pile

143

of A4 on her desk – here her broad bony fingers thrummed, intermittently – as for the matrix of book spines ranked according to size on her shelves. Craig liked to point out, in the first in a big batch of television autobiographies (this about a decade later), that he was still able to recite all her pet authors' names, and was a mantra he liked to chant in reverse alphabetical order. You can count the narcissi, planted in a vase at his elbow – Sheridan, Susan; Russo, Mary; Moi, Toril; Hesse, Carla; Grosz, Elizabeth; Fusco, Coco. My only comment, Craig, is this: Ms Zinine, who smoked an American brand of cigarettes (called Buffalo – they came in a crush pack – she inhaled very deeply), and by her own admission a caffeine addict, though she never moved publicly to rebut your claims, so far as I know hasn't yet had the opportunity.

Zina. She was Zina to her friends. To Craig she was ZZ, who, once he was shot of Exe, liked to invoke the flat world and successive frames – a cause, an effect, a closure – of broadsheet comic strips whenever alluding to her. How often you'd see him sketch, retreating from his lecture notes, an arc of diminishing zeds, then someone snoozing, then a crescent moon, finally a housetop dressed as a silhouette. She wanted to know just why he'd abandoned Exe, whose professors of English, not nearly so rustic as Craig had imagined, Ms Zinine knew socially (through academic functions mainly) and got on well with by and large. Craig thought the answer was obvious, and that the question merely patronised. He said something like it's all media now and the Internet, and smirked. A week later Ms Zinine, hugely endowed with a sense of fairness (yet with no particular sympathy for the hordes of fellow-practitioners) sent him his assignment, in a crested envelope, printed on recycled grey paper, in ghastly Eurocopper twelve point. We'd better note that crest, since it's going to become familiar: this was the Benbrook shield, an old and modified antiquated medieval thing, topping two horizontal ferns.

By now of course (I mean the 'of course' of autobiography – this a lodestone gleaming with fatalism)… by now Prince Craig had resigned himself to future days as a freelance proofreader, in his own mind already permanently destined for those long

long tobacco nights gassing in the cyber cellar. The assignment was due to be completed, or so Zina insisted, over the next ten days, since this was the final point on which his entry could be judged. Its overfed wording, under whose fusion of paragraphs an indecipherable signature apologised for itself, with a *per procurationem*, asked for an essay, of no more than two thousand words, under the title 'Concrete Art and Realism'.

Craig thought himself canny when, planting himself at the librarian's desk, some way over the valleys in Modern College, Exe, he glanced up at that bust – by which I mean that marble I feathered and dusted in the section above. Now was it Glaze, or was it Arnold, or was it Eliot? Perhaps it's as well we shall never know. Craig paid his book fines and handed in his photocopy card.

4

His 'Concrete Art and Realism' – essay that bore a secondary title, 'Ich bin ein Quotidian' – was a world of self-parody, all to do with power. The particular power he meant serenely clung to life in the naturally occurring reliquaries of post-cultural life, such as museums, art galleries, old-style places of learning, town and city squares. It signified itself in a phylum of bronzes and busts. Often these were stern, sometimes bedizened, sometimes they capped a roll of names.

Eerily, a whole century had come and gone. We knew this, he said, because 'all of us' had sat and watched. Remarkably this had taken place without so much as a vanquishing sword. By this he implied that 'realism', or rather 'reality', consisted of no more concrete – and here I invoke Craig's own examples – than the screen flicker of a Chaplin or the Keystone Cops. He pointed out (he often pointed it out in conversation too) that only since the ever spreading ripples of political conscience had artists felt the need for guided tours round workshops and factories. At this point (in his essay, it never occurred in conversation) he summoned what ingenuity it took to bend those two parallel shafts, those two unrelated lines of argument, to a single arrow-head – asserting that what the bronze or bust inveighed was an organ of abstract invention. Invention much like the 'verist' novel or 'social' play, or the tottering uncertainties in all that zany, piano-accompanied slapstick – all cloudy castles fabricated in a climate of questionable expertise.

Could Ms Zinine now begin to guess why Modern College, Exe, was impossible for Craig? He hoped so, though of course this didn't prevent the deceits and oppositions he knew he was likely to bring to the studios of Benbrook (would, would he, smash that shield?) – should he find its doors ajar. He didn't rate his chances of being accepted. Therefore to Craig, a partly beheld Zinine couldn't seem more than the lightly textured presence, with weightless intellect to match, that his own thoughts made of her – distantly, in a mild dust of Buffaloes, in a drench of caffeine. He pre-empted her 'no' by teasing out a *political* 'no', having wrongly calculated a hard shock for a soft college leftism, in pinning his own colour (a blue rosette) to McGregor. It was by that man's authority that Craig declared that the 'concrete' and 'real' existed *under* the level of the satellite transmission. McGregor seemed to him to ask the question was our relationship to things really subject-object? Did the way we encountered the world involve subjective experience? McGregor knew (because McGregor knew his stuff) that programme-makers everywhere kept urging on everyone a way of allowing things to show themselves as what they were merely as a screen manifestation. But. When McGregor troubled himself with how people were related *to* 'things', he found it wasn't as subjects to objects. At this point, conversationally, one always expected an ambivalent Craig to introduce the various schools of realism as no more than schools of 'conscious' art, while according to McGregor consciousness wasn't the necessary instrument for dealing with an everyday world. How so? Well, in terms of our being, we don't find conscious subjects directed towards independent objects. Our being is only the dune on to which our tents of reality are pitched, and what wind of epistemes fluttered in our desert breeze just then (as is much the case now) was the one convected by the engines of McGregAir – media construction Craig Diamond didn't want to miss out on.

Arnold, Eliot, Glaze, were dismissed. Craig rested his case.

5

We turn to crested envelopes again, and Zina's political 'no'
cleverly concealed as an apolitical 'yes' – a surprise
communication Craig found closely tracked by a wodge from
admin. Zina he next saw sad-eyed, and on a breezy day, all
set to zoom from under a canopy of oak and ash (beech also
dotted the campus), yet lavishly at halt in the sheen of her
sports car, which was purring. Its red was just her shade. She
applied lipstick, with a not too expert touch, and not at her
most relaxed with the angle of her rearview. In her letter – for
whose changed typeface (a dull but sober Univers) she had
chartered a complex punctuation – she offered a round-up of
Craig's philosophy. She cautioned him that here it had always
been in the Benbrook ethos to probe the creative impulse with
a range of deconstructive tools. Then she talked about some
of his contemporaries, at whose core we shall find (we shall
find in due course) Lisbeth Fatualli (in a tight handclasp, which
lasted for eighteen months, with Gavin Smayle), a reluctant
William Tropecale, the more arrogant Lorenzo Constant,
Dondie Millar (sculptor), colourfully the flighty Chelsea de la
Mare – all of whom had already spent one academic year in
learning studio set-up and getting to grips with equipment.
Craig's mild riposte he didn't deliver (technology would serve
him, *he* wouldn't be its slave). With a smile he waved her away
– all five of her forward gears in a drive into town – and
continued his trudge uphill, to the Bauhaus cubes of the admin
block. Curious to note that in passing, that was a herd of
Herefords – chewing things over – just there, in the field to
his right.

6

Late September. England, no more mirthful than its new mint
and pan-Europeanism permitted it to be, rendered its sporadic
sons and daughters from all its four quarters, little silhouettes
grooming the mists and dew-sugared dawns. Craig at this
time wore fell boots – a light tan and only slightly scuffed –
and walked. This was a fair few miles, from a room he'd got

above a video club, whose cargo was art movies mainly (tortuous relationships, stylish blue-lit boudoir scenes), to the rounded double peak for centuries known as Benbrook – now the rural preserve or home to one of Europe's foremost talking shops. The walk had its bough-enfolded backway – this a gravel cycle track whose slow bend round the foothills of Benbrook followed one of the Dwar's tributaries, a meek stretch whose opposite bank was overhung with willow trees. From a mild day one (and perhaps I surmise) Craig wouldn't have remembered the cautious Tropecale, under whose powerful calves his dark green mountain bike swept him past, to that distant point on the track where it petered out dramatically. Ahead was a yellow water meadow, in a prolonged sweep to a single, sluggish blue wisp of woodsmoke, whose origin was somewhere beyond a premature horizon. Sharp right was the narrow sealed road snaking the hillside climb to that dual summit, whose appellation lends our college a name, and that tributary below, tinkling through the valley. Would Craig have caught the bob of Tropecale's mustard-coloured crash hat when, with no loss of speed, that strong-limbed cyclist skirted the hillside?

Lisbeth found *her* fitness in the warmth of a private pool, and therefore drove her daddy's land cruiser (daddy's gold-encrusted handshakes wagged with the world's trade fairs), and did so practically everywhere (she'd rise to second gear in a blur from studio one to student bar). I might as well suggest, since no narration ever sustains its fictive bond of trust, that from day two her rural fly-past routinely clattered to a pause, in a blare of jejune radio jingles. She parked and lit up (cheroots is what she smoked) always at the same rain-blacked fence post, one of several staking a notional perimeter round that dappled yellow water meadow. Here she also opened her nearside door, where Craig appeared promptly at roughly 8.45, and accepted, then expected his morning lift.

Back then to that quixotically named Tropecale (yet it was Craig who wore Hawaiian shirts), in whose silences and sullen looks you'd suspect *something*, a plot, ways to save his world of words – man who consistently lagged at the rear.

148

You'd see him flushed, rather that gang of five would see him flushed (Diamond, tacit, elect, and a leader: only Diamond made them six). A restless half-dozen, with a collective glance, all heaving fumes through a fug of mingled smoke (fags and faddish cheroots), whose eyes through the glass of the coffee lounge fell on and mostly ignored the ghost of William Tropecale – he who beheld in a multitude of outlines his own, anonymous reflection.

Tropecale, whose crash hat dangled from his handlebars, wheeled his bike over a last few metres, up a step or two, over flagstones, the staff parking lots. Flanking these was a depth of cold soil and a grave of hydrangeas.

7

I have had to ask for another room, here in the Pine Lodge Motel, on the straight and sometimes potted road, into, then out of Paeroa. It isn't due to that praying mantis, since to the contrary I have come to anticipate its stolid gymnastics – up, down and across the mint stripes of the wallpaper (broad bands grading to narrow, in an endless repetition, cream and diluted green). It's all down to the adjoining laundry room, where an all-day char isn't at one with the hum, those plastic and metallic wingbeats of her machines, and so is plugged in incessantly to an open can of muzak. This is a medieval diabolism. It conducts itself in ragged waves from the reverberant depths of her cavern, into the sophisticated voids of my own, whose ambiance tends to be monastic. Do I dare flirt with its elemental clash? This was a collision that, at its most tempestuous, clanged in synchronistically with that of Lisbeth Fatualli, just as my murdered pen opened her cruiser door. Nevertheless I have had the presence of mind to contact Miss Ashley (who by now probably knows all about Fräulein Buxt's secret box of tricks, in New Bayreuth). I asked her to send me profiles of *all* the Benbrook BA courses, circa 2010–13.

I note with some suspicion that there is no sign, anywhere in the motel grounds (all coarse grass and radial pathways), of a pine tree. There is a Douglas fir. And a rata. Some silver birch. There's a bamboo hedge. There is a cabbage tree. No pines not nowhere.

8

In fact Craig's 'Editing, Performance, Media' he reinterpreted, and as such produced his own separate agenda, which as a document, published more than once in its many metamorphoses as manifesto, Ms Zinine responded to with silence (as was her policy with all statements full of holes and hoaxes). She did once say this, or something like it – 'I don't, Craig, have a sense of your absence' – when for a tenth or nth or umpteenth reveille, the missing name was his. You can, Craig, insist that it wasn't an act of spite, nothing personal at all, though that's at odds with the facts. Most will recall to what extent it tickled the vicarious Fatualli, who from all four corners of campus exile trumpeted your routine boycott of Zina's 9.30 lecture. I, however, remain unconvinced.

At that time (or nearer midday) Craig made much of his institutional need to test the equipment, yet found through the daily booking forms that the recording desks and edit suites were assigned *en bloc* to the then prevailing *Übermenschen*. By that is meant the hierarchy of staff and associates who were themselves engaged in film-making. It was rumoured, across quads and in the refectory, that Ms Zinine had a Stateside distribution deal, having already paved the way with a lecture tour – itself dated to the start of last semester, when a doubtful lull in her student curriculum signalled no other plausible sense of her own absence.

In my opinion, here was just another theatrical smokescreen, dry ice for a dry-eyed audience. So too can I speculate that Craig couldn't waste his nights (not here at Benbrook Height), when, under golden beams, and a transformational moon, that equipment was magically free. I even guess that his stock at Exe's only galactic venue, his Cyber Cellar Nought, had somehow risen, while carefully gauged was that den's wide-eyed proprietor, who I am told was well connected.

9

I am speaking (this new room's no good either) of an embryonic Craig Diamond, whose full profile hadn't yet slimmed to its present manifestation. Nor can one discern his height from the handful of student photographs his aged ego has allowed to survive, since these are all 'action' shots. In one I recall long tartan socks, a tan boot to a grey boulder, other grey boulders strewn among straw-coloured hillside turfs, a sleeved elbow cocked to that one raised knee. Lisbeth, who in the same shot wears a pair of voluminous cycling shorts, and has the back of one weary hand to her forehead, the other pocketed, does appear taller. Yet this wasn't so. I will plump, Craig, for five feet eleven (you who refused to be metricated).

That's his height. His weight I can't approximate, but am aware that tentative though his student budget might have been, he did at that time quaff down a hearty Bass – or a stout if that ran dry – in foaming quarts. He was slightly rotund, a poundage he's tended to lose, in the years since and his media evolution, what with the interdicts and screen prohibitions, and whatever needles to his vanity (I can think of no one more conscious of his public image. And what a racket, coming from outside!). For a damp climate his hair was dark – he said himself, his was a genetic soup peppered with Mediterranean spices – but also thin, and straight, two attributes that haven't at all changed (by which I mean that unlike me, he isn't inclined to baldness. I know that some day I'm going to be domed). On days rolling with r's – Thursdays, Fridays, Saturdays – he lightened his crop with lemon juice and parted it to the right, otherwise the left. It was neat and attractive when short, straggly when Craig was in need of a haircut. What else? Oh, well – complexion, sallow. Jawbone inclined to shaving rash. Apparel – that was bourgeois: slacks, open-neck shirts, all vaguely expensive. I could, amusingly, contrast that with the cargo pants and cable-knit sweaters another kind of student, in a declining day of road-protests, favoured and preferred (but after all these years it's got beyond a joke, so I pass

151

on that). In official photos, notably a "Class of '13", Craig did go in for structured poses, all hurt and intelligent. In his life though he smiled a lot (it was, Craig, a smug smile), and usually had a glister to his eye. Face was round, which with the punishing diets of his manhood I note now as longish and hollow. Tanned easily – just stood in a vernal breeze, to turn a shade of autumn oak.

I think that covers it.

10

A first sortie, cleverly, into the Benbrook library, uncovered for Craig the 'blue book' – which had nothing to do with Wittgenstein – in whose night hushes all assessment criteria had been meticulously set out. That was as true for Craig's 'Editing, Performance, Media', as it was for Tropecale's 'News, Information, Diffusion'. In fact it was true for all major and minor pathways.

There were no exams. Marks were awarded for essays, showings, and the quality of debate – the latter demonstrated as an interior monologue, each student expected to keep a log of work in progress. Attendance of lectures (I'm finding this tedious, but there we are – there's nothing else to do) didn't necessarily contribute to marks, and since a transcript of every lecture was posted on the intranet, non-attendance didn't automatically result in loss.

11

I find I shall have to retouch with certain other details later. And dammit I didn't bring a dictionary.

Now there was one, I shall learn [but here I make mock of my tenses], strategic October day, a blurred sun hazing a dust of high cloud, which in its vats of liquefied crimson overspilled itself into an Indian summer, lasting a whole afternoon. Lisbeth, prone at her poolside, with Craig doing deals on her cell phone, hooked an arthritic-looking hand to the last of her encumbrances, and undid. Craig remained calm. In any case he had always been flabby – and in instances with Lisbeth (whose Valentine's correspondence once filled a postbag – but that's to rush on) turned each situation to nothing but economies, as a man at peace among all those hormonal pyrotechnics. He rubbed sunscreen between her shoulders, to the small of her back, without a twitch. That as her one tactile sensation with the young Craig had to make do with a poor climax, his suggestion that now was the right time to sell her telecom shares. These, in a confused impulse – of paternal relief, and perhaps also of joy – her father had bought almost twenty years before, when the FTSE blipped and the price just dropped a little.

Clouds begin to thicken, which a pale, indifferent and distant sun can't now burn off. Tropecale pedals hard along his cycle path, in a swirl of yellow leaves. There's a blackbird, a bell, a plash of airbrakes somewhere. It's intermittent, but sacks of dew either sieve or blow through the trees, which here on Benbrook's declivity are an assortment. Tropecale numbered oak and initialled beech, spat at a punctuating chestnut, pedalled more slowly past a succession of maples. Craig is already ensconced. Hill cyclist looks up. Zina, the silk of her head-scarf prinked in the breeze, zooms by in her shiny red Élante (this I think manufactured by Peugeot, or sporting its badge). There's a ladle of mist constellated round those Castle Heights, where in the fluorescent gloom of the library, in an ante-room off, up a tottering stair, Lisbeth's old telecom shares are dissolved into malleable enterprise. She thinks: "Hope he knows what he's doing."

Apparently he did, and was here, most weekday mornings, day-trading Euroshares across the Internet, while never far behind, and now in part concealed among the limbs of a yew – her car parked, its bonnet cooled – Ms Zinine stirred up the exotic scents in her lecture room. One just about saw through its glazes, already darkened by the satin of their window blinds, where, today as every weekday, she patiently rehearsed her communications models. These were private elaborations on the theories of a man called Jacobson, all for a fullness of students (bar one).

I have since measured out the six or so diagonal paces a sloping floor allows in that tiny square chamber, in whose computerised labyrinth Craig unravelled his fibre optic threads (his Ariadne hardly wept at the loss of her shares), and in a daily, two-hour heat of high-risk buying and selling, nevertheless coolly underwrote his two-year student enterprise. There is a sash window, which even in the years I'm forced to discuss, was barred, college equipment routinely open to theft. I can look down and imagine all those episodes Craig, in his various media memoirs, has found so amusing. A drollery that, from the glitz and perspective inherent in that golden perch of his, was no more than a cloud-covered midnight, whole counties and cantons awash with fee-paying students – all clueless, according to him. The best of them, here among the mazy paths and pines and studios of Benbrook Height, lumped along with outmoded TV sets (off to some practical showing or communal work-in-progress), and were all destined for a world of shadows, and a life in work as tedious as any you'd imagine. Sometimes I can see a Wm Tropecale, a light-weight video device tucked under one arm. I scan all around, insofar as those bars will allow, from a quad, just here below my elbow, where a yew remains (where, Ms Zinine, are you?), thence over all the unlikely habitations the centuries have accidentally conferred. What is this seat of learning but adapted barns, shippons, billet huts dated WW2, and still not bulldozed... bits of old Bauhaus bequeathed to the admin and archive block (paint, it needs paint), a 1970s refectory, halls from the 1960s (all orange brick in a vortex of wild garlic), a timeless laundry room (a black-walled basement lined with silver pipes), an open-air theatre, an ornamental pool, whose slither of koi is really the gold and copper rainbow reflected off a bed of coins.

12

And I find I have to wake up. It's all because of the room I'm in, complete with twin beds and vanity desk. My sinister reflection has an awkward hand poised, as it writes. One other attraction is its convenient proximity to the bar, whose creek wines or light beers I haven't yet sampled. The problem is its geometry, whose angles of reverberation are in an L-shape off a capacious trellis across the courtyard, whose sharp red diamonds I see softened slightly in the leafy multivectors of a vine, which I don't think bears fruit. Here in its shade a fervent youth – her pockets a jangle of keys – is valeting whole fleets of customer cars. In progress is a large silver Chrysler, whose thickly carpeted maw she is prodding with a powerful vacuum. Drowning *its* noise is the subterranean thrum of that filthy vehicle's in-flight radio. I shall have to speak to the proprietor, again – a lean, silver-haired man with a stoop, and one lazy eye, and whose dentures don't seem to be his own. On the last, and depressingly similar occasion, he outlined pacifically how all of us had to be tolerant, a point I debated philosophically.

13

There have been quieter moments, notably one night earlier this week, when – still mulling over a first drive to McAndrew St – I sat out under the Southern Cross, just me and my papers. Not much goes on, there among the slanting shadows, sometimes dark feline shapes in the half-light, the light itself in an acuteness of frayed angles, and hung from the motel windows over the newly painted decks. By now Miss Ashley had processed my request, with the result that here I cast a long last look over Diamond's 'Editing, Performance, Media', to discern not at all clearly its parallels with Tropecale, whose 'News, Information, Diffusion' in that year attracted only eighteen other students, three of whom dropped out. One was a fatality. The second was a transfer to the University of North London. That, I might add, proved a transition not without unnecessary pain, over whose gored entrails a trio of sympathisers prognosticated bitterly (these three did complete successfully, here at Benbrook Height). The third was a crisis of confidence, a tragic diminution, with an initial aim high into the vaulted skies of movie direction, thence to the clay soil of camera work, finally (and graciously) to a six a.m. start-up firm, supplying sandwiches to office folk.

I contacted Miss Ashley again, this time asking her to delve into the Benbrook archive, where I hoped she'd uncover that vintage blue book – this as an emblem tucked under Craig's

155

arm, and there newly incarnate as so much the symbol of student disobedience. To some that rebellion was tame, *some* being a rogues' vista full of codgers sucking straw. Having rolled back the concrete of Europe's dead decades, you'd incriminate our nows as source of nothing like the amulets of '68 – an era I personally try to envisage solely for a certain May evening at Wembley. I now feel fairly sure that the rules set out for the blue book's final assessment – a mark contributing almost a third of the degree – Craig subsumed to the moving shapes and changing silhouettes in his own nocturnal plush. In its chinks and chiming midnights he drafted, each of his pencils newly sharp, a uniquely successful plan.

Take my hat off.

14

I do sometimes think that here I *ought* to be dealing with a catalogue of failure, since Craig never learned (and said this with a smirk) to use a camera. Craig also fought shy of all but the most basic instruments of sound recording. He resisted involvement, however slight – and with it hours of laborious toil – with all that hard graft in the cutting rooms. His essays – not that I'd say I'd necessarily predict it, Craig an ex-Exean – were well turned and reflective. Conversely his log books – those dialogues with self, conducted on a tufted summit, whose jagged flints provided whatever dull sparks in a privately dark heaven – these were no more than a cut-and-paste of Ms Zinine's disseminated lecture notes (this to Craig a kind of rendering unto Caesar). His zoom and talk-back subsisted only through those windows-into-windows, in his den of electric networks – with an arc, a rainbow, a sweep of pixelated spectra – a remotely fuelled roam over the European stock exchange. Out of that, and its day-to-day payola, Craig manoeuvred himself to the hub of at least one important substructure, whose charter was economic. Lisbeth Fatualli got back more than her telecom shares (a whole bagful of blue chips, he gave her). Gavin Smayle, a bearded, stocky, bristling little man, couldn't easily bear the weight of Diamond's largesse. Lorenzo Constant – who could *smell* money – invited him to half a dozen late-night raves (all a drone on Metaxa, or supermarket wine, or for the elect little sachets of gold dust – all mixed to a paste in lots of ghoulish chat on the Brit Arts Scene, or BRATS). Dondie Millar, who several times asked him to sit for her, in the end posed for him. Chelsea de la Mare starred in his final show (by which I mean final showing, or assessment, that determining mark in the life of any Benbrook bachelor). William Tropecale, social ethnographer, watched. And he watched. And was watched.

15

Too much of this I am bound to reassess through the dimmed optics of retrospect, in what seems a lifetime from Pine Lodge, whose painted timbers I did eventually leave, snugly cocooned in its radio daytime (then with the onset of summer its nights of sizzling cicadas). Only faintly do I now recall a trail of dust, a whole country remote beneath my elbow, in its shroud or long white cloud. I wipe the lens, which is just no good, and am left – here in so vast a canopy of late and fruitless hours – to a long and abortive search for the last John Frame. No sign of him here (this 'here' is his Omani fortification), where I have sought him high and low – above, in those crenellated towers, or down below, in that crystal honeycomb of secret passages and interconnecting tunnels. Ironically all I am left with is this catalogue of Diamond's works, and the puzzle as to how exactly I should have come by that...

16

Also I think even Craig thought most of his ventures banal. A first presentation piece, which his student budget didn't finance (he scripted, he choreographed, he stumped up cash), was marked down – its yield a stunted percentage point, which he beheld through a cloud of bottled rage. Nevertheless he went and traded shares – I wonder through what polar frosts – his gaze an icy blue, and predatory (it was predatory even in its most relaxed).

Generally all such sediment drifted to the shallows. His own glass was quick to clear, and once among his cohorts his vatful

157

rapidly cooled, and thereafter ritual took its therapeutic course. Individual moratoria took place in the damp afterglow of the refectory, whose tables were newly wiped – solid surfaces all in a briefly worn nimbus or blur of moist amber. The next round occurred during late afternoon, and ought not trouble my refining sense of posterity. I call it a ball game, played among makeshift caravans, haphazardly grouped at an accidental oasis, whose palms and blue waters were an archipelago of foyers and institutional niches, all with a beaten pile to the tints of a snack dispenser. This is where marks were exchanged.

Alas posterity has to fight another day. I find myself coaxed to that same era of inward mirrors, a time and location undone helplessly in the sheen of its own reflection, and obsessed with any least change in its patina – a world where all human thresholds long to be discovered anew. Therefore I'm not surprised that for Craig's next contribution, with a microphone and camera, veiled between a Coke and a soup machine, he recorded just such a grades-day post mortem – one of those moments in social history he found the right name for, this his *Dell'arte Tirade*.

After that came *Put Your Hands Together Please*. What Zina most criticised, that whole year out, recall, was what she termed its tentative camera work, for which Craig had paid – and graciously not demanded his money back – a brimming Gavin Smayle. One has only to imagine Zina's partly muffled tone of triumph, a muted trumpet – offstage perhaps – but revealed as pepper on her stave, where an assessor's grace notes normally might go. The piece incidentally found Craig on safe home turf, a glib and glittered compère hosting one of the many cabaret slams that at that time took place under the desert awnings of Cyber Cellar Nought, a venue smoke-filled, and on this occasion spangled with laughter.

Diamond requested a tutorial. Ms Zinine granted it, but then failed to turn up at the appointed place, at the appointed hour. These were, respectively, that book-bound office (Sheridan, Russo, Moi, et al) – place whose door was locked and glass was dark – and a very specific 16.20, all inauspicious under a pale gibbous moon. Craig left a note, pinned to her outer architrave, to which Zina didn't reply. (Though Craig said nothing, here began his meticulous incident log.)

Craig found one other faultline, when he heard, or was rather regaled of Dondie Millar's most recent stunning success (a mark in the high seventies) – to him the wrong reward for what has since become her famous filing cabinet. This (the cabinet, whose drawers and carcass were made of tin) for its years of bureau service bore its dents and superficial wounds in two-tone grey, and having lived long, and grown useless, was just the immortal office junk Dondie liked to stumble on, in this case in the lumber rooms of Benbrook. Things – all things – under Dondie's caress were art, a point of particular emphasis for the sites she often chose. We know that for Zina, current co-ordinates in Europe's high culture demanded these sites were 'liminal'. Therefore for that fossil of office life, student Millar enveigled an overalled peon, who shipped it miles across campus, and parked it at the foot of a basement stair. Important too was how she filmed: *objet* starred under a jaundiced light, with its dead drawers hanging out. Accompanying soundtrack made mantras of or mystified the recorded squeak of its drawers, where the essence of lubrication was really a lost rite, doomed to a previous civilisation, and long engulfed in Egyptian sands. This was looped endlessly.

In the borrowed debates that followed – from the Futurists, who dreamed a machine age – from the Surrealists, who machined a dream age – or from André or Andy Warhol – Craig saw only retreats into cowardice, Dondie's bits of detritus plunged into a shade-crossed half-world, into whose violet flickers human hands cannot set a visible template. Yet, in the years of her first fame, that thing, *objet*, charade was regularly screened, and I think even today you can check this out, in the Millar Film Archive, Lausanne, where all you'll need is an idle twenty minutes.

I don't pretend that what I here have following comes in anything like its correct chronology. At one stage Diamond did prepare a hoax, using Smayle again (important vote of confidence) with his camera, sound and editing equipment. I add caveats, first that it's only now, in the closing days of Ix, and

159

through the prism of his adult glee, that I learn that Craig appropriated texts. For example here was one from La Fontaine, which Craig even passed as his own through the pages of his log book. Solely for Ms Zinine, who liked her candy fonts, it was done in staid Courier, selected from his Toshiba, a laptop he had somehow acquired from the language labs of Exe. Short film apparently showed Craig in a sloppy saffron jumper reciting his, or the Frenchman's fable – all human horse play, you'd think – to a class of infants. Alphabets adorned the wall, as did certain incidentals from various world religions (a prayer mat, yarmulka, a rosary). Two books not in use, but with spines carefully catching the silver gleam of Smayle's umbrella, not ever moving on the speaker's lap, were these: *The Name of the Rose*, and *The Genealogy of Power*. In my second and only other caveat, I, Anno, just don't care – though regrettably this isn't all. For in fact Craig confesses never to have entered any such classroom, addressed, spoken to or entertained its now mid-life pupils, this being an illusion with camera tricks. Point is to look closely, over towards that wall with its carefully rounded alphabets, mortal faith in global harmony, and so discover one other premeditated fake – discreetly a Foucault's pendulum, a sphere hanging from a wire set in the ceiling, quietly swinging in a filter of crimson light, children's mosaics all over the windows, our world and all we learn or teach just a coat we're told to wear.

17

Nor was Craig's sole mistake the lazy distemper he asked his man in technician's white coat, his Gavin Smayle, to apply through the soundtrack, so making his La Fontaine incoherent as words, sentences, or series of acoustic syntagms. All this of course he intended as a sarcastic doff to Zed Zinine's artistic van, in truth an ancient jalopy (so unlike her red Élante) as this and all who sailed lumbered on its metalled way. That, in a spectacle of sun-crossed dust, was a highway leading nowhere.

She brought to bear through all her wise words the surprising powers of convention, pointing out that had she been able to hear… well, his mark might have improved (for still Craig hadn't yet touched the 2:2 border). Did Craig suspect that the largeness of his error lay in that irreversible decision to abandon the sun-warmed colonnades of Exe? (At this time Dondie was doing amazing things with lard on concrete, in a fanfare of firsts.)

If I hazard half of this correctly, a string of visiting lecturers – all of whom had failed in one practice or other – now entered Craig's curriculum, Ms Zinine by then too busy to deal directly with students. Stupendously she'd swung a script deal, for a firm in Soho Square. One such, a journeyman poet, and a great deal less mobile as broadcaster (for so bragged his CV), took over her Naturalism class, and began that campaign spontaneously with a sculpture. This it later transpired he'd conceived on his train out of London (the polluted grime of Paddington, which does affect the grain of our mind), and was an exercise calculated to question our basic assumptions.

What basic assumptions were these? Well, says Journeyman X (or do call me JX) – not as to the nature of reality *per se* (that *per se* is not a beast I know), rather (and this a philosophical rather), our common perception of it. JX therefore wanted, from the start of his five-week vacation, a written description of his sculpture – a still-born, freestanding tower, constructed as an interlock of haphazardly arranged chairs – and anyone who'd got it would find him in the bar. Craig hadn't got it, but found him in the bar anyway. "You serious, JX?" He was – and wanted every detail, every nuance tended to, its focus of reality exactly reproducible for any given reader. A lot of discussion followed, to no real purpose.

At the close, after five fabulous weeks in rural England, noted especially for the puma-spotting on Dartmoor, JX revealed the answer, in a summarising lecture, whose tenor I don't attempt to simulate – all overarched anyway in the authenticating narratives of science. Firstly the second law of thermodynamics (now where had I heard that before?) forbids any return to previous states of matter, ergo no focus of reality can ever be exactly reproducible for any given reader. Then there's the problem of what it is about our universe that makes us think

161

it's real. In Berkeley's view, for example – though why JX chose it, isn't quite clear – there can be no essence of reality without a conscious agent to perceive it. Therefore if the room were emptied of students, who do sometimes behave as conscious agents (JX's joke, whose apologies I now convey), these lovely art objects would cease to be. For Berkeley, this state of affairs can't exist, since God as an omnipresent consciousness is the perceiving agent of All. However. This does open certain opportunities to the atheist – or should we read sceptic? – who, in denying the existence of God (father not merely of JX, but all artistes), by Berkeley's method can also deny the existence of practically any object or phenomenon – which is fortunate for those preferring trash to be trash. JX even devised a personalised jingle to score his point:

Reality, philosophically,
In the JX play totality,
Is not in fact an actuality…

an outburst JX also parodically part-frenched:

Realité, philosophicalé,
In the jeu de JX totalité,
Is pas in fact an actualité…

JX next went on to Kant, wherein certain rhyme ends spring to mind (I can't, he Kant, you recant, we all read Kant), though I don't think I shall go into that.

18

What does Craig now see, when the lights are out, and glancing back? I answer so: in each college semester a windy stream of coloured hats and flying scarves, into the breeze of whose whirligig – that revolving wheel of five-week projects – came new guests or visiting jesters, who bore their wares. Craig did begin to see the possibility for better marks in group liaisons, with Smayle a man for current affairs (who wished to do something 'topical'), and with Dondie, who at times *could* be coaxed from her lard plateaux. Interestingly that was a material from which she had birthed, among other odd trinkets, a Bible. It was symbolic, she said, to raptures of applause. Craig produced a script – this was called *Robbie 'Socks' McGregor* – and took certain soundings, and finally persuaded the henna-haired Chelsea de la Mare, still partly domiciled in a rose-tinted cloud (some eighteen months *after* her school Ophelia) to take part. Let me just scan this disc. Ah yes, here –

Robbie 'Socks' McGregor
a short symposium
produced, directed and filmed by Dondie Millar
written by Craig Diamond
additional script material, Gavin Smayle

Cast
Robbie 'Socks' McGregor,
a media mogul played by Diamond
Simon Parker, MEP, Junior Heritage
Spokesman for the Opposition, played by Smayle
Angela, Government education advisor,
also Parker's wife, played by de la Mare

Scene: McGregor's dining room – mahogany, walnut, glittering candelabra – in his penthouse suite, London's Barbican Centre. The remains of a dinner for twelve, though only McGregor, who is host, and two of his guests – Parker and his wife – still seated at table. Angela is slightly the worse for drink.

MCGREGOR Now look, before we join the others next door, why don't you tell me, Simon, how's that new job of yours… [He lights a fat cigar.]

ANGELA If you can call propping up the bars in Brussels a job!

PARKER Now, now, Ange…

MCGREGOR Another pina colada, Angela…

PARKER Better go a bit easy…

ANGELA Shut up!

MCGREGOR I'll mix it myself! What shall I get you, Simon?

PARKER I'm still nursing this cognac.

ANGELA Actually he's still smarting from this afternoon!

MCGREGOR [we hear him mix Angela's cocktail] Yes. I heard you asked a question.

ANGELA In his short trousers… with his hand up…

PARKER Angela!

MCGREGOR [handing over cocktail] This needs a bit of a stir, Angela. Here's a nice cocktail spoon. What question, Simon?

PARKER Right up your street. More on the latest moves to appoint a network censor – sorry, I mean 'monitor'. 'How do we guarantee equality of expression if we're not prepared to allow basic market freedoms?'

ANGELA Don't you think 'equality of expression' disappeared a long time ago, precisely *because* of Robbie's network!

PARKER That's no way to talk about your host.

MCGREGOR I am certainly NOT offended.

ANGELA 'Host', Simon, and generous contributor to Opposition coffers. He's bought you. You and that angelic leader. What a disgusting smile…

MCGREGOR Angela. Allow me to give you a fresh straw.

ANGELA That's really very kind, Rob.

MCGREGOR What, Simon, was the minister's reply?

PARKER Oh, you know, the usual –

ANGELA A lot of waffle – what they're all so good at in that particular chamber.

MCGREGOR Waffle nevertheless almost always carries some kind of message. Simon –

PARKER Well of course, those ragbag Libs – shall they soon rest in peace – always want to put their prissy hands on everything. They rage against what they say's a mania for control, and call it 'responsibility'.

ANGELA You can't hold up the march of Commerce, as Rob well knows – as Rob is trying to teach you.

PARKER Just drop it, Angela! This *has* after all been my first day in school, I mean Brussels… Doesn't it mean *anything* to you…

ANGELA It means the end of all intelligent debate.

PARKER Angela. You're just upset over that report.

ANGELA Not a bit of it. It's what I expected.

MCGREGOR What report is that, Angela?

ANGELA You wouldn't want to know.

MCGREGOR Oh but I would. I want to KNOW everything.

PARKER Angela's done some consultancy work on the harmonisation of Europe-wide vocation skills, though her key recommendations were turned down – on economic grounds.

ANGELA What he's really saying, Rob, is this: just at the moment, the pax Europa can't afford to offer as one of its essentials anything so costly as an education, at least for the plebs…

MCGREGOR What exactly is *meant* by education? If merely a foil for problematic unemployment figures, well…

PARKER That's just *our* party line, Rob…

ANGELA Now why is *your* party line always somehow identical with his!

PARKER I take it that's a rhetorical question!

ANGELA Oh for goodness' sake! Education isn't a matter of cost and social adjustment…

MCGREGOR Interesting! What, Angela, would you say education *is*?

ANGELA Proper human development.

MCGREGOR That's a bit vague, don't you think? After all, what is 'proper', and what is 'human development'?

ANGELA What is 'proper', for European society, is an efficient functioning of the whole, without trampling on the sovereignty of individuals, for whom 'human development' is all to do with personal talent and ambition.

MCGREGOR Bravo!

PARKER That's very eloquent, Angela. Perhaps you should go easy on that stuff.

ANGELA *Au contraire.* Let's have another!

MCGREGOR Another pina colada. But Angela! Don't let me interrupt. Education *is* –

ANGELA As it's practised, Rob, education is an economic exercise, one that fits flesh-and-blood components into commercially oiled machines.

PARKER That, is not exactly a revelation.

ANGELA Then why isn't it obvious to everybody!

PARKER Not everybody shares your ideals. Politics, commerce, are driven by pragmatism, which I'm afraid is unavoidable.

ANGELA Simon Parker, member for Wenham East! I never thought I'd live to see the day! WHAT were you saying just now, about those ragbag Libs...

PARKER It's one thing to have aims, another to know what's possible.

ANGELA Hypocrite!

PARKER Angela, I really don't think you should drink any more of that stuff...

ANGELA I shall drink what I like! Pass me that here, Rob, you old bastard!

PARKER Now that *is* beyond the pale! I'm sorry, Rob, she...

MCGREGOR As I said before. I am NOT offended.

ANGELA I don't need another spoon. This one's fine.

MCGREGOR You just do as you please.

PARKER Or maybe we should get next door. The others must be wondering where we are.

MCGREGOR Let them wonder. After all they're grown-up people. Now – I want to press your wonderful wife on this question of education.

167

ANGELA I can honestly say I'm glad it won't be Simon's portfolio in the next administration.

MCGREGOR Ah, touché! A riposte, Simon?

PARKER My 'wonderful wife' has had rather too much to drink.

ANGELA *You* don't like to hear the truth.

MCGREGOR Oh – so now we have education *and* 'truth'! What *are* these two things?

ANGELA Very simple, Rob. They're a state of enlightenment, a natural resistance to all that debris broadcast over your satellites.

PARKER Groan!

MCGREGOR Well, good… I do see how some *might* call that education… What about truth?

ANGELA Truth is, no Australasian ever had the least idea of culture!

MCGREGOR So truth is qualitative. And so is education. Though only if they coincide with your notions of them.

ANGELA They're certainly not your notions…

MCGREGOR Here again I disagree. Commerce with all its acquisitive leadership is merely the barometer of society, which in itself is a phenomenon I and my colleagues are powerless to change.

ANGELA But you have influence.

MCGREGOR Not at all. I simply provide what people ask for – which makes good commercial sense. Now, if really what they wanted was Shakespeare by satellite, or Hegelian refutations as a daily editorial, then these are the things that a humble merchant such as myself would provide…

PARKER It's commonsense, Angela…

ANGELA There's nothing at all 'humble' about him.

MCGREGOR As things are, I wouldn't quite be telling the 'truth' about society if suddenly I swapped all my soaps for Shelley, my movies for Mauriac, my chart-toppers for Bartók…

PARKER Just wouldn't wash…

ANGELA With power of influence do come certain duties…

MCGREGOR Which I discharge. I never conceal the paucity of modern life, never flinch from that particularly sordid truth.

PARKER One might call him a reformer…

MCGREGOR A great educator…

PARKER A colossus in the advancement of human understanding.

ANGELA Oh for God's sake! This is unspeakable…

PARKER It isn't!

ANGELA It is!

PARKER 'T isn't!

ANGELA 'T is!

MCGREGOR Children, please! Now why don't we talk about the cricket…

ANGELA, PARKER Groan!

169

During these five weeks, the meads and stone villages surrounding Benbrook received as Zina's special guest her friend and colleague Sibyl Sear, who already knew the well-tramped tourist haunts. Sib had long douched her stardust in Zed's metropolitan broadwalks, as a theatrical dancer – proscribing ballet as prime among all ancient forms. Perhaps only Zina understood the rationale of Sibyl's professional work (not I mean her teaching work), knowing as Sib also did the peripheries of film and distribution – a cold grey wash whose shores were the dotting isles beyond the blurred margins of McGregAir. I'm sure we shall soon appreciate, via the Benbrook *Book of Rigours* – an unwritten code that some day Craig would write – that Chapter One insists there is no right way, other than ascetic, and that the golden path of art is small in succour, tractable only to the few exponents whose habitat *is* these distant lands.

Sibyl's recent acclaim was a choreograph, for which one cold Sunday, over a ploughboy's pickle, she produced a handwritten notation, in several sheaves. She did this for Zina. She did it for a departing JX, who nodded excessively. She even did it for a lonely-looking barman, a clean, combed, bewildered youth, who otherwise quietly polished his hand pumps, yet whose occupation demanded a smile (an action he broke to too systematically). This she saw through, in its sparkle of falsehood, its twinkle of troubled amusement, and so folded up her new symbolics – in all honesty a revolution, for all that elegance of line – and returned to her lunch.

Her choreograph (as did all Sibyl's pieces) wound itself to a clockwork taut with potential – *limbful kinetics*, she called this – and used several trios, sometimes a quartet, often a sestet, drawn from a student team of twenty-five, all barefoot and in the same house stripe, Sib's insistence at this time being Lincoln green leotards. As a group or sub-groups, to the frenzy of Sib's metronome graphemes (perhaps no barman *could* understand), these plied their programmed mimetics through the corridors, interconnecting offices, and over the shopfloor of a condemned, by now wind-eroded factory. Just the spent husk of human toil Sibyl had always tended to as backdrop, this

170

one a wharf property (its listing revoked), whose brick windows were either barred or a mesh of shattered glass, and whose sole remains were a corrosion of twisted machines (production had been: she knew not what, cared less). What would the avant-garde and prophetic Sibyl Sear understand by Diamond's *Robbie 'Socks'*?

She did don studious glasses at the showing, light-catching and penny-round, yet missed overtly given clues, in particular the choice of form – 'short symposium' – and the spurious appellation granted the world-wide McGregor (surely Sib knew about McGregor!) – 'Socks' an epithet derived from Socrates. Here in the *crème* of Athenian society, no longer concerned with Love, but rather the narcissistic wastes of capital and power, Sib it seems didn't read, translate, or whatever (whatever, Craig, you meant her to do). That triumvirate of Western rule, though the emphasis has since shifted, even then was Politics, Commerce, Pedagogics. Significantly Craig will not invite Art to his table.

In her four separate assessments, Sib gave to the producer, director, and above all to the *technic*, a customary first – art-chick-siblings Sib and Zeen having nights ago downed a Spanish plonk, a bottle or litre or who knows what (all this being guesswork), their Medusan eye running its expertise over Dondie's first-year résumé. That went back to her polystyrene phase. By contrast a pen-poised Sib tired to the point of bedtime an already fatigued vocabulary – 'minimal' the most careworn, and not surprisingly the first of her plodding adjectives – in her hosannas for Dondie's camera work, described as 'heroic'. That, she said, was despite the constraints a collaborator has to accept, and did at times spark up in a firmament of instant stars – quite an achievement, given that frankly limited text. By this she meant a series of close-ups, whose binding semiology encompassed: McGregor's dining-room mahogany and walnut, and over his shoulder his glittering candelabra (meaning wealth); a plate crossed with cutlery, with its smears of dried gravy (those absent nine, of the original twelve); a glass ashtray, whose sole occupant, a cigar, waits to be re-lit (I'm talking, that can wait); a freshly made pina colada (good

171

clean fun); a brandy glass, the base of its bulb the changing hues of warm honey cooling (bourgeois stolidity); the sheen in Angela's henna-coloured hair (she really *is* a firebrand); the tic in Simon Parker's nervous eye (*Simon Parker, member for Wenham East!*).

To de la Mare Sib apportioned a fair 2:1. Loved, she said, that way you had with a cocktail spoon. And that bit about 'sovereignty of individuals' – real fire there! And that *so wise* shake of the head, as McGregor wins the day – swapped soaps for Shelley, movies for Mauriac, something about Bartók (pity that couldn't have been developed, Bartók...). For Smayle, an unfair 2:2 (did what you had to do); and for Diamond, an unprecedented lower second. For Craig this was disappointing, recalling how meticulous he'd been, raking the ash of group discussion *after* the show. Sib Sear chaired, and what she lacked as a gavel she reclaimed as Stentor, ignoring those great pains he took, explaining just why that Platonic trope suited his purpose. In writing she couldn't help point out that he alone had refused the unique opportunities her class-based sessions had opened up. His failure to explore the voice/body in space/setting had meant an awful waste of time with outmoded techniques. He'd got this need for complex ideas, yet took an approach that was over-dry and just too brief. Finally his argument that Socratic dialogue was page-based, to her was plain perverse, given that Socrates 'stood' by the spoken word. A conventional script was a dead and private place, she said, and all forms of resistance a predictable tactic. He should ask himself: was he too settled and certain about his limits and interests? Could he not push himself into new areas, and learn? Above all, learn...

Through his log book, a shares-rich Craig felt the need to reply. It was wrong, he said, to say he'd refused an opportunity. Merely he had chosen to present a conversation piece in the style of an after-dinner debate, intending to show that even here at Benbrook debate *was* still possible. Also Craig wished to correct certain misapprehensions as to the historical figure of Socrates, and pointed out sarcastically that the words attributed to him were all written by a writer and philosopher called Plato (circa 427–347 BC), a well known historical figure whose work went on for some fifty years after Socrates's death. Plato, for so Craig's lecture continued, was a disciple of Socrates, whose question-and-answer style of inquiry into a range of prevailing beliefs he (Plato) greatly admired. It was now generally agreed among scholars that, using a fictive Socrates as the focus for all his *personae*, Plato developed these same techniques in a form known as dramatic dialogue, for the purpose of presenting his own philosophical ideas (which of course may in part have been derived from the real Socrates – who himself had left us no written testament). To dismiss as 'perverse' Craig's argument for Socratic dialogue as page-based was frankly not supported by the facts, since practically everything attributed to Socrates had come to us *as* dramatic dialogue.

As for Craig's 'need for complex ideas', all he would say was this: the fact of power invested in a commercial élite was a straightforward observation, and one with important implications for anyone involved in the arts today. Concerning limits, he set himself none, and 'resistance', he said, was a two-way street.

I myself might add that if all this wasn't provocative enough, a young Diamond, bolstered by his winning pontoon hands each weekday at the shares baize, had chosen just that didactic tone unlikely to win him friends. Vis-à-vis the staff/student relationship, Ace Diamond couldn't desist from teaching *them*.

19

And yet. In spar contests, gunslingers past had met an unruffled Sibyl Sear, whose personal completeness hinged on an unchanging regimen of fruit, pickle, rye bread, or on cold days soup from the country kitchen – thick pea or thin minestrone. I know this as central to her life and health, when double-S was once the cause of quite some purist commotion over French onion soup (as I scratch my head, as I try to piece together all these fragments in my lap...).

Her mornings in Benbrook had all so far begun with a mud-splashed little jog, the lanes and Sib herself a thin wiggle threading those spiky-looking hedgerows, or the heaps or then the dilapidations among a maze of dry stone walls. Sib's intervals – her pauses for cold damp air, and breath – I tend to think of overhung with misty pines, oaks pendulous with dew, maples in a breeze of fluctuating greens. All anyway was so much the mid-earth pleasance where, with shielded eyes, I imagine her gaze across the hills and quilted fields, I would hope thinking, just thinking. On her 'last' such day, or – due to Craig (Craig likes to think) – her *next*-to-last – Sib and Zed met privately for talks. Sib bowled up in the palpable radiance of peach blossom, gelled, showered and flushed. Zeen was unusually pale and, Roger thought, slightly hungover. (Meet Roger soon.)

The meeting took place at the White Harp. Diamond, Dondie et al, and even William Tropecale, knew it well, a stone, timbered, revamped coaching inn, several miles away by road. That road in question was a snaky, tree-canopied backway, winding in the skirt of Benbrook's two peaks. For Tropecale, the Harp was a venue close at hand by virtue of the cycle track, whose radial auxiliaries marked out a pattern of declivities, in dizzying zigzags, these cutting across or through the mountain's banks, and all tightly bound in a criss-cross of tree roots. It had a barn door, whose hinges I oil, then open. Inside you'd find it quietly resonant at ten a.m., littered with a lot of rustic pine. There were two or three heavy tables having scattered round them one or two stools and several austere-looking pews, all thickly carved. There was a slate floor and an open fire. That latter had (and I get this from Pevsner) two fine corbels. Beams, everywhere, were varnished, and the walls were limewashed. Hangings were dikes, aqueducts and Isambard bridges, all done in silhouette (or something along those lines). A log in the grate exhaled sheets of blue smoke, which the fire's dimpled copper canopy hoisted into the flue.

Our two sat at a window, under its stone casements, where Zed had a frothy cappuccino. Sib preferred a herbal tea. This, when it came, came flavoured with orange peel and cinnamon, with a hint of fennel, and an aftertaste unmistakably

174

chicory. She complained (Roger, she complained), finding a dehydrated blade of salad cress stuck to her saucer. But to business… (So, Roger, what was that?)

What would Zed feel if Sib offered individual, debrief tutorials, to put certain students back on track?

"Oh. Well. That's fine by me," said Zed. "Not all will come."

20

Craig incredibly did respond, finding Sib's notice superimposed on a year-one reading list. He read them both, and found that the latter must have been pinned there as long ago as late October. That apart, this was the unimagined end to his morning, among whose pink electric flickers a creditworthy Craig had sold over a thousand shares, waifs whose whirl of numeralised abstractions merely rumpled a distant reality – some dead world somewhere, ranging from glass to gravel to powder-room ceramics. He also once invested in pneumatics.

I bid her snore. I bid her nurse that lobular pain, in intellectual cottonwool, for generously Zina Zed had given up her dungeon, all for cousin Sib and her debriefs. Into that hallowed arcade, coz Sib pitched her nomadic tent. This, Craig couldn't help but note, was a coffee-table biography. An elastic Merce Cunningham was the glossy biographee, who as book wasn't more than a constructed solid, unperturbed under the watch of Zed's womenonly wall – her *my Moi*. (Only sleep, Princess.) Onto that Bible or bibelot, Sib had put down her glasses, whose arms were homesteader crossed, whose lenses blew into blue ovals two shadowy pools of light, and whose bridge *I say off, short-sighted Muse! Be off! This is a debrief!* Now then. Let me see. Sib had Zed's Z chair, on to which she'd planted both buttocks and the sole of a foot, whose Roman toed sandal she'd left groping on the floor. Palms shall we say crossed, over the raised, trousered knee. She did, what? by now in a levitation of herself, her plane the plane of phantasy… Well. She placed an intense chin in the cradle of her hands, which even Craig could see were strong pianistically, and aristocratically sculpted. Her gaze, which without glasses lacked penetration,

Craig saw wander in a wash of fishbowl curves all over his head and slightly stocky torso. Tell me, her gaze said, her posture said, finally her whole being given voice said, tell me, Craig, what sucks... Me? The place? The course?

Craig clearly detested all this chatty socialism, its amateur therapeutics, and in its worst moments (all glue, sobs and saccharine) found easy retreats into the hard lights and loud sirens far to the right.

"*Rob 'Socks' McG*," he said, "I believe is misunderstood."

"The man, or the play?"

Craig saw the possibility (the play, why no the man of course): "The play."

"I want to know, Craig, why did you write that play?"

"Isn't it obvious, once you've read, seen, heard it?"

"Don't you think, Craig, it bears too much of Exe, and brings with it the baggage of Exe?"

"I see you've delved into my background."

"No further than Exe, Craig. Why don't you tell me more about that."

"Excuse me? More about Exe?"

"More about your background."

Oh. Well. Chance here for borrowed garb, an embroidered thread unpicked from a plain calico in someone else's biography – so where should he begin? There were huge complications, he thought, in the fact of his American father, and his own Canadian birth. He remembered his infancy as a cross-hatch of ice, infused with an autumn sun. Later, with an end of talk talks, whose monsters were sovereignty of being, came a long and agonised prayer, or really smoke from a pyre, its brown clouds puffing up to the secular deities of Fortune. By now all the money had gone. Then came his parents' separation –

"Ah! but I, too, have been through this," Sib simpered.

You don't say. Well. For Craig (I mean for that fictive Craig, that simulacrum swimming in Sib's confused field of vision), that left him *in vacuo* emotionally, and living, materially speaking, among the relics and fast fading glories of an impoverished gentility. Nor could he summon much retrospective strength, to harp on all those problems of school – English snobs inveterately so, bullies ditto, and all of them plummed, plumed, prudish. Craig boasted an arduous adolescence, warmed only in its winter vales by the hand-rub of art warfare, his ardent ambition, a passion for self-promotion, for polemics, and this all concocted as a deadly elixir – one certain to put him off-beam here (at Benbrook). Benbrook, where art is a puffball, patted round insouciantly at the edge of everything.

"So is that it, Craig? A mistake coming here?"

What's a mistake, other than an underworld of moonlit possibilities? Craig, a man always quick to point out the therapist's mistimed hour, embraced his life's gaffes. Art, polemics, had no other possibility, since the age that spawned them in itself was an age to negate them (was not now 'notoriety' a commonplace?). Craig filed rights to dramatise *himself*, a prickly brooding presence, who in the depth of his metallic vault conscientiously tasked himself to a lifelong insurgence against this edifice called Benbrook – its decades burnt by a desert sun and whipped in a drying wind.

"You'd like, Craig, to be a man apart…"

A man errant. One who, for example, couldn't ever share in Benbrook's teenage tantrum, a squall disabling metaphysically, and borne out of narratives always demanding cowed disapproval at any last flame, fume, spark (or what) into the tangled night of artistic liberation. Conversation also wasn't possible. Nor the inclusion of any last object (meaning 'art object') – since objects stood to be defiled. A good Benbrookite regarded careful non-alignment, a negated past, shrunken ambition, in fact all forms of self-nullification, as the ultimate good bad end of social progress – perhaps feasible only through the privilege of lottery and arts council handouts. Craig knew well enough that that was a trench from behind whose sandbags our journeying Sibyl Sears made easy sneers at an arts-rich boy like himself, in whose person they'd wrongly suspect – that crime of all post-Marxist crimes – gold brocade and velveteen luxuriance.

"You finished now?" she said (for she above all bore the taints of Gestapo state handouts).

177

No, he hadn't (though really he had), for to join that pomo merry-go-round, in Benbrook, in books, in community nooks, was to live a dishonest life, and to lie. Schoolmarm Craig didn't mean *not* to show how fully that is done. He told her how his weekend London life centred on the small studio he and his poet friend Lou (a ghost, spectre, fabrication) rented in Adam and Eve Mews. All who came found a new manifesto nailed to the door each week, whose focus till now was Exe, that palaestra whose cloisters thrummed to the lost, lame, limpid scions of a dead Professor Glaze (busts of, laurels on). There they still equated manners with mannerism, in *their* case callous and refined – yet these were just another artificiality, thinning at the seams in a puffed-up world of art.

"There they rehearse," he said, "a bluster of affectation as justification of their work."

"If I may say so, Craig, that does come across."

Oh. A broadside. Come then and see his next manifesto. It's under construction, it's here.

"Why not rather tell me, Craig."

Well. If we have to go on with this (and we do). Craig's concept of art was less to do with Benbrook and 'the scene', and everything to do with power. At that time the power he sought was no less British and insular than Sib's, or Zed's. I quote him, or rather paraphrase at length, as a man (and as unofficial censor) only too familiar with his manifesto – not that he ever did commit this to print, if metaphorically Craig did go on nailing it to doors:

What is an artist? It's someone who, when irksome politically, our spoonfed lobbyists dismiss as irrelevant, a plant palely nurtured in a soil that centuries of unquestioned tradition have eroded. Tradition itself is a weed with blasted roots. A novel is simply the repository of accepted social convention, as are plays or poems. The fact that all of them persist as forms is merely an act of self-parody.

Here Sib was with him, well briefed herself as to convenient targets, when whole fraternities of big-booted minorities shook off the snares of social inequality, and fired torpedoes *somewhere*.

178

Typical 'intellectual' (at least according to *this* configuration), whose vilification can't be complete without a committee, Benbrook proscribed as 'socially irresponsible'. That was because in an art world controlled by its new oppressors, one saw very little point in all that 'cultivation'. Benbrook had you tumble over fresh cadavers every day, into a media lens or the columns of a highbrow rag, with all the commercial advantages such an enterprise conferred. No other values meant as much. Alongside that any intangible, non-commercial, and as yet unquantified type of art looked hopelessly inept. On Craig went with his masquerade:

"Did you know," he asked, told, instructed Sib, "Stratford-on-Avon was once the most celebrated birthplace in the western hemisphere…"

Neither the materialism in all our petty democracies (or dull-eyed committees), nor the dialectical materialism in the dispensaries of Marxist prescription, cares overmuch for that particular type of fact, an order of prestige likely to interfere with all Karl's and Zed's and Sib's and Benbrook's brand new dogmas. Nor would Craig quite let it go with his soap-box sinners, those bad advocates tipsy with decline, unless putting up as counterpoise his own pet saints, his rebels against a new map for Europe – not *quite* those setting off bombs in French and German cities, nevertheless persons full of zeal and resistance.

"You see the artistic impulse is fundamental, yet isn't bound by pragmatism. I might say it's of almost organic importance. How do you square that with the version of *corpus juris* all institutions nowadays impose…"

People in general possessed an uneasy conscience where art was concerned, and so made it subject to capital, and through a labyrinth of regulations turned it into standardised produce.

"Are you really content," he asked Sib, "to sacrifice the highest ambitions of art (you could say also the highest ambitions of society) to a turnover in ephemera, all heaped to a merchant's altar?"

Sib, of course, led an avant-garde in scored mimetics, and so made no such sacrifice herself. She put away her specs and walked off gingerly with her Cunningham under her arm, and in a private memo to Zed offered the following advice (whose wording I don't attempt to imitate):

Zina, you'd better look out – this Diamond's a man to watch, a misogynist, a fascist (*if* you want my opinion).

It wasn't hard to see how a man who faked some fervent belief in the aristocracy of art might one day turn to political extremes. This of course was the likely outcome, knowing as we do Craig's opposition to the institution that enslaved him. Yet, it was *that* institution's supreme indifference to him that was really the source of his pique. Benbrook imagined *its* as a liberal voice, when in fact it was reactionary – or so he rationalised. In my own view, Craig was a frustrated man of action, who hadn't properly understood the idea of leadership, other than forming however loose a confederacy (which didn't include Tropecale), and who hadn't yet plunged as group commander into anything so formalised as an art war. For the time being he drew up his preferred rules of engagement, and a role. That hinged on the theoretical love of power, one always at odds with the levelling forces of democracy, and detached from the common mass. The mass had no relish for proper communication, a sub-hum no longer regarded even as a luxury, or as an element essential to life. Here all magic or poetic activity disappeared, our long night and party over, no more games – now was the reign of the stereotypes – a 'new' and unreflecting sovereignty whose envoys rode out over all that traditional soil.

"The People?" as Robbie McGregor might ask (you can see him open-handed, at the head of his table, intoning these words as a plea). "They tell me what they want, and I give it."

Opposed to this but party to joint status was our Siamese she-cat Sibylline-Zinine, who suffered the organs of government to dictate what Robbie's masses *should* have, more as an education thing.

21

I shan't, in my tired role as graphologist, infer any admissions from the sweep of his student pen, an implement plump with

180

vitriol. I guess only at the margins he drew, or at what was implied as their meaning, finding (as I do) two broad bands, in poisonous blue-black blood, grid lines unable to fix his page outside or beyond the naïve exhibitions of Benbrook. Nor could Craig see much beyond the lower second (the class of his degree), attainable only at best – or so, for a time, he thought. By contrast Tropecale had no interest in the world as a personalised aftermath, smouldering heaps, humanity's ruins, battle scars, an innocent pall of smoke, as it hung, as it capped those naked poplars – a tree-topping air whence all that acrid dust lifted slowly from the scene. He did though venture into Diamond's playful shellfire, weaving through his landmines, in a chance moment when combat crossed their minor pathways – one of those five-week idylls, whose sky was quicksilver, and whose passing clouds graded into the rain-edged gaze of a myopic Angela Roth. She was scrawny, sadly dressed (all bags and bunches), and had plain bad teeth (yellowed pearls a barring light on an anthracitic cave). It seemed, from the way she put it – coffee slops, fag ends incandescent – that a long, sullen career subediting *ArtKart* (an unspeakable magazine) lay some days behind her. This was a quarterly publication, a grey glossy, whose cover design almost always implicated the theatrical guy, or gal, or both, unvaryingly limboed to a precise sequence of debilitating poses (a fat toe probing a not too committed ear lobe, for example), or failing that maniacal torsions facially (you've seen, have you, that Maori jig, the haka…). Against Diamond's flak – all in the cache of metaphor, you understand – you will allow me, please, to size Tropecale's holiday garb. He was a student, yes – but a cyclist trussed in outdoor rambler's gear – for so I track the deep impression left by the stride of his boots, in its double line across that marshy campus grass. There was also William in shorts, and a truck-driver's shirt – here to learn, and understand, the making of propaganda.

Ms Roth maundered through her programme, which she quaintly titled Narrative Technique. She led by crude example – long line of exponents late from an arty vomitorium – slashing an anaemic torch light into the blooms of her medieval forests. Floors fell away, in a tangle of quackish Viennese idioms. What, she asked, do we make of this (holds up obscene art work – engorged Gentile phallus, planted in an infant's ice-cream cone, infant unsuspecting)? Answer: could that be shock of the new less as wearisome, more as work of art (and a whole ragtag of art history dragging behind)? Ms Roth thought that a 'good' attempt, failing to see the joke, yet went no further than to say: we *aren't* talking text, necessarily (these her own hip-slang Americanisms). She invented exercises, likely to last whole evenings, and all through those sunless afternoons. In one such her class of twenty-six she addressed as individuals, asking each to find a random object, and turn it into narrative. Tropecale made afflatus with his bicycle pump, and invited a now unwilling twelve (for so that twenty-six had rapidly dwindled) to report on its new, and perilous hanging – as mobile, that was, cord for which wasn't strictly speaking 'found'. You cheated, Will, and sought it out.

I dare also suggest that Chelsea, whose Eustachians were inflamed, and ears plugged with cottonwool, performed *Hamlet* as a six-minute mime, a moment in group consciousness a wrathful Ms Rothful preferred to see excised – for its flagrant return, she explained, to grand narrative philosophy. Had Chelsea learnt nothing? A more cautious Lorrie – incidentally baptised Lorenzo, and at Benbrook registered as Enzo – what did he, Lorrie do? As always Enzo unclasped his gem-encrusted watch, and set it beside his notepad – ponderous – and deliberating – and pinned by a smile I find it not now possible to describe. For Enzo however this *was* an auspicious start, clean-shaven as he was, and preened, and the one *rara avis* who'd trained himself to grasp that essential separation, Art *vs* Science. He asked *was time a sequence* (Hawking), or was this only a subset of conscious association (Proust) – and even so would our certain answer help to determine the kind of narrative each could engender… That made her think. But only through that briefest slur of plasticised flywheels, a stuck machine once our natural leader, a slightly older Craig – and a man forever tapping at Zina's sleepy door – had brandished the rolled tube of his newspaper. This was, provocatively, Tory,

182

and a broadsheet – Craig an informed yet scornful reader of the city page.

Angelic Ms Roth raised an interdicting palm, gesture reiterated in a slaver of canine dentures, their human pretenders framed in a disaffecting smile. She couldn't, she said, begin to count the times she'd seen this done – no real imagination in all those tedious reworkings of the day's (if one may put it so) emboldened, and lurid headlines. Well, actually, Ms R, that wasn't quite what Craig had in mind. Moreover we're talking here an enraged undergrad, who try as he may just cannot smooth the serrated edge unsheathed as his own defining narrative, whose prompts and urgings drive him to repel *all* Benbrook's patronising patter. He unrolled that tube (*Telegraph*, even then a repository of specious editorials). Out of it dropped an A4 sheet, its watermark a hart and a gargoyle. From it Craig read (exact wording I cannot actually vouch for):

"Zina, you'd better look out – this Diamond's a man to watch, a misogynist, a fascist (*if* you want my opinion)."

Friends – you tenacious twelve, thirteen counting teach' – what narrative shall hap to make of this?

"There's no *hap*," said Roth, "if the narrative is you. You have to tell us what *is* you."

Now that was a bad mistake by her, who wasn't fully apprised of Zinine's arts policy. Craig set off, with those slight complications, he thought – for parents had he many – in the fact of his aged father, or that and the fact of his own American birth. (Did Sibyl, I wonder – fleet-footed and oracular – and Angela – certain and heaven-sent – ever compare notes?) Proustian vistas – for so Craig doffed his cargo cap to a beamish Lorenzo – he beheld in a faintly nocturnal vision, whose black, cross-hatching drizzle was a rain of Wall St lucre, important where life remained untouched by the English notion of 'class'. Later, when his father remarried, then his mother too (childers had they one), the new monsters of his child nights were inevitable – a slightly story-forming instability. That left him *in vacuo* emotionally, and living, existentially speaking, among the relics and fast fading glories of infant love. In the end love is all. Nor could he summon much retrospective strength to harp on too easy a life in school, where what he lacked as a warm fire of family being, he naturally compensated for as an all-round excellence academically (Exe, Benbrook, to so hyper-trophied a mind – which held all around it tamed in orbit – were a huge anticlimax). Craig boasted a violent adolescence, cooled only in its simoom-blown oasis by the anointments of art, out of whose ambition, and a passion for self-promotion, he was certain to leave all others he came across scaled in the elixirs of sleep. So here he was at Benbrook, where art was a puffball, patted round insouciantly in the skirts of each new and newly threadbare theory.

"Tell him where he's wrong," said Roth, her pale visage inclined only slightly to those stone statues or other twelve (but disciples had she none).

"Well," said Craig, "what is *wrong*, or rather *what* is wrong? What, other than this, here on our terrace of brimstone, so dead-and-alive in its evils of probability – what?"

"You tell me."

"Is fiction circular?"

22

Roth finally scratched about among the butts in her regulation ashtray, which the pantries of Benbrook ensured in a range of fruit tarts, foil cups flavoured apple, apple stitched with cinnamon, or cinnamon laced through sugar-coated mango. For Craig, as in fact for most others, she hauled out from all that charred debris another lower second, and I imagine turned promptly to her cell phone, to discover, in a single, sweet, and cathartic exchange, a new welcome in the cave-dweller homefires of *ArtKart*, where her sub-plot, or job, had been kept open. All good then. And ciao! Although, in pinning that now usual score to Craig's lapel, she did comment, in a scrawl of neurotic pen loops, blue curlicues, elevated crossbars, each dot a dash, that, laudably, no lack of passion had she found, but at the same time lamented a regrettable incapacity to operate outside the narratives he knew and felt comfortable with. Who dictated her script? Well, *I* don't know. But I can say who fared better. For one there was Tropecale, that breeze-clipped bike pump leading him, late each moon-flooded night, back to the sound studio, where he cobbled together an over-long talk on the velocipede, all overarched with anti-Gallic bias, its narrative a glow of pearls, all threaded on a string of sound effects. There was also Constant, who now abandoned that Proust-Hawking axis, finding so much more in Heisenberg and Roland Barthes. A first and an upper second, respectively.

From this time approximately, Craig and his five globe-destined cronies – Lisbeth and Gavin – Lorenzo, Dondie and Chelsea – together passed cloud-covered hours lolling in the pews, or stoking that open fire, miles across those green English hills, the White Harp a plotter's home-from-home. Craig, in these days heavy-eyed, and slightly glazed – and with his pockets full of loose change – had already primed his barboy Roger. I don't doubt Roger's thin bowtie, in its shading a cherry red, nor his several identical cream-collared shirts (their names were Monday to Friday – though the waistcoat always was the same), neither do I disagree that his provenance was somewhere near Stamford Bridge – bloke famed and framed for a long rectangular face, permanently lit by a lopsided smile. Craig quaffed his pints of Bass, while Roger worked on with that immaculate napkin, the bar bright and brassy, his pump handles plushed. Here, because nothing quite *is* that funny as folk, Craig (demanding whole histories of Roger's one-sided eavesdrops) got his defining insight into Sibyl's diet – that fruit, pickle, rye bread, her thick pea, thin minestrone or French onion soup. Re this latter she'd almost effected a citizen's arrest, detecting the none too slick infiltration of a manufactured stock cube (Rodge conveyed it, gravely, to Cook). But what else but? Well, Sib jogged in each weekday morning, meticulously wrapped in a scarlet bandanna (its design, Rodge, I think you must recall as Egyptian interlocks), and here plopped into a glass of boiled water a lime, or a rosemary, or a peppermint tea bag. On one occasion, Roger served them and oversaw, when Sib and Zed met privately for talks – Sib in the newly showered splash of peach blossom, Zeen more than usually pale, and perhaps slightly hungover. Rodge took no cash – for

Zed never dealt in cash – and as usual put the bill on Zed's account (for Zed, a frothy cappuccino, for Sib a herbal tea). Sib though complained, finding a dried blade of salad cress glued to her saucer. Though never mind that. To business... (So, Roger, what was that?)

"What would you feel, Zeen, were I to offer individual, de-brief tutorials, to put certain students back on track?"

"Oh. Well. That's fine by me," said Zed. "Not all will come."

(No, Rodge – what was business *really*?)

Oh, that...

"I want, Zeen, to put together a promotional video. Can I use the film labs?"

"Sib. You don't have to ask."

Although Craig only laughed, here was yet one in a crowd of dated entries, so meticulously set down in his incident log.

23

The tricks, trips and traps of arts management blew their old new methodologies in sudden tempests through all such institutions just at that time. Central to satellitic Benbrook were its pagan standing stones, whose chisels and fiery incisions were the freshly applied glyphs local to the Brave New Business School, in a bush life of whiteboards got up to look sportive and jargonised. Its was the burning rock, a reptilian shore, from whose shivering ambiance – hot, daytime thermals rising – team gurus, damp-browed and deodorised, legged it in to Benbrook, having finalised their portfolios in the sway and muffled clacks of the London-to-west-coast train.

In the snares of his adulthood, Craig remembered one particular Bible tome, whose bulleted agenda mapped a long, unwavering line through base manifesto to cloud-capped sponsorship. It was advocacy – even in his days at Exe – even through those pyrotechnics underground in cyberspace – that Craig had always sought (and was sinned against not to have uncovered at Benbrook). He and a rapier-waving Enzo hatched up a Wellesian cutaway. Here there were certain shades, as Craig has since explained, of *Citizen Kane*. I can't help thinking it is apt.

186

The thing I now know encompassed impressive camera-work from Lizzie Fatualli, who panned in through one of Benbrook's billet huts. First off she came in over a grey-roofed townscape. Then she hovered over the surrounding squared fields, chromatically a ploughed red and unripe maize. Then came a brookside willow, its tears and its shudder musically a polyphony of dawn-bright droplets. Aurora's rural sky had only hours ago unfolded its snows of mist, so that finally Lizzie came in through a roof light.

Interior shots, to the naked eye the same, *were* variously scripted, and darkened our single, unassuming gaze onto a semi-public cubicle (by which I mean college lav). This was old, and outside lean-to style, its planked door a surface shred of peeling caramel. Cautiously Lizzie's only light was a tarnished light, an embarrassed, aureate glow, whose flakes or fragments fell from a double, and sanctifying nimbus – which hovered atop the cistern. Don't ask me how she got these effects. All I say is that the point of all this puerility – an arts dimension a beleaguered Craig now felt himself obliged to explore – was what occurred *inside* that cubicle, from which Craig and Lorenzo never emerged (not at least for the film's duration). In its bass booms and bombardiering echo that chamber yielded all the plenitude our creators deemed necessary. Craig, Lorenzo, intoned their dual and alternating rail at all those historical convergences one supposedly assumed had brought them, their two lives met, to a point of mutual leg-cross, or rather blared as a mantra, its monotony slightly relieved with tonal colorations. This took its course via *Dada* to *Différence* to *Fictive Self*. The whole thing ended with a toilet flush.

To Tropecale this, when screened, was merely reminiscent of a crowded, and partly asphyxiated occasion at the White Harp, whose lounge was loud with chat and festooned with cigarette smoke (a lunchtime). Tropecale, a sackful of golden drops – he dousing the Harp's urinal – knew whose they were, on hearing two plangent moans, a short then a long one, two curling whispers let loose in an adjoining cubicle. He only smiled when later, affixed to the bar mirror, he tracked first

Craig, then a fresh-faced boy he'd never seen before, from the door of the gents into the normalising wrap – of what? Of a dozen cross-conversations.

24

Craig wearied visibly within the first week of his final semester, yet forced himself to inhale the tobacconised ether washing round those two cloudy peaks. There is a film memoir, whose locality its makers term 'anonymous', or 'megalopolis by night', its world a world of sugarstick. Its feature is Craig, in a diary discourse. Watching it I am taken back, to a season sheeted in English rain of more than thirty years ago. A clip I have in mind is its montage of time-lapsed head- and tail-lights, a mingle of crimson speared with unfocused streaks of silver – all of which an appallingly media-thin Diamond fronts in real time. Provokingly, that backcloth isn't meant to be his Exe or Benbrook (these the subject of his memoir). This instead is a distant counterweight – a fool's Utopia, a lead-based Elysium, with fast cars, balmy nights and palm-strewn beach hotels. To cluttered minds, these are the potent indices of life's success, just the cold shower a dollar-rich Diamond thought befitting those Little Englanders (the scions of Glaze – the Zeds, Sibs, the brothless breathless Angela bleddy Roths – no doubt other caravans in train) – all of them the flesh-and-blood marionettes Craig still loved to villainise. Arch arts bureaucrats, is what he called them – whose only ambition, a not noble one, maintained them nose-down in the defilements of Academe, a place thick with blue conspiratorial shadows, where every cloak concealed a knife. Craig was certain they were watching.

So why, Craig, plump for this moon-phased metropolis, and gladiator's bench, its bowed slats bent to the body weights of a later, and much more mature confession? These were frankly idiotic admissions, whose essence he made all the more tawdry by that defiance of his, his arguments dogged, dull and secular. He couldn't suppose that Benbrook alone had depleted him, those tragic, but really comic years ago. Added to all these complications, he underwent enforced domestic change – not

once but several times – all in the space of a last doubtful year
ascending Zina's summits. (What anyway were these, other
than two English hills folded in the lazy blue tinge of Zina's
faggish dreams. Hers was a vision long ensnared in bindweed,
fuel a hubble pipe, itself too much the joint property of a flat-
footed avant-garde.) It became impossible to remain in his eyrie
above that video shop, because of its proprietor – this a man
with a grey goatee, who for the full twenty-five years of his
previous working life had done things unspeakably hush-hush
at a place called Fort Halstead, in England's southeast. This
man was also Craig's landlord, and a protector – crank who
rumbled out from an electronic press, and into the vales of
dew-sopped England, a limpid, limping, lit-and-politics
Internet mag, which in a rush he'd baptised *Brash!* Craig he
did eventually get to contribute, at a low point in that student's disaffection – a time when Tropecale found him searching Benbrook's drama archive, doing some research into twentieth-century performance models. Craig, who offered a retrospective, and one free association, rendered up part of this for
Issue One of *Brash!* It was I think a reworking of some American hack or other, and jangled along like this:

what happened in Act One was: first, audible
; fifth, arithmetic, and was it a sultry
afternoon, and was there commerce (?), blessings but not
priestly, a surface, fenestrated – though this wasn't quite clear,
more commerce, tyger tyger burning blight william bleak, what
is just what is lineation, note an Amerigo she say eraser
not a-rubber, commerce in laughter, c.i.f.,
a cake is a rose is a cake no it's worse it's
verse than that it's riverrun, let's shut out xmas for
once for twice thirdly to that gentleman in the tall
dictionary thats right you sir (but I I I I – I digress)
what, synaesthetically is color colour really rarely, dont
shoot because – big horse – I shant riley hear, and shall
be (chorus) shallow shallow shallow beeeeeeee ESTABLished;
second, good gracious a pressing a depressing need for
clocks tocks lochs waterweeds i mean wheels, silence, a
whole shaving foam of silence; second, syllable as
pillable, now look here henry james didnt i know your
brother; third, a happy thanksgiving, what is a lecture a
lecture is that poet of the aluminium or should we say Al

189

Oominum or wouldnt any pencil sharpener do as i said poet
waxing anthropologic the logic of anthropos i knew a man
called Antrobus would be funny if that was Anthrobus,
water water all a rOund, shady spots, practical humours,
every man in his, you know to be honest ive even
less latin than Billam Spokeshave and practically no Gk
apart from that Anthrobus, i have to say the nostalgia of
ancient photographs of ancient poems pasted in notebooks
its all such a bore bore bore
hurry
hurry
hurry roll up to my un winding:

                    :
                  :
                :
              :
            :
          :
        :
      :
    :

:stare at me
wont you wont yo
ho
ho
ho% what is the late nova ember
o lud thou twangst
and is it angst
edicated fleas do it

    ho

This the kind of thing that once enjoyed the dignity of
experimental literature, but hasn't endured. *Brash!* (crass)
didn't strike too many hits, though its goatee'd parent did
forge on for five more quarters. Craig lost interest long before
that, and couldn't be coaxed, badgered or bullied into
contributing more. In fact when its editor got to his most
insistent, Craig quit his lodgings and moved to a quieter, tree-
lined part of town. Therefore it's all the more surprising to
me that Craig did bother to recite the thing whole in his *film
moi* memoir (as probably befitting that brand of garbage
Benbrook was willing to applaud, samples of which never
smuttered his work books).

His two-hour morning trysts playing shares roulette continued to bolster his student exchequer, a practice Craig enacted
daily – this jokingly his one religious discipline – which latterly he plugged (whenever there were lulls) with part-digested
snatches from whatever book he'd plucked from the library.
One such was Robbe-Grillet's *Last Year at Marienbad*, which
came his way translated by a man called Richard Howard.
Howard's author's introduction explained that the tempo of
life's emotions quite often didn't correspond to the linear rig-
ups of fiction. Phone rings, man answers, two converse, first
man hangs up, leaves his apartment, drives, etc. I, Anno, now
in a sense entrapped in Diamond's temporary Marua, am
meant to identify this (and this alone) as the seed of a last film
project he and Chelsea worked on jointly, our pair casting off
that same straitjacket Robbe-Grillet had worn out and thrown
away before them. Craig, in white top hat and tails, and im-
maculately gloved to match, appears first on a sunlit balcony,
then in the slanted depths of an empty blue swimming pool,
then hand-in-hand with Chelsea, who is masked, then suddenly nude, then not Chelsea at all, but a tub of enamelled
hydrangeas – and so on. I don't know what marks that piece
achieved (I imagine for Craig a lower second), but I do begin
to guess at this as the point where Diamond ceased to discuss
the likelihood of an overall 2:2.

I am tired. Craig too was tired. I shouldn't be surprised if
Zina also felt tired, who by chance placed Craig and Tropecale
in the same dissertation tutorial group – as did she Lisbeth,
Dondie and Gavin. Here, in the accumulated fatigue of its next-
to-last stride, was a reasonably free hand, given to research
and an answer-like conclusion (though as we all know there
are no answers in the arts). This was in respect of any chosen
writer/performer/producer/director. Craig, after a week's
head-scratching, looked back to Stanley Kubrick. Dondie chose
Duchamp. Gavin chose a man called Russell Dibbs, who at
that time an inept bourgeoisie bore shoulder-high, all for his
rugged interview technique. At his scowls whole armies of
European commissioners blustered or squirmed. Lisbeth chose
a theorist, called Thalia Krzyzsteva. Tropecale, who all this time

had effected his own rebellion, in a subtler, quieter style than Craig's, looked through a reverse temporal telescope all the way to Chaucer, asking was it Geoffrey who mis-directed the poetry of myth into the swamps of social commentary... Craig, abetted by Chelsea – these two planning to form a film company, after their life at Benbrook – stitched together a few pearls of satirising verse – *O amber light, whose cloistral beams*, etc. – whose recitation ceased on Tropecale plodding into the coffee lounge (behind-the-hand giggles were all he ever caught, and a rustle of paper as that was firmly entombed between the covers, not of the Robbe-Grillet – but Raymond Queneau).

Craig moved house again. This only indirectly involved the landlord, a man named (coincidentally) Benbrook, whose trade was antiques and memorabilia. Benbrook lived behind his shoppe (called Memories), and let out his ancestral home, a large, Edwardian, riverside dwelling – its gables all carven fascia, its façade a painted stucco, its colour a steely blue – its ground floor going to Craig. Craig remembered a filter of green shadows, which in May-time filled his drawing-room – through a fig tree grown too large for the tiny courtyard garden. This in itself wasn't the problem. The problem was, a too close proximity to the mazy river Dwar, which regularly breached the stone bridges linking the narrow streets and medieval walks. The town was small, and these were its cobbled remains. A weekend of incessant rain, which semi-permanently lacquered the town's pine-blue roofscape, and completely engulfed the surrounding fields, and rose high against the hedges, left its mudded silt, when the flood finally receded, and a thick layer of sludge throughout the whole of Craig's ground floor. This hardly helped him plan his final assessment piece, whose mark would account for a third of his degree, and in the handbook of rules was stipulated as strictly performance. Craig, who still considered that *he* was teaching *her*, informed Zinine that a performance *per se* was not the appropriate conclusion to his two eventful, and difficult years at Benbrook. What, she asked him, did he mean by this? He meant, he said, to give a lecture (a plenary), in Benbrook's central theatre, having already sent out invitations to the English

192

Arts Establishment, some of whose members had replied, and would attend. Among these was a trio from McGregAir.

"I'm sorry," said Zinine, "you can't give a lecture."

"But I insist."

"You're in no position, Craig, to do that…"

"Actually I am. As a fee-paying student, I this morning instructed my lawyers to initiate proceedings."

"What proceedings?" (A naïve, and incautious question, to which Craig responded with an over-fed dossier, detailing cancelled lectures, attenuated tutorials, the non-availability of college equipment, plus a whole string of litanies besides.)

Generally the lecture he gave was entertaining and informative, though didn't demand the full hour Craig allocated. Its title was 'Remaking Public Opinion', and the gist was this: remove books, magazines, newspapers, TV, film, radio, the (then) world wide web, electronic mail, and what in fact you remove is the anthropological structures inscribed as the norms of society (which anyway are arbitrary and wholly related to power). Applause. And yet, I fancy, Craig could still be disappointed at the 2:1 he was finally awarded. He put it behind him, with the fully made intention to write his own person, and inscribe his own simulacrum, into those 'norms' of society – which after all he'd taken so much trouble to prime, prepare, and lecture to receive him.

Wm Tropecale could also be disappointed, since he too received an upper second. And yet, as all of us by now should know, he – an unworried anagram of someone else – was intent to sell his soul in quieter, much more subtle ways than his binarism Craig.

Marua

One more slight twist in Diamond's zigzags across the continents is one he called Marua, a word in Maori meaning pit or cavern. That's his hideaway, high above the spangled marine of the Tasman Sea. I got there belatedly, for too long having sat out under the point of the Southern Cross, still choosing my best moment to drive to McAndrew St. That was just me, my papers, and an ice box blooming with stubbies. These I had watched transplanted from the motel cooler, doing all I could to ignore incessant plaints from a nearby radio. At times I'd see a vague insect flicker in the slanting shadows, or a dark feline shape in the half-light, the light itself an acuteness of frayed angles, light almost a substance, hung out from the motel windows over the newly painted decks. Courtesy Miss Ashley, I mustered a long last look over Diamond's Benbrook curriculum, his 'Editing, Performance, Media', then returned – wearily, it has to be said – to the angles and mirrors of my motel room. I was clear at least in principle. Now *was* the time to abandon that cargo of bottles dotted round my outdoor lounger.

1

In the morning I had my car valeted, then picked up the keys in the lobby, where I settled the bill. The motel boss – a lean, silver-haired man with a stoop, and a lazy eye – offered me three alternative routes into McAndrew St, all of which I muddled and discarded for the map. I got there shortly before eleven. An intense maize-coloured sun had just begun to burn away the Melba cloud-cover, which a moment before was prinked in a couch of satin pillows over the eastern spine of the mountains. It was here, in the naked gold approaching noon, that I found the McGregor neighbourhood. It was tucked away behind a brightly coloured filling station. Adjoining that was a truck depot.

McGregor's was one merely in a linear rank of clapboard

framehouses, each in its acre plot. A double stripe of concrete banding one of grass formed the driveways running front to rear. An adjacent lawn had wire screens slung with netting, and the one beyond that a child's trampette. Across the street a whole frontage lay marooned in the cannibalised remains of antique motor spares, all in a sun-bright coat of orange rust. That was the house I parked outside.

McGregor's was number twenty-five, whose territory was bordered by rose bushes, these all blanched and void of perfume. That boundary I traversed, without much sense of having found the right place. Here there was no sign at all of that broadcast jamboree, the McGregor/Diamond link-up, a satellite soirée whose rose-tinted hub was Robbie's backyard birthplace, a grandpap they'd have to wheel out across the decks into an orbis of lights, lens and microphone. In fact what I found was a last lick of paint, one little patchwork gummed to those homy suburban timbers, as old as Robbie Socks himself – a peeling, cinerary grey.

Then fatefully I caught the invasive hum of a radio. This one was planted under the eaves of McGregor's old garage. Its gluts and glitz abruptly crumbled in deference to the frenetic whirl of hourly news, whose solemn reader offered another senseless fatality out on the Desert Road. I was tempted to turn this off, but involuntarily found myself intoning surprised hellos. This was to two be-shorted workmen, one Maori, the other much younger, and a junior partner, and Pakeha, who flicked at the talc of sandpapered paintwork flaking his hair. Both lounged in the evergreen shade of a feijoa tree, whose fountainheads had begun to conceal the corrugations of a sleepout. Part-striped myself, half in and out of the shadow slanting off the roof, I asked was this really the McGregor monument. Well – it was… in all its cracked glazes and rottenness of window frames, what with the decades of neglect, the property bought then sold by a school, itself now no more, and last in the hands of a global adventurer, who left the country back in the topsy-turvy forties (politically speaking). Some Western media mogul – this my binary star, my own Craig Diamond, man trading from Malibu in long-distance real estate – had bought it up, as intended set, scene or what-you-call for a world-wide TV show, all to celebrate local hero and dollar zillionaire McGregor, whose own empire was inter-continental.

And what about this mogul?

Both said no – no sign of *him*. All their dispatches arrived as abbreviated cell-phone text, from the curator's office – which Diamond's own tentacular networks had, very generously, funded. The curator's brief was heritage, 25 McAndrew St the first address of the first McGregor museum, an institution whose future foundation glugged in the wash and spume of all that TV foam.

2

Not that I had any time for curating, a discipline over-stuffed and -staffed, and a clumsy throw into the murky exteriors of punditry and culture. That though wasn't the point, since according to the latest, and only available text, whose window was covered in thumb prints – or to put it this way: if in this wilderness my only contact with Craig was through his curator – then the name I sought was Pohatu Patarua. Ms Patarua's practice and not well appointed office (all cheap wicker chairs and overhead fans, and a diffusion of stale perfume) was in Ponsonby, on the art-and-crafts side of Auckland – my drive to Paeroa having proved pointless (keep yer shabby schoolhouse). Not that I could doubt the stone-faced Patarua, whose bank troves were newly cached with coins, all from her patron's tamper-proof vault. This was a magnitude of electronic dollar signs. Ms Patarua's instructions were clear – regardless of cost, to renovate.

I jotted down the address – on Ponsonby Rd in fact – and escaped into the cool ethers my bright clean car unleashed as an all-round swirl of air-conditioning. I manoeuvred the whole thing about on the nearest driveway, then jabbed at its powerful engine – a hum then a bellicose roar as I skittered out of Paeroa – that filling station only a blur of pink and cherry hues – and zipped across the Hauraki Plains, where I allowed a hitch-hiker only the scent of my exhaust. Now and here and several decades after that rusty Nissan Bluebird, a point I can't help re-focus in the magnifications of hindsight, I followed a dead slipstream, left there by the young McGregor, in a hop from Highway 2 to 1. McGregor of course was bound all those years ago direct for the airport. Stupidly, *I* had business with Ms Patarua.

On Highway 1 (these crazy NZ drivers): bikes, trucks, a canary-yellow Buick, all swooped up in my rearview – and in tail-lit starbursts slid past in either lane. Bits of old tyre, the shed footwear of heavy goods vehicles over-stretched in the thunders of city-bound traffic, sporadically littered the roadway. An odd arc-shape, here and there an almost circular thread, often the treadless article itself, entire. I slowed down. Over Newmarket I switched on the automatic guidance system, with no useful result. Fact is I got enmeshed in a temporary contraflow, from Khyber Pass to Symonds, a calamity that put me back on a road towards Mt Eden. I pulled up. I tried again. I switched the guidance system off. Eventually I parked, alongside a garbage lot in Napier St (Napier, with all its Art Deco), a flushed walk and some way from my destination.

3

Illogically a not fully enthusiastic Art Deco punctuated the depletions and makeshift of Ms Patarua's office, itself a breezy summit that I tottered to uncertainly. I had my doubts as to this as a business address. There was I recall a party stairway, wedged between the sunny glitter of two anonymous shopfronts, in breadth over-proportioned, and swampish to the tread – all down to its rich carpeting in a flame-coloured pile. Couldn't help think of that as garish, at a first few steps above the sidewalk – here where the sun's yellow glaze shrink-wrapped the windows, mid-afternoon – yet penetrated to a murky velveteen in the higher altitudes of the stairwell. I tested various corridors at each elevation. A film agent's door was one, and alongside that a sports physio's, until finally I found and was ushered in to Ms Patarua's, her den a torrential swish of air. Vaguely I puzzled, but soon then identified the audible ripple of desk memos. I glanced up, was mesmerised

197

briefly – then in a drone of office etiquette naturally detached my gaze from the rotating blades of her ceiling fans.

Her partitions were calico (I mean in wash and not material), and her hangings were Maori. Central to these was a minutely carved waka, a canoe with broad oars and warlike figurehead, moored in a bay, whanga or inlet. Another was a hilltop pa, a fortified settlement, positioned above the reception desk – a station that remained unoccupied. Its stain was a glossy walnut. There was too (somewhere) a grass-skirted warrior wielding a spear, while incongruously all her light fixtures were capped Art Deco – shades or mosaics of coloured glass veined with lead. I told her I was trying to locate my old colleague Craig Diamond, and was obliged to do so above a tinkle of semibreves. These when I looked about (again) were consorting with treble clefs and grace notes, a music alphabet cut from tin and strung in a window as wind chimes – vanes that caught that incessant breeze while the motors whirred above us.

For the record (and what record do I write?), I now no longer suspect an unwillingness to help on the part of Pohatu Patarua, who did seem obstructive at the time. This was a very large woman, dressed for the shot-put, into whose formidable hand I followed the fate of her fountain pen – a trinket in costly greenstone – object she blurred, and twirled, and flourished *majorette*. Must she do this rather than answer questions? She excused herself. Then of course she *had* to answer that phone, which all afternoon had shrilled too often and too impenitent, and which she hadn't the courage to keep switched off. Here was, I knew, as I creaked in my wicker chair, the surface of workaday crisis, for don't you think, Ms P, that Anno is immune and therefore can't understand (as I write, and as I write…). In a few short eternities I did elicit certain facts already known to me, and to the department – i.e. that Craig was here to pre-record an interview with McGregAir's grand old man, under the tin roof of his old family home, place even now undergoing its facelift.

4

I asked if Craig had inspected the site, to which currently the answer was no – blood from a tapu stone. She explained it so, as a bottomless trough, and the cultured Mr Diamond's public munificence – a man awesomely busy – whose acts of intent didn't necessarily involve personal participation.

"It's true then that Craig is solely responsible for the Paeroa reconstruction…"

Pohatu wouldn't put it in quite those terms. What I'd failed to understand was the role of Heritage, a revamped department whose new dynamic rendered it pro-active in the negotiation of all such projects – in fact any renovation on this scale.

"But you're not Heritage," I said.

No. She wasn't. Advanced capitalist thinking had forged certain possibilities in areas of public accountability allied to private enterprise. At some point Craig was certain to undertake a guided tour of 25 McAndrew St, fruit of his US dollars. That seemed most likely when the roof went on, which if newly manufactured – my probes, questions evidently *too* direct – nevertheless was sure to be authentic. Now hadn't she somewhere got that requisition…

"But is Craig here?"

Her phone, flying memos, an open drawer (which she shut, and which she then re-opened), a twirl of her jade baton, that glassy chime in her suspended treble stave – a finitude of things whose short stumpy lives served only to conceal a simple, and at that stage monosyllabic answer.

Mr Diamond, she believed, was based in Titirangi, having a penchant for street awnings and open-air cafés, not to say its proximity to Waitekere's rainforest (temperate), where any thinking man (also she thought temperate) would want to hike. There were, she said, spectacular views to the Tasman Sea, a duality of calm, which was emerald and surf, and was soap suds. These were niceties not normal to Craig in, for example, his smoke-tints, at play in Exe's off-campus caffs, all kitted up with his cyber visor.

"Okay," I said. "Titirangi." Then I got up: "E noho ra."

"Haere ra," she said, putting down that pen, in a beat of rolling r's.

5

Exit stage stairway, a blood-red plush turning to honey, in just a few gasps to spare. My knockabout Ford – new import, note – had turned the garbage collector sour. Couldn't get his truck sufficiently close to the skips – booming yellow tents – because blocked by a Mark I Espadon, model *passé* in the North (I meant the northern hemisphere. In Northland I learned they are common). I'm sorry but the waves of heat, here a persistent pulse in Frame's Omani fort, at certain moments do undermine my train of thought. The trucker called someone in uniform, who in turn dialled for a clamp, a claw-like structure that in engineering schools is considered a paradigm – to do with certain morphisms at the concept stage, a brightly rotating mesh on an inky blue depth of computer screen. The key one needed to unlock it was a thousand dollars, or slightly less depending on the time of day – sum I disgorged without much protest. Just then a tow truck arrived, whose fee to take a harbour drive, *without* catch, booty, swordfish, Espadon, or whatever, was another fifteen hundred. This was a sum I also paid, and did so good naturedly, saving my heartiest wave for the garbage man, and having got myself comfortable at and behind the wheel. By the way he *did* reply, with a sneeze of brakes, in triplicate, followed by a crumpled smile.

In the belly of that Espadon, in-car guidance gave me a Map 30, then a Map 53. Map 30 was soft grey cashmere as backdrop, sprinkled with shards and large green polygons, with park or school or reserve as appellation. A long meandering thread of ink followed the contours of Manukau Harbour – itself a serene sky blue – from Inaka Place to a Steiner school. Inland a web of yellow roads connected all possible locations from Glen Eden to the eastern fringe of the Waitakere Park. A proposed route bordered itself in broad black stencils, which in overview lazily sauntered back to Ponsonby through Avondale and Western Springs.

I drove out. Furthermore I drove out without getting lost.

Once there I parked in Park Rd, narrow and overhung, then strolled to the street life humming at the roadside cafés. Cream and orange stucco, a glass front tinted maroon, awnings, parasols, round plastic tables, slatted wooden chairs. I ordered hot latté, topped with froth and crumbed with chocolate, and asked the cashier if Craig had been for *his* cup. This was a youngish man with impeccable skin, Latino rather than local, who plunged both hands into the pockets of his apron. Ah, him media. This was not his patch, though just once or twice the world famous Mr Diamond (amazingly a man, as opposed to icon or construct) had picked at a lentil bolognese, at that table there, checking or sending his email.

"I remember the ruby coloured cell phone."

It was said among the kitchen staff, who catered for the home entertainment trade, that Craig had got a place out towards Huia. That meant Map 53, pink roads and rainforest. He couldn't guess where exactly, and suggested I check with Harcourts, a firm in real estate, who must have shown him several.

There the window was adorned with photographs, exclusively hillside frame houses, all with their pools, views and dry anchorage. I roved round among the painted eaves and brightly varnished timbers, and picked out one in particular. This in the lopsided precision of its sold sign boasted its millions, its modesty a legion of trailing noughts. I went back to my swordfish, resetting the guidance system vaguely to the limits of the Huia Rd – a dam, a track, the Karamatura Stream – and drove south slowly, just as it started to rain.

The road, in places no more than a track, threatened several times to peter out. Too often I found myself testing some innocent driveway, intruder in search of a house, only to turn about, puzzled and slightly despondent, thence to press on on a more uncertain road to Huia. Then startlingly the acuteness of his roof line and the height of its ridge were instantly recognisable, in a clear view over the tree ferns greening his decks. The gable was smoked glass and lacquered wood. The sign, also of lacquered wood, and framed with grey bark, named the house Marua, word that from Maori I translate to cavern

201

or pit (as I am sure I must have said). I parked up off the road, not in view of his windows, and made my way to the end of the drive, the rain splashing in the pines, the pines in a deep blue shadow slanting across his porch.

6

I rapped my knuckles several times on the grooved panels of the door. I turned my back, to look out at the patches of mist, at the thin film of rain suspended over the mountain, at the mountain smeared in a cloud of evergreen. I heard, from the bunched shadows, a faint ring of raindrops, then just occasionally the cry of a bellbird. I tried that door again, and this time found movement in the brass of the handle. Gently, I pushed my way in.

I paused, and in the dying echo of my footsteps gazed up into the shafts of sunlight twisting in the vault above, where a mass of architectural timbers soared to a single point. I strained for the hum of conversation where a series of balustraded galleries trained my eye all over them and back downstairs. I went up, that hum getting louder, and found behind a door a blacked room banked with TV screens. All were devoted to the same repetition, a Craig younger than now, in the first of his two autobiographies.

I watched. Those squares in a larger matrix receded simultaneously, as the camera (in fact it was Fatualli's camera) slid from close-up. That gave the florid rash and a deep shadow left by his morning shave, swiftly followed by Diamond standing on a rock. There was a breeze in his hair and the Tors of Dartmoor distantly behind. He talked about what he'd achieved, and of how he'd learned his trade. Surprisingly none of that was at Benbrook, but at NatKnotNite (a point, Natsuki, I feel this urge to talk to you about).

Here again he couldn't leave alone those two-and-a-bit bad years, spent with his thumbs to his tutor's throat. His Zinine he painted in curdled hues, against the zest of her little red runaround. In what she viewed as work, he called her a fag-faced Cinderella, who had somehow got her hands to the knobs of academic power, where haplessly he too had mired himself

202

in the slops of Benbrook's art wars.

There was a story he liked to tell, and re-told here, obsessively (it was one of his cocktail asides, spiked with broken glass). It centred on the graduation ceremony – a stuffy fanfare, according to him – and the decision he made to boycott. The problem here, so far as *I* know, is one of semantics, where 'boycott' is not the term you'd use. Truth is there came at that time an ad in the film press, for extras and beach bums, and the lure of California, and nothing to stay his departure. That, I learn only now, was under the blue smoke and scatter gun of Zina's last farewell. She had, inept to the end, tacked an endnote to the final transcript of Craig's degree, as the official response to his own summing-up. That he'd delivered as the supporting statement penned for his final project – his address to the whole of Benbrook.

He did grudgingly concede that in his last days there, coaxing on Zinine's part he had found patient, polite – even friendly. Yet if all this underpinned her series of tutorials, a combative Craig simply reissued it as one of his project's sub-texts. Zeen asked more than once: *Why's the guy so anti? What exactly's he trying to say?*

Craig attempted to answer both these queries. He had spent a great deal of his time, he said, tracing his ancestry, in vague hopes of identifying precisely what it was that throbbed so violently in his blood. There was, in the mid-nineteenth century, an unusual family conjunction, when Catholic and Jewish lines combined, and that he thought proved some heady cocktail. In the last century the Diamonds dissolved again, this time through the domineering spirit of Craig's paternal great-grandmother, whose evangelism that doyenne could not have made more severe. Through her came zealous proclamations, for so a few odd fragments revealed – a collection of letters mainly, and snippets here and there by word of mouth. She read Galsworthy, on whom a life had been published in 1976, written by someone called Dupré. Active in Galsworthy's high moral purpose was a secret respect for the structures of power his novels satirised. Some such can, I think, also be said of Craig.

To whatever extent his great-gramma shared her model's moral purpose was, so far as Craig saw, idle to speculate. For her, as for far too many during that English era, everyday life was simply too grim for the luxury of satire. No more a child herself, she bossed and brought up her three orphaned siblings, and showed the same ruthless streak with a hard-working husband, come that time. Nonetheless there is the cotton thread of farce, and the smuts of bastardy, when neither she (by marriage) nor Craig (by birth) was a Diamond at all. One twig of their ancestral tree was a hapless country Diamond girl, whose flame-haired lover, having once implanted his seed, scuttled back for a colder clime (some distant Nordic shore). The fruit of that seed was a boy, whom the Diamonds quietly gathered into the arms of their own. It was to *his* line that great-grandfather Diamond (white-haired and genial) belonged. Craig reiterates several times that his was a family van rumbling or grumbling on, in the ever thinning shadow of a Zion embraced by Rome. Therefore all his open emblems belonged, he said, with the engines of persecution driven through the tents of opulence – in essence that was his whole life's ritual. Needless to say, that point sat at the heart of his plenary lecture.

Yet was that really his purpose? Publicly Craig looked back to that first academic year at Benbrook, and still identified no more than a teenage playgroup, its undergraduate practice at times only a pale-lipped mockery of the theoretical structures put there to support it. Endlessly that had set the tone. In his worst hours Benbrook had been his spectre and his foe. Zed, Sib, Angela Tombstone, the top two per cent of fellow-students – all in the mad sad hours of his nights, all fluffed themselves up in his lamplight, as an institutional opposition. So then what, Craig, if you felt an opposition, was an aim – what *was* that aim? These for Benbrook were central questions. Craig however only ever took the word 'aim' as the play of one *ism* attempting to outgrow or depose its predecessor. The one inbuilt proviso that made any genus unique was its cultivator's rake, a tool turned to the ashes of all things past. What an ex-Exeite preferred was the measured transformation to bright new desert blooms. In the first frictions of the various enterprises setting themselves against the tyrannising canons of art, the commonest spark was the spark of negation, whose exemplars were themselves far from ignorant of the canonisation process. Negation, as the force you'd accept as a tool of social agitation – process not unrelated to art – in his own opinion couldn't alone become *viable* art. Lacking were vital ingredients, or the distillation of all our human impedimenta – and that had much to do with thoughts, feelings, blood, passion and poetry.

For himself he refused the suicide pact that, consanguineously, the institution and the institutional artist had drawn up together – parchment signed in a scarlet flourish, under the sputtering lamps adorning our last remaining cul-de-sac (all our dead ends a dull new millennium). Craig still fancied you could hear a last faint tinkle of test tubes, shaken about in the ballroom masquerade of pseudo-science, where the Herr Professors (a Herz and a Merz and a Holz and a Schmaltz) tested and compared solutions. A droplet here, a pipette-squeak there, and lo! the enchanted bright carmine of a lone linguistic compound. Presto! Machiavel! New strong chemic the negation of negation! This enabled almost any argument against the straitjackets institutions like Benbrook wanted their students to wear, in whose structures of power was the assumption that it and its tutors were fully representative of all that was innovative and new. Counter to this Craig Diamond proposed the heart, rigour and pulsing good health all sceptics knew, and assimilated all such freaks as the cold grey ashes of so many basement experiments long ago seen to have failed.

You detected a certain relish in all these asides, in his jibes at Benbrook's various ideologies, which he now began to list. Imbecility number one was Zeen's pet procedural method – practice vaunted in the many avant-garde filmshops where she'd wasted so much time… This was, under the absolutes of logic, only a systematisation of what already existed as chance combinations, and was therefore only an attempt to control the inherent dice-throws of life. *That* Craig would call *self*-negation. Imbecility two was Zeen's other tame crock, art object taken and defamiliarised. This was also a self-negation, since mounting a cabbage or flume pump as formal exhibit only asked the question *what is a gallery*, a line of investigation that planted us gumbooted in the muddy fields of social inquiry. Myself I can't go on with this, so graciously I'll skip the three, four, five, however many dozen, and cut to Craig's conclusion, which was this, that not much 'originality' was ever what it claimed (i.e. wasn't originality). Craig for one couldn't accept into his own aesthetic, which he still regarded as pristine, the crude transferences of arbitrary centres – for example artefact-to-originator, or artist as abdicant – or that cult of personality we're apt to smile at knowingly when observed in mud-hut cultures. Much the same medievalism clung to that other icon, the 'installation', lump of old machinery douched in the mystic mantic magical fragrance of its creator. In Craig's view, you took this no more seriously than the follies of an Exeite.

As a last jibe outwardly at all our media Gestapos, Craig addressed himself to Zinine personally. He pointed out that Benbrook's quest for novelty had been the shedding of art as such, and in its postmodern hue, the colour jaundice, lay slumped in an adolescent stew of rebellion, its sheepish adherents able only to dismantle 'the received idea'. (*Dismantle*, in a new lexicography Craig wished to propose, was an *intransigent* verb.) Student Craig (or so ran his own propaganda line) had never been permitted to speak for himself. His fleeting simulacrum was a flicker of unwritten text bridging a handful of desultory inscriptions. There had been – and this he couldn't forgive – an authoritarian remoulding of his page (technically known as 'peritext'), at the hands of an institution. For the Craig of the here and now in celluloid (or rather of the then), that institution had receded as only a syntagm – a few written edicts and a series of footnotes – nevertheless in his sleepless nights he was still obliged to deal with the blind limitless curfews of the Benbrook Height College for the Performing Arts. Constructs and con tricks. Or should Craig say that by his watch this was already one minute to eternity…

Tock.

7

Then finally the only charge he levelled was that of incompetence. By then Zinine functioned rather against the dust of her own cremations, the defiles of ash and cigarette smoke, a long history permeating every nook of that cramped office space she alone ruled. Anyway a whole new world of summer she felt in its first perfumes, as an intoxicating radiance, a brilliance stealthily making waves across the water meadow, then up over the maple trees. I have already mentioned her note. This, as a self-therapist's act of closure, she clipped to the thin transcript of Craig's degree, having somehow melded its two loose scripts with those she had written to another student. That other, still yet anonymous, remained an untroubled, moreover untroubling undergraduate, whose own page two, delivered erroneously into Craig's slightly trembling hand, glowed in Benbrook's twilight.

Craig, whose strategies so often hatched themselves in the velvet interior of an ammunition box, decided not to broach this at all. Then at the pre-graduation shindig, annually a drunken boat trip – this in an open pleasure craft – up and then back down the mazy river Dwar – he found her portside the bar, listing somewhat, having turned briefly from her own social set (Sib, Dib, Glib and others) in order to light a particularly pungent cigarette. "Hate to talk shop," he said, and talked just that. I personally *am* prepared to accept that the razored asperity, that astringent blade slashing practically everything he said and did just then, wasn't down solely to the stresses of student or artistic life. The Dwar, serene, placid, and moonlit tonight, and snaking through those softly crescent hills, nevertheless regularly breached the grey stone bridges dotting the medieval walks and cobbled relics that characterised the town. Not that long ago a weekend of rain had completely engulfed the surrounding fields and hedgerows. A thick layer of silt cascading over the gully stones eventually slimed the whole of his ground floor *lebensraum*, a natural mark of *écriture* he'd still not fully erased.

Zeen mused that his missing paper was one of those over-sights the demands of her office were likely to see her perpe-trate from time to time, and a clerical error she personally was unprepared to rectify. She knew well enough her own page twos – she'd got a curriculum of these – and might not easily forget that among those sheaves was the one she'd assigned to Craig. Craig liked to speculate on this – as an operation undergone in the torments and practical jokes of an enchanted English summer, its shadows, flickers and night imps very slowly extending its influence. All this quite rightly occurred under a pendent blue mist, Zinine's ashtrays filled with the butts of those appalling cigarettes. A key phrase her vagrant document returned to again and again was one that in part mummified student Craig, whom she described as a man driven by invective, ooze of fire, heat and magma fuming away at the very structure in which he had to operate. If she couldn't quite recall this now, amidships, then schoolboy Craig she di-rected cap-in-hand to the programmes office, on campus, where for a few pence or photocopy fee a duplicate could be made. Quirkily this in itself constituted the long lasting pos-terity Benbrook implanted in Craig's foggy reflections – and at that time his weary brain – and was the point on which that first film autobiography ended.

Tropecale remembered one other climax. All night Craig had drunk whisky and Coca-Cola, thinly iced and sprigged with mint leaf – one of those concoctions Craig was at that time partial to. Having chugged and washed both shorelines for ninety minutes or more, the *Dwar Princess* turned in the Dwar's estuary and embarked on the return journey, by which time Craig had had a good half-dozen too many mixers. Tropecale, himself soberly dressed, his own sweet temper fuelled by still water only – this he sipped, from a cloudy tumbler – observed that at one point Craig had turned a bilious shade of grey. This was in the bowels of the *Dwar Princess*, cocoon vibrant with conversation and the drone of engine noise. Craig propped up a post in a head-to-head with his buddy Lorenzo (Lorenzo Constant), man equally soaked. Constant knew that the *Dwar Princess* was in fact Scandinavian, whose first and authentic name was the *Saxo Grammaticus*, appellation made official in a quaint ceremony under the green tinkle of bottled *brut* – this in a cold harbour somewhere on a Baltic coast. Craig laughed, only then turned green himself. "You, Craig, okay?" No. What had bothered him was Zeen (Zeen had made him green), in whose superficial reading of his text she identified a last apologist for modernism, position we all knew as untenable at Benbrook. Benbrook, one of those early millennial playparks, where that particular rationale (modernism) had been sealed in a crate and fork-lifted to the lumber room.

Constant, a man true to his name, now assured 'acknowledged legislator' Craig that his two-year Arthurian quest – a sort of kitchen drama, where the smash of utensils was all of it a sacrifice for the student soul – just hadn't been in vain. Craig only smirked, confidentially. More generally that student soul was the soul of millennial man (Craig's woman, the Mill Enemy, he'd already cast as Queen Zinine). "I," he said, "pronounce it *solde* – and so would that goddam Tropecale, eavesdropping again, I see…" Fair point, Lorenzo had to agree, since the spoils (that student soul) came packaged as a short, small-framed, pustular fellow-grad, all amber lenses in a thick black spectacles frame, whose name was Abb (contraction of God knew what). Abb, a murky 2:2, was certain already of media stardom. He knew, in his blood, bones and sinews, that the *Zeitgeist* wore winged sandals. There was one specific reason for this – to bear Abb up and deposit him atop a plaster pedestal, of a kind ritually shattered under the rampaging lump hammers issued with every student start-up kit at Benbrook (but never mind). Abb wanted a future biographer, and wanted one now.

"Craig, allow me to introduce you to Abb, an admirer…" Craig's green visage was turning slightly puce. "Let me tell you, Craig, your reputation precedes you…" Lily handshakes.

Tropecale was there at disembarkation too, with his arms folded. Craig was close by as he, or I, breathed deeply all that night air. I was with him too looking out under all the lamplit hillsides. Already a procession of college profs, who for once led from the front, had got their charges under careful watch, that waddle of newly hatched chicks, as all went that mercurial way. Who knew how many versts inland? or where? A far manured country. Land of oxen and a thousand torchlit shippons.

Craig threw up, a thin brown treacle whose gobbets of brimstone I saw instantly cooled in the crests of sea and river water slopping on the harbour wall. Abb said he knew the venue of a really man like funky 'sworray', which after a long trek turned out to be a double-fronted terrace, low lit internally, and here on the outside a frosty glitter of small square window panes. It nestled among the darkly marooned droplets of a fuchsia bush, at the remote end of a car-lined lane off the Church of St John, and not out of bellshot of that holy place. Abb Hi'd and Hallooed on the doorstep, when his ring was answered.

A dark-haired, round-faced, dumpy researcher from Benbrook, whose notices and catalogues I dimly recalled (a video and installation artiste) ushered in first Abb, then a crapulent Craig, then a reluctant Tropecale, all in a single file through a billow of hashish dust. A dead debate was already underway, in a tiny square sitting room, where the few sticks of furniture had been pushed to the walls. The walls, Craig, were thickly coated in a sickly egg-yellow oil paint – décor your hostess later had to sponge. In the TV corner the TV had its face contritely to the wall. In another a lopsided yucca grew almost to the ceiling, fruit of a glaucous bell pot.

Abb, the Bedazzled One, added his own small change to the tarnish of debate. This was a usual line, art and its social import, or the artist's 'special' place. The door bell sounded and in walked Lorenzo. Craig, now shading at the jowls, the colour jade dulled under the slants of a table lamp, said *Hie thee, Horatio!* – and without pause dreamed a different philosophy. That was not a nut but a seed, whose humble bound bore potential for ripeness and sunshine and plentiful harvests, and therefore harnessed most human stock to the condition of work – an unending sow, nurture, reap – with not much scope for play. Generally gulls, hucksters, fortune-tellers, and more spectacularly Abb's supremely elevated artist, had escaped that wheel, turning play to work, and in the latter case the process

210

of being into a mystical rite. That brought with it starlit status, the thing Abb really was attracted to, and therein lay the path of decadence and self-destruction – "Really what every *ism* is, ism't it, Lorenzo?"

"Absolutely!"

The doorbell again, a boy on a flimsy moped, gloved, helmeted, here to deliver – and what had kept him! – a stack of late-night pizzas. Said Rhoda the researcher: "Do help self!"

Ah only if deep pan and pepperoni would Abb accept a slice. He said so both palms raised.

By now Craig's jowls had turned to a tinct of jade tinged with the darkness of blood, a brooding exterior under which a fatigued Tropecale watched him prepare his retreat intellectually from Benbrook, its shoddy populations now despised without reservation – its preachers, teachers, the caught and the taught. He picked up a Latin phrase book, no doubt Abb-inspired, and found here what (?): *ab uno disce omnes*. That seemed to content him for a few quiet moments. Then abruptly Craig stood up, that greened complexion as suddenly floured. What had passed in a whirl of hands all round him, those wedges of pizza, stray capsicum, a rogue thread here and there of hardened cheese, had left its mires in the twitch of his nose-thirles. A hot viscous bile recumbent in his stomach, having once acquiesced under a first purifying eruption, now stirred volcanically again. He tangled in a sprawl of limbs – those many lolling students on the floor – but a touch too late for the bell pot, which he missed.

Result was a passable parabola adorning a yellow wall.

8

A creak of timbers in that wooden architecture overhead meant that the clouds had passed, that the rain had ceased. A mid-November sun was pouring golden honey onto Marua's roof, while here inside, the marine of Diamond's television screens had dissolved to black crêpe.

In an adjoining room I found books in a packing case, a manual, papers, scripts. Amazingly I went unchallenged, permitted to wander all over the control suite, circumadjacent to

211

which was a newly built dome and projector. No electric locks, no bars, no ID device scanning for biometric data.

Was there a reason for this? I supposed that in the remoteness, Marua's mountainside dotted with playboy baches, Craig could anticipate few if any unbidden guests. Yet *where* was he?

A few programme slots existed in prototype. I discovered this sitting at the control desk, alternately pushing buttons and leafing through one of those manuals. First fruit of that investigation came in a brief melodic line, and a blare of trumpets, heralding a pull-down window, followed by several others suspended at various points in the dome surrounding me. A travelogue, with the working title *McGregor Country*, arrived on a flat screen, in a short film scenario whose end it was hard not to think of as tourism. Its backing was an ensemble of ocean strings, laced with a twinkle of woodwind. This in an opening sequence serenaded an aerial sweep over McGregor's native isles. No voice had yet been added, though a script had been worked on. This appeared through one other aperture (fake worlds in a labyrinth of pull-down windows), its plum-blue border banded in inky black. I read, but inattentively, and in the end abandoned the immobility of text for that flicker of moving images, where the roll of a timpani marked each little crescendo.

Two hikers, one wearing orange, one in a yellow cagoule, emerged from the fringe of a pine forest, and in the haze of its evening shadow posed for the camera. Partner in orange, who was a man – large-framed and leaden limbed – bent to untie, then retie a boot. Yellow waved, was slight, and slightly shrank to a pinpoint, then disappeared altogether as a succession of new panoramas wound their way in. First a limestone outcrop, its jags soft-edged under the stray beams of sunrise. Then a rocky foreshore, its boulders an elephant-grey, and steeply banked, and overhung from a low cliff by the limbs of a pohutukawa tree, in its full flower or flames of crimson. Lastly that airborne lens arced over a big-game fishing vessel, lines cast from all open sides of its deck, swishing for tuna, marlin, blue pointer shark.

212

Plane and camera landed, seamlessly – thereafter McGregAir Information took to firm footholds. For example a meander through scenic reserves, over boardwalks, in and out of observation points, among the groves of what remaining kauri trees there were. With the bob of bush hats went the measured strides of a bush walk, among fallen trees, a swipe of ferns, the tangle of undergrowth. This same roving optic rescreened itself through an abandoned gold mine, the flash or wing of a mynah bird, a glass beehive, the bubble of mud, steam and sulphur Rotorua-style. At this point the music stilled to a low hum on a cello string, alone and mysterious, then rose in a spurt of piccolos and the spray of a sun-filled geyser, the surrounding landscape dotted with clumps of tea tree. There was a hot-water beach. There was an archipelago of thermal pools, hand-made and kitted out with poolside entertainments (more screens – screens in a world made screen). On a beach at sunset, silhouetted surfers parked their boards and nursed their tins, the sea spangled, the sky streaked in copper and blossom pink. Then fade out, on violas.

Craig's one other film autobiography was more pronounced than the first, in its deceits. Somehow he'd resurrected old footage, and perhaps even enjoyed commercial ownership of Hahn's historic signing-up, that wholly stage-managed protocol that swore him into office. As you know, Europe's first was a Berlin-based president, Hahn a home-town boy – *Ich bin ein Berliner!* – then in his early fifties, but youthful in appearance. He was slim, with closely clipped hair, and careful in his range of suits, expensive but always understated.

Craig had had this key moment remastered holographically. What resulted was its hybrid, here in virtual 3D, where his technicians inseminated Craig's own, and interactive image. He appeared, a famulus, who sidestepped his way through a background press corps, then swaggered to the foreground (I beheld him, here in Marua, just an armstretch away). I watched as he perched, here on that long table where a world of negotiators raised pens or rested elbows – Hahn, Hahn's party chairperson, his party manager, his future Minister of State for State Affairs, likewise Foreign Affairs. A short pensive hush went with the graven lines tugging down and up – a man in two minds – or pulling at the corners of Herr Hahn's mouth. Hahn unscrewed the lid of his fountain pen, with care and deliberation. In stretching for the blotter, someone jogged a water jug – the result a reflected pool of light coruscating all over the domed ceiling. Other wrists raised other nibs and other fountain pens. One man I recognised as a McGregAir representative, young and fresh-faced. Others were here wing-footed from McGregor's main rivals. Of these one with a snazzy breast-pocket handkerchief I thought I vaguely recognised, but couldn't place the name (it wasn't Steven Hart).

Craig's coy little smirk, and what was for him an ingenuous palm – his palm was open honestly – co-ordinated all these clever intricacies to the surrounding sound-track, at that moment an unbelievable roar of nib tips. Successively these scratched at the same fateful treaty, in a first and last accord – expansive, right-hand sweeps, i's either distantly dotted or dotted not at all, trailing t's in the comet tail of accelerating crossbars. Craig, whose plasticised flesh turned from a burnt sugar back to white, thence to the ache of lobster, suffered the break-up of his image, stray limbs, a jacket pocket, a mouth no longer synchronised to the noises it produced, a whole man adrift on a south sea, sea sprinkled with multicoloured islands, coins, a rollerpoint, Craig's left sock floating to the ceiling. From somewhere, from inside a shoe, or a trouser leg, he did manage to say that the system hadn't been fully tested, and in circumstances such as these I would do best, Will, to reboot.

9

I rebooted. In five minutes or so the system rekindled itself, in sputters and a flash of chrome, but began its whirr from a newly chosen entry point. This time the McGregor introduction zoomed in on McAndrew St, its famous framehouse now newly renovated – a tin roof painted peach, its clapboard a dazzle of freshly sunkissed white. A cragged, servile medic wheeled the grand old man himself out on the decks, where Craig – his hair gelled and wearing a tuxedo – awaited, an avuncular smile pinned to his face, and wielding a microphone ('In tonight's linkup,' unquote). Then that scenery infolded itself and fell away, leaving for Craig his one other theatrical change, his flesh more naturally human, his natty house garb set off with a silk cravat. Again here were those about him, whose throb of life the software froze or cast in stone. These were Hahn and his entourage, with flanking Machiavellis, who remained in an endlessly flashlit moment – urbane smiles, warm friendly handshakes. In truth it was a ragbag of Right and Left, whose improbable cohesion McGregAir's, and later EuroSHart's history-makers patiently glossed – decades of broadcast propaganda inching our first president, a man doomed and yet civilised, helplessly into office.

10

Craig snapped fingers, restarting not the whole, but one only among those mummers – a man incredibly young, in fact almost schoolboyish, until now seated at the heart of those several McGregAir aides. He stood and was suddenly transformed, into the same man if slightly older – medium build, large-framed, blue-eyed and open. He and Craig exchanged a few words I wasn't meant to hear, then Craig turned to where I still sat at the control desk (by then I controlled nothing).

"Now Mitrovich you've met," he said. "No need to introduce."

Mitrovich, now sandalled and leather-thonged, a youth deeply tanned and bearing an alpenstock, grinned. I tried to smile back, but mustered a slight twitch only. Mitrovich for one moment was, then wasn't a pale New Yorker.

Craig – a new rabbit, a brand new hat – motioned my gaze to a pull-down window behind him, screen through which a second Mitrovich on a henna-burnt afternoon drove into Ix. Here was some business he'd got with Frame, all to do with the French Revolution. The grey-black curls of Mitrovich's newly advanced age, and sagacity (as once I had hoped), swirled in the breeze. Young at heart, he clattered round the cobbled bends of Ix, turning the wheel from wall to turreted

215

wall, a manchild fast, loose and gleeful, bearing down in a borrowed convertible. Then that duplicated second disappeared round a bend, and the screen went blank – then as abruptly burst into microcoloured light. Another of Craig's aerial sweeps, this time over the broad streets and high roofline of Singapore, a zoo, a night safari park, a system of cable cars. We swooped in finally through a hotel window.

11

Through that hotel window, a large dining room – mahogany, walnut, glittering candelabra – and a private function, in fact a toast to Diamond's sixtieth birthday, which happened to fall within the same twelve months as McGregor's ninetieth. The remains of a dinner for twelve had not yet been cleared to the kitchen, with only nine of those twelve identifiable by me, and even so with varying degrees of difficulty. Here was Diamond himself, at the head of the table, waving, demonstratively, an unclipped, unlit Havana. Ruts I knew to be deeply etched in his face, and the emaciated pallor, had all been brushed away with digital makeup, as was not quite the case with McGregor, a lapdog at Craig's right hand, a man trying hard to disagree with his host's expostulations, playful though these were. A thread of saliva, silvered in the candelabra light, dangled from a corner of McGregor's mouth, whose lips were a pale blue. Sitting opposite one another were Lisbeth Fatualli – her gold encrustations, just like her daddy's, and her wizened neck – and Gavin Smayle, whose eighteen-month liaison all those years ago had been tucked up in a warm sty of reminiscence and allowed to sleep sensuously. Cheroots a hoarse-throated Lisbeth smoked no more. Lorenzo Constant, a pan-Europe patron and now strictly Stateside critic (of the visual arts), and a socialite, had reinforced that student arrogance as pads and wads of wealth, which he wallowed in, and appeared to be comfortable. There was Dondie Millar (sculptor), whose large eyes were puffy at the lower lids. This lent her being a fatigue or sadness, which her bright cheeks and the ring of her laughter insistently contradicted. Also the flighty Chelsea de la Mare, also Wm Tropecale, or rather

216

myself, or rather some filmy graphic rig-up purporting to be me. Then there was Mitrovich again, in yet another replication – large, close-set eyes, still youngish, and still wearing his hair relatively long.

"Sorry," said Craig – the Craig with the cravat, and not waving the Havana – "about that waist-line. Had only Morwena's description to go on. Suppose I should have spoken to Mitrovich."

The bitch Morwena – the dirty bitch Morwena – had tensed her flesh and mentally shut her eyes each time the flab of my mid-life body pressed itself to hers, a younger, satin fruit.

"She's somewhere here but you've missed her. Retired to the drawing room with Chunk – a lovely boy, by the way, and thanks very much!" He hoped Morwena had been carnally as powerful.

"She has had, Craig, the measure of everything."

"Now William that is just what I'd expect! It's a pity Zinine couldn't accept my invitation. Wouldn't she love Singapore… Wouldn't she, Anno?"

"Don't think I don't know, Craig. Natsuki. Technically, that's a breach of security."

"Now don't you worry about security. All she said was this. There's a funny chap, in that hush-hush place where she went to work, who sometimes sprinkled his mail with bits and bobs from Chaucer. Now naturally I wondered who that could be."

"Naturally."

"Since you left it, Anno, things have been well taken care of back at Ix. You are Anno, Anno?"

"I was, and am. Tropecale only by adoption. After that bomb in Berlin."

"Ah, yes – quite understand…"

In Singapore, that other Craig looked distantly into the nutty hues of his brandy glass, but left it there twinkling on the linen of the table cloth. He steeled himself, then began, monumentally, the task of trimming, then lighting his fat cigar. He drew, puffed, and was content, and in a hail of blue smoke and bluster turned to McGregor.

Others were leaving the table – Lisbeth, Lorenzo, Chelsea

217

de la Mare – in fact all but a last sad trio rose and drifted off and joined the others next door. Craig suggested that before joining them, Robbie might take this opportunity to reflect that here in person was the BDP's first and last monitor, a post whose existence Frame and Mal de Fak had publicly denied.

"Well well!" McGregor croaked. His voice was cracked and thin.

"Another glass of port, William?"

"No. I don't think so."

McGregor, who at ninety allowed himself moments of sentimentality, drooled into the creases of his chin. In reaching for his serviette he knocked his fruit knife into a debris of peach stones surrounding his plate.

"That's right, Robbie. William Tropecale. A Benbrook old boy."

To Craig of course all Benbrook ever was was typical of any institution, prone to consign to the recycling bin everything preceding *it*. It 'called into question', a phrase Tropecale remembered on Zinine's lips particularly, practically everything but itself, an ethos central to the BDP's own sense of purpose.

"Having said that, Robbie, we're all right now – now we've got our EuroSHart."

"Full circle then," McGregor said, who even now would live to see the reinvigoration of that first and 'only' monopoly, his own.

"Though we haven't quite bought off William here, who's still hanging on to his Chaucer. I've never understood that, Will… Chaucer."

"It's something you never will." Tropecale pushed the remains of his one glass of port firmly to centre-table, a man as small as Chaucer in his Englishness, yet whose limits had brushed the universe. "Conversely, Craig, for you and McGregor, and that globalist ethos generally, the force driving all things on is narrow, and petty, and self-interested – and full of spite."

"Will, we have to be safe, here in our dangerous world. All of us have to be safe. And what you say isn't entirely true. Another glass?"

218

"No."

A projected Craig reminded the vision Tropecale, while McGregor as cartoon cutout sucked at his teeth and oozed goo onto his lapels, that Ducane had unwittingly helped him reconstruct his own Chaucerian plaint, whose hybrid began:

O amber light, whose cloistral beams
Have ravaged my empyrean!

Craig might as well confess that here in that ditty scorning a fellow-student was the essence of his youthful art, not he thought lost, but merely stifled. Now that he was 'safe', he was tired, and wanted certain mental freedoms.

"I want, William, to produce something meaningful. Just once. Could it hurt you if I managed that?"

By now McGregor's chin was propped on his pigeon chest, and he dozed. Tropecale looked first at him, then at Craig, whose lips were pursed. Two concise smoke rings were already beginning to crumble. Tropecale considered his glass of port, and the film on McGregor's fruit knife. "You have, Craig," he said, "no chance…"

Craig only smiled, then gently stubbed his cigar. The screen and with it Singapore went blank, then that floating hologram also dispersed, leaving only Mitrovich, who now wore a long grey coat. His mousy ringlets fell darkly on its epaulettes. The department, he said, was now under control, which meant that Frame had gone, and Two and Six had begun the process of removing all the old guard. Soon this would find itself supplanted by Mrs Quinn's hand-picked personnel.

My hand hovered over the reset button, at which point codename Mitrovich metamorphosed again – turning stocky, with cropped red hair, his complexion a bowl full of tulip petals.

"Just one other thing before you go," he said, and by now he was aging, sallow-faced, had a faint lisp and a trace of Eastern European. But that is not how I remember him, my head in a whirl, here as I stumble from Marua, me myself Anno blinking in the bright November sunlight, the sands around me blowing up, a storm concealing all in the world that there is to conceal. Mitrovich was calm, measured, wore a broad hat, was gaberdine'd as a sleuth, was someone who struck a match, was a man with a pipe in the winds of an English summer. Under a vortex of damp tobacco smoke he buried his face in a cross-slide of shadows. I drove, I boarded a plane, I marched into Ix, where Miss Ashley, Frame and Luis had gone, and Two and Six were in control. I drove out, in a blaze of dust, to John Frame's fortress, and there found its chambers stilled, its escape routes deserted, their openings all looking up to a cloudless blue sky. I sat down. I opened these handover notes. Slowly, and very carefully, I began to write. Now, meticulously, I at last lay to rest that monster, that screen flicker, that construct, that invented Craig Diamond, that little man who claws away at everyone's frightened soul. For one tiny eternity the world's wide screens went blank, our bitstreams high and low all ceased to chatter. A gentle flurry of sand reclaimed its last little inch of desert. Therefore I too shall disappear, and again shall call myself Anno, or Anon, that ghost who walks in the twang of English words, in his universe built on a narrow village life…

A good night now for nothing.